Glass & Sin
The Shattered Crowns, Book 1
Cordelia Cross

Bold Bandit Books

To those who survived their glass coffin and found
safety in the forest.
It's time to shatter expectations.

* * * * * * * * * * *

Content Warnings

AUTHOR'S NOTE & CONTENT WARNINGS

Glass & Sin is a dark fantasy romance and a reimagining of classic fairy tale elements. It contains themes and scenes that may be distressing for some readers, including:

- Some graphic violence and bloodshed

- Dark magical elements and psychological manipulation

- Toxic familial dynamics (specifically involving maternal figures)

- Explicit romantic content

Please read with care.

Contents

Chapter One

Once Upon a Nightmare

"ONCE UPON A TIME," Snow White whispered to her own reflection, "a princess forgot how to breathe."

Moonlight pooled across the stone floor of her tower room, silvering the edges of the heavily cracked mirror nailed crookedly to the wall. In it, the girl who stared back at her looked more like a ghost than a princess—pale skin almost blue under the night glow, black hair falling unevenly, in jagged clumps just past her jaw. The last time her mother had taken scissors to it, she'd promised it would keep her safe. Her mother, the queen, always chopped it so short, but she must have lost track since it was starting to grow longer now, silky and reflective in the moonlight.

Snow White's fingers rose to the hollow of her throat, tracing the line of her jaw, then lower to the tender swell of her collarbone. The mirror had once been part of a grand wardrobe; now its surface was spiderwebbed with fractures, slicing her reflection into shards. In one shard she caught only the curve of her lips, stained naturally deep red as if she wore forbidden rouge. In another, a single eye stared back at her, wide and too knowing.

You'll never be as pretty as her. The thought wasn't hers; it was a distant echo. Her mother's voice curled inside her head. In her eighteen years of life, Snow White had never seen anyone more beautiful. Her father would tell her repeatedly how Liora won his heart with the first look. He used to recall their eyes catching, and he couldn't look away, entranced, hypnotized by her beauty. *Someday, I will find a man who looks at me the same way my father looked at her.*

She let her hand drift down, over the thin linen of her nightshirt, skimming the curve of her breast. Her nipple tightened under her palm at the light contact, and a slow burn traced its way up her throat. She swallowed, half-ashamed, half-defiant. But when she closed her eyes, the feeling rose anyway.

In the privacy behind her lowered lashes, he appeared again. The boy. The prince. His highness. Strong but gentle hands cupping her waist through the coarse fabric of a stable girl's dress. A mouth hovering close to hers, hesitant and reverent, as if she were something precious instead of something to be hidden. She never caught his name. Only the piercing blue of his eyes and the way his blonde hair had fallen over his forehead. Only his gentle touch and his kind laugh. Only the way he had looked at her like she was a miracle, not a mistake.

In her daydream, he leaned down. Soft lips touched hers, not demanding, just asking. His kiss was soft and sweet, yet unexpected. She had never kissed anyone before and longed for her first real kiss. Warmth grew low in her belly as she imagined his fingers slipping beneath the edge of her stays, slowly tracing the swell of her breast. She ached for his touch. The racing in her chest blurred with another ache lower down, a restless, tingling hunger that made her shift in her seat. Her real fingers followed the path of the imagined ones, gliding over the thin cotton to her chest. Her eyes closed tightly when she grazed the sore spot beneath it—dark, blooming pain radiated from her ribs, stealing the air from her lungs. She hissed and pressed more firmly, feeling along the curve of bone. The pain was ugly under her nightshirt—she knew it would be a blotch of sickly yellow and purple when the light came.

Why...? She felt small in the empty room.

The memory came back in pieces. Her mother's hands, deceptively rough, tugging the laces of the corset. The queen's perfume—juniper and something harsher, like crushed mint. The world narrowing as Liora pulled and pulled, voice light and sharp while Snow White struggled to breathe.

"You want to look perfect for the ball, don't you?" her mother had said. "Beauty is pain, my little snow-thing."

Then the comb, gleaming in the morning light like a jewel. A gift, a kindness so rare Snow White had almost wept with gratitude. Then the sting against her scalp, the sudden, drowning darkness.

She pulled her hand away from her ribs, fingers shaking. *She had seemed to change, turned colder since Father's death, but could a mother do this to a daughter? How could she? Why would she?* Snow White's thoughts faded into the darkness. The realization washed over her like a crashing wave. *It was her. I don't know why, but I can't ignore it.*

Moonlight carved harsh angles into her cheekbones. For a heartbeat, her reflection blurred, and she saw not her own face but her mother's—the same black hair, the same red mouth, the queen's beauty honed into a weapon. The thought made her chest seize. She looked away from her shattered mirror and wrapped her arms around herself.

Her gaze darted to the narrow window, to the slice of night beyond. Somewhere down below, beyond towers and courtyards and locked iron gates, the royal stables huddled against the outer wall. She could almost smell the sweet, familiar scent of hay and horse, feel the velvet brush of a muzzle against her cheek. It was the one place she truly felt seen. The horses, their keen sense of connection, almost as if they knew her heart. She spent hours in the stables, sitting in the hay reading. She loved to read—not that she had much else to do—stories of faraway lands, young love, and happy endings. The books gave her comfort and occasional hope. Sometimes she would read aloud to her four-legged companions or snuggle next to her gallant, dependable steed.

"Grimm," she whispered. Just saying his name eased something clenched inside her. Her father's last gift. Her only real friend within these stone walls. If she pressed her forehead to the cold glass and squinted, she could almost imagine him: a dark shape shifting in the straw, ears pricked as if he sensed her watching. His glistening black mane, which Father said had matched her own, and the way she knew Grimm would do anything she asked—he would even try to jump the moon for her if she asked him to.

I should leave. The idea was wild and impossible. *I could climb down, get Grimm, and go. Ride away, far, far away. Find a nice village, a place I can live. I can be a stable keeper. I can be okay. I can be okay without her.* She thought of the queen's hands on the corset laces. The comb's teeth biting into her scalp. The slow, dawning realization that these were not accidents. Not motherly mistakes. Intent. The room seemed to shrink around her. The cracked mirror, the narrow bed, the single candle sputtering on its stand—this tower was a gilded cell, and she had been pretending not to see the bars. *I've got to get out of here. And it has to be now.*

Snow White's gaze returned to her reflection. The girl in the mirror straightened her shoulders just a fraction, lifted her chin. Her red lips parted, not in fear, but in something like quiet defiance.

"Once upon a time," she whispered again, "a princess ran away." The words hung there, frightening and thrilling. Much like the wild plots in her books. Runaways, star-crossed lovers, knights and maidens, sirens and dragons, and everything in between. The candle flickered. Somewhere in the castle, a clock began to strike, each toll rolling through the stones like a heartbeat.

The sound pulled her backward, down, through years of layered memory, back to a time when the castle had been full of light instead of shadows, and she had still believed "once upon a time" always led to "happily ever after."

• • • ● ● • ● ● • •

B IG FLAKES OF PUFFY white snow began to fall on the morning of Shay's eighth birthday. From her bedroom window, the world beyond the castle walls looked like a storybook illustration: rooftops dusted in white, the distant forest softened to pale gray shapes. Shay pressed her nose to the cold pane, leaving a round, foggy print. Shay's black hair was long and silky; her rosy cheeks matched her cheerful dress.

She was petite for her age, shorter than most of her peers, and she smiled as the snow fell, thinking about how much her parents loved the snow. She had been told often that her name, Shay, came from *Schnee*, the German word for snow, because of the blizzard the night she was born. She liked the idea that the whole world had been wrapped in a blanket just to welcome her, as it was again today, eight years later.

"Your Majesty," a warm voice rumbled behind her, "if you smudge that glass any more, the servants will revolt."

Shay whipped around. "Papa!"

King Wilhelm stood in the doorway, already wrapped in his heavy fur-trimmed cloak, cheeks pink from the draft. He was not the sort of king bards sang about—he had a round belly and a nose slightly too large for his face—but his smile lit the room brighter than any torch.

The king had longed for a boy, a strong heir to take his place on the throne one day, but Liora was firm from the start that she would only give birth one time. Wilhelm loved Liora, and when the nursemaid announced their baby was a healthy baby girl, Wilhelm smiled, knowing he was blessed. Times were beginning to change in the kingdom and Wilhelm felt sure his people would bow to a queen as their leader on the throne one day.

"Come here, birthday girl," he said, holding out his arms. She ran to him. He scooped her up with an *oof* and spun her once, her laughter tangling with his. When he set her down, he held her at arm's length to look at her properly. "Look at you," he marveled. "Pale as the first snow, hair black as the raven on my banner, lips red as the apples in the south orchards. Every day you look more like your mother."

Shay preened a little under his gaze. "Do you really think so?"

"I know so," he said solemnly, then ruined the effect by tweaking her nose. "Only you're kinder. Don't tell her I said that; she'll have my head mounted over the hearth!"

She giggled and covered his mouth with both hands. "I won't tell."

They walked hand-in-hand through the corridor toward the great hall. Servants bustled past carrying trays and armfuls of linens, and everyone they passed smiled at the little princess and dipped quick bows or curtsies. "Happy birthday, Highness," gushed Marta, the laundress, as she hurried by with a basket of steaming linen. "Eight already! Oh, the years do fly."

Shay liked how they looked at her, with simple fondness. She liked how the castle felt in the chilly mornings: fires crackling in every hearth, the air scented with baking bread and roasting meat, voices echoing as people called greetings across the vaulted space. She wondered about the cake she hoped they'd bake for her that evening and the music that would surely fill the hall before the feast.

All through the castle, servants had hung garlands of evergreen and pale winter berries along the pillars. Tapestries depicting ancient battles glowed with reds and golds in the torchlight. Above the high table, the royal banner drooped slightly in the still air: a large purple and black raven, flying over snowy treetops.

"Your mother insisted on extra candles," Wilhelm said as they walked. "She says they make your skin look luminous." He rolled his eyes fondly. "As if you needed help with that."

"Where is she?" Shay asked. "Mama promised she'd braid my hair before we go outside."

"In her chambers," he said. "No doubt arguing with her mirror."

Shay laughed, because that was what he always said, and because it made her feel grown-up to joke about the things adults turned into whispers.

"I want to see the horses," she said. "Can we, Papa? Before breakfast?"

Wilhelm's expression softened. "Impatient, aren't you?" He pretended to sigh. "Very well. I suppose we can let the cooks wait a little longer." He led her through a side door, down a narrower corridor lined with portraits.

Shay skipped ahead, reading the plaques under each frame. "King Erich the Iron," she recited. "King Roderick the Wise... King Alaric the Cruel." She made a face at that one. "Why would they keep his picture?"

"So we don't forget what not to be." Turning, he added, "Come, little scholar, I'm getting hungry."

As they reached the turn toward the courtyard, a familiar young man stood—tall, broad-shouldered, barely twenty and dressed in the dark livery of the royal guard. His hair was thick and curly brown, and his muscles bulged out from under his light armor.

"Captain Hunter!" Shay called, delighted.

He bowed with a smile that creased the corners of his eyes. "Your Highness. Happy birthday." His stance was easy, confident. He reached into his belt pouch and drew out a small object wrapped in cloth. "For you," he said, holding it out in his palm.

Shay unwrapped it with eager fingers. Inside lay a tiny wooden raven, no bigger than her thumb, wings spread as if in flight. The carving was simple but careful; someone had taken time with the feathers.

"I made it on night watch," Hunter said, and smiled. "Thought every princess should have her kingdom's bird close, even when she's not in the great hall."

"It's beautiful," Shay smiled. "Thank you, Hunter."

Wilhelm clapped his friend's shoulder. "Glad the night watch is on such high alert," he teased.

"Nobody would dare while I'm alive," Hunter joked back.

Wilhelm chuckled. Captain Hunter was the finest swordsman in all the land. Years ago, in a skirmish on the northern border, he had dragged King Wilhelm from beneath a fallen horse and taken a spear meant for the king in his own shoulder. Wilhelm liked to tell that story at feasts, smacking Hunter on the back and calling him "brother." He had named him captain of the guard not long after, making him the youngest to have lands and a title. Hunter had earned the king's trust a dozen times over.

To Shay, he was simply Hunter—her father's most trusted swordsman, the boy who had taught her about horses, who gave her riding lessons while he told her tales of far-off battles. She grinned up at him now, clutching the little raven. "We're going to the stables before breakfast—since it's a special day," she informed him. "Come with us, please."

Hunter turned. "I'm afraid I have other duties this morning, your Majesty."

"Come along, then," Wilhelm said, winking at Hunter.

Wilhelm and Shay stepped out into the courtyard. Snowflakes kissed her cheeks and melted in her hair. She tipped her head back, laughing, and stuck out her tongue to catch them.

"Careful," Wilhelm warned, though he was smiling. "If you slip and break something, your mother will say it's my fault and forbid you horses forever."

"She wouldn't," Shay protested.

He didn't answer. Shay chose not to notice.

They crossed the courtyard and ducked through the larger of the stable doors. The smell of hay and warm animal musk enveloped them. Horses snorted greetings from their stalls, ears flicking forward.

"Happy birthday, Your Highness," called the stablemaster, bowing awkwardly with a pitchfork in his hand.

"Thank you!" Shay chirped, bouncing on her toes.

Wilhelm's eyes sparkled. "We do have one small surprise," he said, nodding to the stablemaster who grinned and opened the door to the last stall.

A black head poked out, nostrils flaring. The horse was young, not quite fully grown, with a glossy coat like polished obsidian and a mane that fell in a wild curtain over one eye. He nickered softly, curious.

Shay gasped and let out a soft "oh." She whispered, "He's beautiful."

"My princess," Wilhelm said. "Meet Grimm."

She inched closer, extending her hand the way Hunter had always taught her. Grimm sniffed her fingers, then lipped at her sleeve. She giggled as his warm breath tickled her wrist. "Does he... does he belong to me?" she asked, hardly daring to hope.

"He belongs with you," her father said. "His coat matches your hair, after all. It seemed only right."

Emotion flooded her eyes. She blinked them away and threw her arms around his wide middle. "Thank you, Papa. I'll take such good care of him, I promise."

"I know you will. The two of you will grow together." He kissed the top of her head. "You have his feed and training to worry about now, so you'd better eat a very large breakfast. Can't have you tired in the saddle."

They spent a few blissful minutes there, Shay stroking Grimm's nose and whispering secrets into his twitching ear, Wilhelm watching them with a softness on his face he wore for no one else.

From a high window in the east tower, another pair of eyes watched a very different scene.

Chapter Two
A Mirror and A Murder

Q UEEN LIORA'S CHAMBERS WERE warmer than any other room in the castle. She had sent her attendants away shortly after waking that morning. Braziers burned in all four corners, filling the air with the scent of juniper and mint. Thick rugs muffled the sound of footsteps, and heavy curtains billowed faintly around the canopied bed.

The only truly cold thing in the room was the mirror. It hung on the far wall, tall enough to show a person from head to toe, framed in dark, intricately carved wood. Its surface, when Liora was not speaking to it, looked like still water in a deep well: reflective, but with a shadowed depth that made it hard to look away.

Now, the queen stood before it naked. Her skin, warmed by candlelight, was the color of cream. Lips plump and crimson beneath two perfectly symmetrical almond eyes, veiled in long dark lashes. Her hair cascading down to the small of her back, ebony and glistening. Her backside was round and full, curving up over flared hips before turning sharply inwards to a narrow waist. Her legs and arms elongated and slim, leading to pointed fingers and toes. Her breasts were full and high, nipples pink against pale skin. She possessed a body nearly unmarked by the hunger pangs of her poor, peasant start in life. Although childbirth temporarily stretched her skin, her youth and ritualistic oil care cured her of any sagging. Yes, the queen was truly beautiful in face and body. A look that had turned the heads of nobles and peasants alike. And she knew all this. She had studied herself the way soldiers studied maps.

Liora dipped her fingers into a bowl of perfumed oil and began to smooth it over her shoulders, down her arms. The oil glistened on her skin, catching the light as she moved. She watched herself with intent concentration, as if seeking imperfections. Liora turned sideways, running her oiled hands over the flat plane of her stomach, the swell of her hips. Her thoughts flicked back, unbidden, to the winter market many years ago, when she wore rags and had frostbitten fingers and the hunger in her belly had been for bread, not crowns. Men had stared at her then, too. She had learned quickly that their eyes were a kind of coin, and she could spend what they offered.

"Mirror, soul of silver and glass," she said, voice low and almost entranced, "who in this land shall I never surpass?"

The surface of the glass shivered, the way pond water ripples when a stone is dropped. The dim reflection of the room blurred and then sharpened again—into the image of Liora herself. Not a different version. Not a kinder one. Simply her, as she was, flawless and formidable. A slow smile curved her lips. She tilted her head this way and that, admiring the way the light picked out the angles of her cheekbones, the arch of her brows. "Of course," she murmured. "Who else would it be?"

"Peasant," one merchant's wife had spat at her back then. "Shameless." Now those same kinds of women bowed to her.

"The king would give you anything," she whispered to her reflection. The glass did not answer. It never did. It only showed her what she already knew. "A kingdom, a war, his heir. All for this." She cupped her breasts, lifting and dropping gently. "For me."

She crossed to her dressing table, where gowns in rich jewel tones hung from carved hooks. She chose one of dark amethyst that clung to her curves, the color making her eyes look even blacker. As she slid the fabric over her skin, there was a knock on the door.

"Enter," she stated.

The man who stepped inside moved with the easy grace of someone used to wearing steel. Hunter bowed his head out of habit, the deference he gave her practiced but sincere. "Your Majesty," he said.

"Hunter," she said, settling onto the cushioned stool before her smaller, ordinary mirror. "Come in. Close the door. It's cold in the hall."

He did as she asked, though the room was already warm enough that a bead of sweat slid from his temple. Up close, the scars on his forearms and hands were more visible—pale silver lines mapping old battles. It was duty that brought him here now.

"Out there," Liora said, nodding toward the window as she dipped an eye brush into kohl, "your king walks in the snow with my daughter."

Hunter stepped nearer, curiosity getting the better of him. From this height, the courtyard looked like a child's toy scene. He could just make out the portly figure of Wilhelm crossing the yard with a much smaller, cloaked shape skipping at his side.

Liora's mouth twisted. "Such a doting father," she drawled. "I suppose he means well."

Hunter glanced at her reflection, but his gaze was respectful, not lingering. "He adores you both, Majesty."

"Mm." Liora leaned forward to draw a precise line along her upper lid. "Yes, I'm aware." She looked up then, past her own image to the scene outside. Wilhelm had stopped in the middle of the courtyard to say something to the girl. Shay tilted her head back, laughing as snowflakes landed in her hair.

Liora's eyes narrowed. "Look at her skin," she said lightly, though her fingers tightened on the brush. "So pale it almost disappears against that snow."

Hunter followed her gaze. "Aye," he agreed. "Like a little ghost."

"As white as snow," Liora repeated. She laughed, the sound bright and sharp. "Snow White. That's what she looks like. That's what I shall call her from now on." The name tasted bitter and sweet on her tongue—an endearment and an insult all at once.

Outside, Shay laughed again, the sound lost on the wind. Inside, the queen smiled at herself in the glass, at the man who served her husband, at the kingdom she believed rested entirely in the palm of her perfectly manicured hand.

Hunter smiled faintly, because the queen was amused and because he was loyal enough to echo her. He shifted his attention back to the window, measuring the distance between king and guard, between stables and gate, as any good captain would. "Fitting, Your Majesty." Hunter echoed, "Snow White."

• • • ● ● ● ● • • •

THE FIRST TIME SHAY rode Grimm outside the castle walls, the world felt big enough to swallow her whole. Snow had stopped falling an hour before, leaving the sky a pale, watery blue. Sunlight broke through in thin shafts, catching on ice-rimmed branches and glittering the blanket that covered the fields. The air was so cold it bit the inside of Shay's nose.

Grimm stamped in place as the stable boy tightened his girth. His breath steamed in short puffs, dark ears flicking back and forth. "He's eager," Shay said, running a mittened hand down his neck. The black colt—still young, but broadening—arched his crest and snorted, tossing his mane like a proud peacock's feathers.

"He matches you today, Highness," the boy said, grinning. "Black against the white."

Shay laughed. "We'll disappear together." She could feel the eyes of the guards on the battlements as she put her boot into the stirrup. Hunter had doubled the patrols since the last rumors of raiders along the river. But for this one day, no one had tried to tell her no.

"Ready?" King Wilhelm called from the gatehouse arch, his cloak hitched against the wind.

"Yes!" Shay swung up into the saddle. The familiar warmth and breadth of Grimm's back settled under her, comforting as a hug. She squeezed her calves, and he immediately started walking.

"Stay within sight of the walls," Wilhelm said, commanding and protective. His gloved hand closed briefly over her ankle, grounding. "The guards and I will watch you from the tower. Any trouble, you turn and ride back. Straight line. You understand? And stay away from the western ridge. The mining caravans are moving today, and those men are too rough for a princess's eyes."

"Yes, Father," she said dutifully. She liked how he always explained things like she was capable, not fragile.

He gave her a brief, approving nod and stepped back. Wilhelm lifted his hand. "Let them see you, Shay," he said, voice booming through the open gate. "Let them see how strong the blood of this kingdom runs."

She could not yet grasp the politics hidden behind his words. She only knew that when the gate chains clanked and the portcullis rose, something inside her rose with it. Shay clicked her tongue. Grimm surged forward. For a moment they were under the shadow of the gate, stone pressing in on both sides, cold dripping from the arch like water. Then they burst out into white light. Grimm's hooves threw snow behind them as he broke into a canter, then—when she leaned forward and let the reins slip—a full, pounding gallop. Wind tore at Shay's cloak and burned her cheeks. Her hair whipped out from beneath her hood like a black ribbon. She laughed, the sound snatched away by speed.

The castle shrank behind them: walls, towers, banners all turning into a gray line against the sky. Ice crystals kicked up by his hooves hung in the air like diamond dust, pricking at her exposed skin with a thousand tiny, freezing kisses.

Ahead, the field rolled away in gentle dips and rises, dotted with dark, leafless trees. A flock of pigeons rose from a hedgerow, their wings a disorganized flutter. Shay steered Grimm along the edge of the frozen creek. The ice gleamed, frosted white. She imagined they were racing some thin, silent twin of themselves, reflected in the glass. "You're magnificent," she told her steed, leaning forward to pat his neck.

"Faster, Grimm. Show them what we can do." He obliged, stretching under her with powerful strides. Each push of his hindquarters vibrated up through her bones. She felt every muscle moving, every breath. They were one creature: black against white, heartbeat against frost. For a little while, she wasn't a princess in a castle. She was just a girl on a horse, flying. She only knew the fierce, clean joy that filled her lungs like cold light.

When at last she eased Grimm back to a trot, then to a walk, his sides were damp under the saddle blanket. Steam rose from him in faint curls. Shay's toes ached from the cold; her fingers stung as she flexed them on the reins. "We should go back," she said softly, though every part of her longed to keep going, past the line of the forest, down into the hills. "They'll worry." Grimm flicked an ear back as if he'd heard and reluctantly shortened his stride.

Shay turned him toward the distant shape of the castle and urged him into an easy trot. As they rode, she twisted in the saddle to look over her shoulder, committing the wide white world to memory. "Someday," she whispered. "Someday we won't have to turn back." Grimm shook his head and snorted, and it felt like agreement.

• • • ● • ● • ● • •

S HAY HADN'T SEEN THE curtains twitch in the high tower window as she left the castle's safety. She didn't see the shadowed figures watching her go.

Far above the courtyard, Queen Liora did not notice her daughter's joy at all. Her attention, as always, was fixed on herself. Hunter stood in his simple captain's coat, sword belted at his hip, shoulders squared out of habit. The scar at his jaw caught the light. He was a good man. Loyal. Brave. Trusted. Useful.

"Close the windows," she said softly. "I don't like the light from the courtyard on my skin." He obeyed without question, crossing the room with measured strides to draw the heavy curtains. The chamber darkened, shadows deepening around them. Now only the braziers and the mirror cast light. When he turned back, Liora walked toward him—not hurried, not hesitant, but with the slow, easy confidence of someone who knows exactly what every shift of her hips does to the person facing her. "Your king is out in the snow, playing with a horse," she said. "My daughter clings to his hand like a burr. And you"—she let her gaze climb deliberately up his body, from boots to throat "—you come when I call."

"It is my duty," Hunter said, though his throat worked as he swallowed.

She stopped in front of him, so close he could smell the oil on her skin and the faint salt of her sweat. Tilting her head, she studied his face. "Is that all it is?" she asked. He met her eyes then. Too honest, she thought; that had always been his problem. There was heat there, yes, and need, but also something softer. Something that would have to be used carefully.

"I serve the crown," he said. "The king, the realm... and you, my queen."

"Then serve me," Liora said. As she spoke she dropped her dress from her shoulders, letting it fall smoothly to the floor, caught only for just a moment on the perk of her nipples. Her hands rose to his chest, fingers brushing the leather over his heart. She felt the drum of it, hard and fast. She smiled and slid her palms up to his shoulders, then around his neck. The move brought her naked body flush against his clothed one. He sucked in air, and she felt him tense, then give, like metal being heated and bent.

She liked that. She liked it very much. "You talk so well on the training field," she murmured, letting her mouth hover near his ear. "All those orders, all those shouts. Let's see how well you speak for me."

Her hands worked at the fastening of his coat. He didn't stop her. When the leather fell away, she pushed him back toward the open space of bare stone before the mirror. His boots scuffed on the floor. The back of his heels hit the edge of the cushion where she had been kneeling, tripping him. With a small, surprised grunt, he went down. She followed, straddling him in one smooth motion. The stone beneath the cushion was still cold. Hunter felt it through the thin layer, the chill a stark contrast to the heat of the woman now settling over his thighs. His hands came up automatically, hovering at her waist, not quite daring to touch.

Liora took them in hers and placed them where she wanted them. "Do you know why you are here?" she asked.

"Because you sent for me," he said, breathing already uneven.

"Because I can," she corrected. "Because when I crook my finger, even the king's most trusted man comes running." Color rose along his throat. She watched it with interest. "Tell me," she said, arching slightly so that her breasts brushed against his tunic. "What do you see?"

He swallowed again. His eyes flicked up to the mirror in front of them and then back down, as if afraid to be caught looking at the wrong thing. "I see my queen," he said. "Beautiful."

"Not good enough," she murmured. "Surely you can do far better than that."

Her hands slid down his abdomen, slow, unhurried, until they met the stiffness already rising beneath his belt. She pressed the heel of her palm there and felt him jerk. "Use your words, Captain," she said, voice a velvet blade. "You command men with them. Command me."

"Liora," he rasped. "You're... you're the most enticing thing I've ever seen. Your skin, your mouth—" He broke off with a ragged exhale as she ground down just enough to make him feel it. "The way you move. The way everyone in a room turns toward you, like they can't help but look."

"Better," she said, approving. "What else?"

He obeyed because he always obeyed. He described her—her hair like midnight silk, the curve of her hips, the exact shade of her eyes when she was amused versus when she was angry. He spoke about the first time he had seen her, filthy from the road but already luminous, walking beside Wilhelm's horse like she deserved to be there more than anyone.

With each word, she guided his hands, his body, steering him where she wanted him. His praise grew less coherent as she took control, but the meaning did not change: she was everything to him. Beauty, power, center.

The mirror watched them both. It showed the queen riding her captain as if she were claiming a throne: back straight, chin lifted, gaze on her own reflection even as her hips moved. Hunter, on the floor beneath her, clung to her like a drowning man, the muscles in his arms straining. His thick manhood throbbed deep inside her, stretching her with every thrust she demanded.

His sounds were rough, unpolished—low groans, bitten-off curses. Hers were deliberate. Every gasp, every moan was shaped as carefully as her kohl line, calculated to push him further, to pull her own pleasure tight. She ground her hips in slow, teasing circles, feeling the friction build against her swollen slit, her bare breasts bouncing with each deliberate roll. Sweat glistened on her oiled skin, making her curves shimmer in the candlelight that flickered across the opulent room, heavy with the scent of juniper and their mingled arousal. "Tell me," she demanded as his control began to fray, as his fingers dug into her oiled skin, bruising her thighs with desperate grips. "Tell me who holds your loyalty."

"You do," he said without hesitation, voice breaking. "You, Liora. Always you. You are the one I would burn for." His eyes dark with unspoken devotion, locked onto hers, the vulnerability in them twisting something sharp in his chest - a secret fire that fueled his every surrender.

She laughed, breathless, delighted. "Good boy." The words pushed him closer to the edge, but she was not ready yet. She slowed just enough to keep him there, hovering at the brink, her center smoothing around his length as she lifted almost off him before sinking back down, torturing them both with the denial. Her own pleasure coiled low in her core, hot and demanding.

"Look," she hissed, grabbing his chin and forcing his gaze up to the mirror. "Look at us." He did. In the reflection he watched the way her body moved over his, the way her nails raked trails over his heaving muscles. He saw his own face—young, hungry, unguarded. "What do you see now?" she asked.

"Power," he said hoarsely. "Yours." The words escaped him like a prayer, his hands sliding up to cup her full breasts, thumbs circling her hardened nipples, drawing a hiss of approval from her lips.

That made something in her shiver. "Say it again."

"Your power," he repeated, hips bucking up to meet her, driving deeper into her welcoming heat. "You could bring down an army with a look. You could make kings kneel. Your beauty is lethal, intoxicating. I'd die for just one glance from those eyes, for the chance to worship you like this forever." His words poured out, laced with emotion he couldn't hide. His love for her showed in every desperate touch, every reverent thrust.

That pleased her almost as much as the rising crest of her own climax. The affirmations of her allure and command ignited her further, her core tightening around him like a vise, milking him as she chased her climax. She let herself go then, driving him harder, using his body like the instrument it was—her personal throne of youth, flesh, and devotion. Hunter's groans turned to guttural pleas.

When the peak hit, it tore a cry from her throat—a sharp, triumphant sound that surged up from somewhere deeper than her lungs. It echoed off the stone, off the mirror, off the carved beams overhead.

At the same moment, far below, in the courtyard outside the stables, King Wilhelm happened to be walking back through the snow, cheeks flushed from the cold and from watching his daughter ride. He had left Shay with the stable hands, reluctantly agreeing to let her unsaddle Grimm herself—a small taste of responsibility. Wilhelm's boots crunched on the packed path as he made his way toward the main stairs.

Then it came: a sound carried on the still winter air. Muffled by stone, distorted by distance, but unmistakably a woman's cry. Laughter? Pain? He couldn't tell. He paused, frowning, and looked up toward the queen's tower. A curtain fluttered there, briefly, then stilled.

Another sound followed—the faintest echo of something like a groan, lower, longer. Wilhelm's heart gave an odd, hard thump. He had never liked eavesdropping, even accidentally, on other people's privacy. But that had sounded... wrong. Or perhaps it was only that he was unused to hearing his wife make any sound that was not carefully shaped.

He hesitated.

"Majesty?" a guard called from the archway. "Is everything all right?"

Wilhelm forced a smile. "Yes," he said. "Of course. I

thought I heard..." He trailed off. What would he say? That his queen had cried out and it had made something cold slide down his spine?

He shook his head. "Never mind." He climbed the stairs, boots ringing on stone, the echo of that cry following him up and up.

When he reached Liora's door, he did not pause to knock. Some uneasy part of him had already begun to form images he did not want to see.

He threw the door open.

Chapter Three

A Royal's Last Breath

T HE BRAZIERS' LIGHT WASHED over the scene in a hot, wavering glow. Liora turned toward him at the burst of cold air. They both froze.

Wilhelm's gaze dropped, stupidly, to where Hunter's body joined his wife's. The reality of the scene—his most trusted man buried deep inside the woman he had raised from the gutter to share his throne—hit him like a physical blow. His eyes widened, the color draining from his face; he took a staggering step back, his hand lifting blindly to his chest as if searching for a wound that wasn't there. "Liora," he said, his voice a torn whisper. "Hunter." The name tasted like ash. For a heartbeat after the king spoke their names, no one moved.

The enchanted mirror loomed behind them, throwing back the scene in merciless clarity. The intimacy of a moment ago turned to something ugly and exposed under the king's gaze. "Liora," Wilhelm said again, as if maybe this time the name would belong to someone else. "Hunter."

Liora's heart slammed once, hard, against her ribs. Then a strange, icy calm slid in behind it, as if a second self were stepping forward, taking control. She let her body go loose and sated, as if they had been interrupted only in some innocent game. Slowly, unhurriedly, she shifted her weight and began to climb off Hunter's lap. "Wilhelm," she said, voice low and lilting. "You startled me."

"Startled?" His voice cracked on the word. "I ... I startled you?"

She rose to her feet beside Hunter and turned to face her husband fully, making no move to cover herself. A smear of saliva gleamed along her throat where Hunter's mouth had been. In another context, she would have enjoyed the way her husband's eyes flickered over her body, unsure where to land.

Now his gaze was not hungry. It was broken. "I—" He dragged a shaking hand over his beard. Color had drained from his face, leaving his skin a strange, mottled gray. "How long?"

Liora tilted her head, considering. She could lie, of course. She could say this was a single lapse, a moment of madness. But the truth held its own view. "Long enough," she said.

Something inside him seemed to tear. "I am your husband," he said hoarsely. "I raised you from nothing. I gave you a crown, a place at my side, my child." His eyes cut to Hunter. "And you. You were my brother in arms. I trusted you with my life, with my kingdom, with my family. And this is what you do with that trust?"

"Majesty—" Hunter started, scrambling up, hands out as if he could somehow rewind the last ten minutes by sheer force of will.

"Don't," Wilhelm snapped, the word laced with more steel than he'd used in years. "Don't you 'majesty' me, not while you're—" His hand flung outward, as if warding off the image.

Liora watched him with interest, even as a small, inconvenient pang twitched somewhere near her heart. She had expected anger, yes. Hurt. Perhaps accusations. She had not expected him to look so ... small.

"I should have seen it," Wilhelm said. He laughed, an awful, raw sound. "The way you lingered by her chair at feasts. The way she smiled a little wider when you entered a room. The way your eyes went to her, even when you were speaking to me." He took a step into the room, the heavy furs of his cloak brushing the floor. "I told myself I was imagining things. That my queen was too wise, too devoted, to risk what we had built together for—" His voice faltered. "For this."

Liora's lips tightened. "What we built?" she repeated softly. "You think you built this?"

"This kingdom bears my family's name," he said. "My ancestors—"

"Your ancestors . . .sat on cold chairs and played at war while their wives starved in back rooms," she cut in. "You did not raise me from nothing, Wilhelm. I clawed my way here with my own two hands."

"By spreading your legs," he said, and then flinched as though he'd struck himself.

Liora's eyes sharpened. Hunter shifted, instinctively moving half a step between them, though there was no sword yet in the king's hand. "Careful, husband," she said. "You know who truly rules in these rooms. On that throne."

"And is this how a ruler behaves?" he demanded, gesturing wildly at the cushion, the discarded clothes,

Hunter frantically pulling up his trousers. "Like a tavern whore rolling on the ground with the captain?"

Hunter flinched at the word; Liora's expression went very still. "You were always weak," she said. There was no heat in it, just flat assessment. "Easy to guide. That is why I chose you. A man eager to worship is easier to rule than a man eager to command."

"I loved you," he threw back, the words ripped from him. "I would have done anything for you. I gave you everything you asked for."

Hunter shifted again, uncomfortable. "Majesty," he said, to both of them, trying to find some way to stitch this rift closed. "Please. Let me—"

"Be silent," Wilhelm snapped. His hand went to the sword at his hip, the movement half instinct, half something darker. The scrape of metal leaving leather seemed louder than it should have been.

Liora's gaze flickered to the weapon, then back up to her husband's face. His knuckles were white around the hilt, the blade trembling.

"I could have forgiven almost anything," he said. "A lie, a single moment of ... of madness. But this? In our chamber? With him?" The point of the sword lifted, not quite steady, to aim at Hunter's chest. "You took my wife," Wilhelm said to him. "You took my trust and ground it into the floor. By rights I should hang you from the outer wall and let the crows take you." Wilhelm lunged, overcommitting. His weight came forward. For a split second, his throat was exposed, unguarded, the pulse there jumping like a bird's.

Hunter's hand closed not on the king's arm, but

on the hilt of his own dagger. He lunged in behind Wilhelm, his arm snapping around the king's chest and yanking him hard back against his body. Wilhelm grunted in surprise—and then the dagger's edge kissed his throat.

There was a terrible, suspended moment where steel met skin, where both men could have chosen to stop. Then Hunter's grip tightened. The blade pulled across in a swift, practiced motion. Wilhelm's next inhale turned into a wet, choking sound. A sheet of red opened along his neck, blood welling bright and hot. It sprayed in an arc, spattering Hunter's hand, the stone, and Liora's bare torso.

For the first time that morning, the queen flinched. Her hands flew up instinctively, and for a single, terrifying heartbeat, her mask shattered. Her eyes went wide and white, pupils trembling, gasping in sharp breaths as the sheer irreversible reality of the act crashed into her. The gallows loomed in that silence, closer than they had been since she was a beggar on the streets. Then she swallowed and the steel slammed back down over her gaze.

Wilhelm's sword fell from numb fingers. His hands flew to his throat, trying uselessly to hold in the life spilling out of him. His knees buckled. Hunter eased him to the floor without meaning to—muscles still remembering how to catch this man, how to protect him, even as they killed him. The king's eyes rolled, unfocused, toward the ceiling. His lips moved around words that never quite formed. Blood bubbled at the corner of his mouth. Then his body jerked once, twice, and went slack.

The quiet fell, heavy and thick. It was a suffocating silence, broken only by the crackle of the firelight in the corners, indifferent to the life that had just ended. The room was suddenly too hot. The cloying sweetness of Liora's juniper oil mixed with the sharp, metallic tang of fresh copper—a scent that coated the back of Hunter's throat and made him want to retch.

Liora looked down at the crimson streaks across her breasts and torso. The contrast was stark, almost beautiful in a sick way. She touched two fingers to a rivulet, lifted them, and studied the color. It was darker than the wine she'd drunk at dinner, thicker than the oil on her skin. She had grown up around blood—her own, other people's. It had never frightened her. Now, it stirred a complex mix: revulsion, triumph, inconvenience. "Idiot," she said.

Hunter jerked his head up. "I—he—" He scrambled back from the body, leaving smeared handprints on the floor. "He was trying to kill me. I was only—"

"Protecting yourself?" she supplied coldly. "Is that what you will tell the council when they find you kneeling beside a dead king, your knife at his throat, your trousers undone?"

His hand flew to his waistband, as if only now remembering his state. He fumbled to fasten himself, face turned pale. "I thought—" His voice broke. "You said—"

"I said nothing," she cut in. "You acted. Without thinking. As usual."

He stared at her, as though seeing a stranger. "You told him he was weak. You goaded him. You said he would be killed if he fought me."

"Yes," she said with a shrug. "Hardly my fault if he insisted on proving me right."

"Liora," he said desperately. "Tell me this is what you wanted. Tell me this—"

"What I wanted," she interrupted sharply, "was a king who would do as he was told and a captain who understood which way the wind blew. At the moment, I have one corpse and one fool."

His mouth opened and closed. The blood on his hands was beginning to dry, darkening to rust. "I thought," he whispered, "that I was giving you what you wanted. With him gone, you—"

"Would be a widow with a dead king and a living lover," she finished. "How long do you think it would be before they whispered that I'd had you kill him? Before his brothers and cousins came knocking with armies, claiming the throne had been usurped by a whore and her pet swordsman?"

He flinched at the word, more at the coldness in her voice than the insult itself.

She crossed to the door and listened for a moment. The corridor beyond was quiet. No shouts. No running feet. No one had heard. Good. "We don't have long," she said briskly. "Help me."

"With—what?" His voice sounded hollow.

"Making sure I don't hang," she snapped. "Do you want your little act of passion to lead us both to the block? Or do you want me on the throne, able to shield you from the consequences of your own stupidity?"

Something in him rallied at that—at least enough to move. "What do you need?"

"First, we clean me." She gestured at the blood painting her chest and arms. "If anyone sees me like this..." She went to the washstand and poured water into a basin, dipping a cloth. The water turned pink as she wiped at her skin, methodical as ever. "Open that window," she said over her shoulder, nodding toward the narrow casement set into the far wall. "We'll say an intruder came in that way. A hired blade, perhaps. A robber."

"A robber who somehow made it all the way to the royal apartments without being seen?" Hunter asked, even as he obeyed, shoving the shutter open. Cold air knifed into the room.

"The assassin will never be found," Liora said. "We will weep and curse and say he vanished into the night. People will imagine whatever monster frightens them most. The truth will never occur to them." She wrung out the bloody cloth and tossed it into the hearth. The flames hissed and flared.

"Move him," she said.

Hunter stared at her. "He's heavy."

She gave him a look. "You have carried him before."

That memory twisted the knife in his gut. Once, on that northern field, Wilhelm's weight had been a reassurance—proof that the king still lived as Hunter hauled him out from under a dying horse. Now, the limp drag of the corpse was obscene. He swallowed bile and bent to the task, sliding his arms under the dead king's shoulders and heaving. Wilhelm's head lolled, blood smearing across Hunter's tunic. He carried the body toward the bed, as if they were merely putting a drunk man to sleep.

"On the floor," Liora corrected. "By the window. Swordsmen don't usually crawl into bed to be murdered." He adjusted course, lowering the king's body awkwardly near the casement.

Liora crossed to the spot where the sword had fallen

and picked it up delicately by the hilt. "Here," she said, setting it near Wilhelm's outstretched hand. "He must look like he tried to defend himself."

Hunter watched, numb, as she stepped back, assessing the tableau: the dead king in his tunic and boots, the drawn sword nearby, the open window with frost creeping along the sill.

"Next," she started and then said to herself, *Scream.*

He blinked. "What?"

She rolled her eyes. "Nothing, you oaf. Next, you leave."

"Leave?"

"Run," she said. "Far and fast. If you stay, the blood on your hands and the guilt on your face will do more damage than any blade. If you go, I can tell whatever story I like."

He shook his head. "I can't abandon you."

"I already have what I need from you," she said coolly. "A dead king and a hole in the succession large enough for me to slip through. If you stay, you are a liability. If you go, you are a convenient absence to blame things on later, if necessary."

His jaw clenched. "So that's it. Years of service. One foolish act. And now you throw me away."

"Spare me your softness now," she said. "I am trying to keep us both alive. If you ride to some distant border town, change your name, keep your head down, they may never find you. If you insist on standing at my side when the body is discovered, they will hang you by sunset. And I..." She let the sentence trail off, letting him fill in the possibilities.

He looked at her a long moment. He saw no love in her eyes, no trace of the softness he'd imagined. Only sharp calculation. "I did this for you," he whispered.

"No," she said. "You did this because you could not bear the idea of losing what you thought you had. Don't make the mistake of confusing your needs with my wishes."

The words sank like stones. At last, he nodded once, the movement jerky. "I'll go," he said.

"Good. Take the servants' stairs. The less anyone sees you, the better. Wash your hands, change your clothes, don't be seen. Then run."

He hesitated by the door. "What will you tell her?" he asked quietly. "Shay. Snow White." Hunter suddenly felt so used, so dirty.

Liora's expression flickered, then smoothed. "I will tell her what she needs to hear," she said. "As I always have."

He thought of the little girl in the snow, laughing between king and queen, trusting them both completely. Guilt crushed him. "Good-bye, Majesty," he said. Then he was gone.

Liora listened to his footsteps fading down the servant's passage. When she was certain he was out of earshot, she walked to the center of the room and drew a deep inhale. The blood was mostly gone from her skin. Her hair was still a bit wild; she adjusted it with quick, practiced fingers. Then she crossed to the mirror.

"Mirror, soul of silver and glass," she rumbled, eyes locked on her own, "who in this land shall I never surpass?" The glass rippled, showing her what she wanted to see: her reflection. "Good," she said.

Then she dressed quickly, pinched her cheeks hard to bring tears to her eyes, opened her mouth, and screamed. The sound tore through the corridor, down stairwells, into the courtyard. Servants dropped trays. Guards jerked to attention. Somewhere in the lower halls, Shay froze with a brush in her hand, stroking Grimm's mane. Within minutes, the queen's chamber was full of people. Liora knelt beside the body on the floor, her dress hastily thrown over her nakedness, the skirt darkening where it lay in Wilhelm's blood.

"My husband!" she wailed, tearing artfully at her hair. "My beloved! Murdered in his own room! Oh, merciful saints, who would do such a thing?" No one noticed the faint, satisfied glint deep in her eyes.

Shay rushed in to see her father's body cold and lifeless on the floor.

Between theatrical sobs, Liora cried, "It's just us now, my dear, Snow White."

• • • • ● • ● ● • •

SIX YEARS LATER WHEN Snow White was fourteen, she still thought of that day as a sharp, clean wound. She sat on an upturned bucket in the stable, Grimm's warm bulk pressed against her shoulder, and told him about it again, as she always did when the ache grew too heavy. "I miss him," she said, scratching gently along his withers. "I couldn't have gotten through it without you."

Grimm snorted softly, tipping his head so that his muzzle nudged her shoulder. She swallowed. The stable smelled of hay and leather and horse, familiar and comforting. Outside, autumn rain drummed softly on the roof. "I heard her scream," she said. "Everyone did. It sounded like the whole castle split in half."

She remembered dropping the brush, stumbling as people rushed past her in the corridor, voices tumbling over one another—*the king, the queen, blood, murder*. She remembered the press of bodies around the chamber door, the way her mother had clung to Wilhelm's still form, shrieking and sobbing until her voice went raw, the way Hunter was nowhere to be found, but he should have been there to protect her father. She remembered being held back by someone's arms as she tried to push through, crying, "Papa? Papa?" over and over. Afterward, her mother had taken her in her arms, pressing Snow White's face into her perfumed shoulder, and wept.

"He's gone, my little Snow White," Liora had said between racking breaths. "Your poor father is gone. Killed by some beast who crept in through the window. I will never rest until I find who did this. Never."

Snow White had believed her. "I loved her for it," she told Grimm now, voice small. "They said she collapsed from grief. That she ordered half the guard to comb the countryside. That she stopped the investigation only because it hurt too much to keep hearing about it." She stroked Grimm's neck, fingers tracing the familiar path of a scar there. "Everyone said she was so strong. So brave. A queen of iron wrapped around a heart of glass." Grimm flicked an ear back, as if skeptical. At fourteen, Snow White believed that grief made people do strange things.

No one questioned that the investigation had ended with no culprit, no trial, no justice. At least not openly. The few councilmen who dared ask why the captain vanished on the same night were found floating in the moat or retired suddenly to distant estates with heavy purses. Fear, it turned out, silenced a court faster than loyalty ever could. No one remained but the ghosts of what-ifs that sometimes hovered at the edge of Snow White's thoughts at night.

She leaned her forehead against Grimm's neck. "You helped me," she murmured. "When they told me he was gone. You're the only one I could be ugly with." Grimm sighed, his breath warm against her hair. Snow White smiled faintly.

The stable door creaked. She looked up swiftly, half thinking—hoping—it might be Hunter come back after all these years. Some said he'd gone after the assassin. Others whispered darker things.

But the noise was only a stableboy, carrying a sack of feed. He bobbed his head and hurried past. Snow White exhaled, tension easing. She straightened from her perch and brushed straw from her dress.

· · · ● ● · ● ● · · ·

THAT NIGHT, AS RAIN tapped at the tower windows like insistent fingers, Queen Liora stood naked and oiled before her enchanted mirror and studied her reflection. "Mirror, soul of silver and glass," she said, the words like a trance, "who in this land shall I never surpass?"

The glass rippled. As always, it showed her—the same

flawless face, the same ageless skin. Time had not yet dared to leave its mark. "Good," she breathed. But her thoughts did not stay on herself. They slid sideways, unbidden, to another face: a younger version of her own. The resemblance was growing sharper each year. Shay—Snow White, as the servants had taken to calling her by Liora's decree—was no longer a child. At fourteen, she was all long limbs and coltish grace, her features just beginning to settle into the kind of beauty that turned heads in hallways.

Liora had noticed the way a young page had stumbled over his own feet when the girl passed, the flush on an older noble's face when Snow White smiled up at him, innocent. She had seen the way the sunlight caught on her daughter's unbound hair as she ran across the courtyard, turning it into a black river. The queen's fingers tightened on the edge of the dressing table. "Too soon," she whispered to her reflection. "Too close." The mirror did not answer. It never argued. It only showed her what she feared and what she wanted. Liora tapped the table once with a painted nail, decision crystallizing.

The next morning, she summoned her daughter to her chambers. Snow White arrived with her hair loose down her back, a small foolish hope blooming in her chest that perhaps her mother meant to spend the day with her, to talk of Wilhelm, to share memories. It had been so long since they had simply been together.

Liora's ladies-in-waiting melted away at a gesture, leaving queen and princess alone. "My little snow-thing," Liora said. Her voice was smooth, almost warm. "Come here."

Snow White came, her slippers whispering on the

rugs. "You wanted to see me, Mother?"

Liora's gaze swept over her—over the fall of that dark hair, the glow of youth in her cheeks. "You are growing," she said.

Snow White smiled, uncertain. "That's what girls do, I think."

"Some grow into something dangerous," Liora said softly. Before Snow White could puzzle that out, her mother's hands were in her hair. "At least this can be corrected," Liora went on. "Stand still."

A chill skated down Snow White's spine. "What are you doing?"

"Protecting you," Liora said. "There are eyes everywhere. Ever since your father—" She paused, letting her mouth tremble delicately. "I will not see you taken from me by some assassin who caught you in the wrong place at the wrong time."

"What does my hair have to do with that?" Snow White asked, confusion tinged with fear.

"Pretty things attract attention." She picked up a pair of shears from the table. The metal glinted. "Attention can be fatal."

Snow White's heart started to beat faster, and the bile rose in her throat. "Mother..."

"Hush," Liora said. "Do you trust me?"

Snow White did. "Yes."

"Good girl." Liora gathered a thick rope of hair at the back of her daughter's head, twisted it once, then raised the shears. The first cut was the worst. The sound of metal grinding through hair was louder than Snow White would have imagined. She felt the sudden, shocking lightness as a great dark weight fell away down her back. She made a small, wounded sound.

"Don't be vain," Liora said sharply. "It's only hair. It will grow again. Or not, as I choose." More snips followed. Liora was not careful. She hacked the hair to chin-length in rough, uneven chunks, not bothering with symmetry. When she was done, she turned Snow White toward the mirror.

The girl barely recognized herself. Her once-silken river of hair was now a ragged frame around her face. She looked younger somehow, and yet harsher. Exposed. "There," Liora said. "Less... conspicuous."

Snow White swallowed, blinking hard. "Mother, I—"

"You've been spending too much time in the stables," Liora said, cutting across her. "Your gowns are ruined by straw and mud. It's wasteful."

"I'm sorry," Snow White said automatically.

Liora moved to the wardrobe and flung open the doors. Silks and velvets gleamed inside, a rainbow of luxury. "These are no longer appropriate," she said. "For now, you will wear this." She turned, holding out an armful of coarse, grayish cloth. A simple dress, the kind a kitchen maid might wear. No embroidery. No lace.

Snow White stared. "That's... that's not a princess's dress."

"It is a safe dress," Liora said. "No one pays attention to a girl in rags. Assassins do not waste arrows on stable hands."

"But—"

"You spend half your days down there anyway," Liora went on, as if she hadn't spoken. "You may as well look the part."

Snow White's throat tightened. "Are you—are you sending me away?"

"Don't be dramatic," Liora said. "You will stay here, inside the castle walls. You will not leave them without my express permission. Not to the village, not to the forest, not even to the courtyard if I say no."

Snow White's chest caught. "But I've always—"

"Your father was too lenient," Liora snapped, the first real flash of anger showing. "See where it got him."

Tears burned at the corners of Snow White's eyes. "Mother, please. The walls feel so—so small. I can't—"

Liora gripped her shoulders, nails biting lightly into flesh. "Listen to me," she said, each word a slow drop of poison coated in sugar. "There are people in this world who would hurt you just to hurt me. You are all I have left. Do you understand? If I must turn this castle into a prison to keep you breathing, I will."

The words wrapped around Snow White's heart like chains and a blanket both. She nodded slowly. "All right."

"Good," Liora said, smoothing her tone again. "Then we understand one another."

Within a week, every mirror in the castle, save the enchanted one, was gone. The great gilt frames in the hallways vanished, leaving ghost-pale rectangles on the stone where the sun had not touched for years. The little oval glass in Snow White's room was smashed by a silent servant who did not meet her eyes. She begged him to leave the broken mirror, and he obliged the princess.

"Why?" Snow White asked, standing in the empty space where her mirror had hung.

Her mother's answer was simple. "So you will not spend hours mooning over your own reflection like a tavern girl with a new ribbon," Liora said. "Vanity is unbecoming."

The castle changed around her as well. The bright banners were taken down, replaced with heavier, darker tapestries. The windows were draped in thicker curtains, shutting out more light. Music in the great hall grew rarer. Laughter in the corridors died away. Only in Liora's chamber did the candles still burn twice as bright, reflecting in the single forbidden mirror as the queen asked, again and again, who was fairest. The answer never changed.

Even so, sometimes, late at night when the corridor outside her daughter's room was quiet, Liora would pause and peer in at the sleeping girl. In the dim light, with her hacked hair mussed on the pillow and her mouth softened in sleep, Snow White looked heartbreakingly like the girl Liora herself had once been—before hunger and men and crowns.

"She will be beautiful," Liora whispered once, to herself or the dark. "Too beautiful." She shut the door softly and went back to her mirror.

Chapter Four

The Fairest

B Y THE TIME SNOW White turned sixteen, the chopped hair and rags had stopped feeling like a punishment and had become a uniform. It didn't matter. Nothing her mother did could hide what she was becoming. Liora had watched the girl bloom with a small, possessive smile, seeing her own features echoed in the girl's face. But as the courtiers began to look past the queen to the princess, that smile thinned, then vanished entirely, replaced by the cold, unblinking stare of a predator realizing its prey has grown teeth.

Snow White stood in the shadow of the stable arch, rubbing a handful of straw between her fingers, and watched the thin line of light slide across the yard as the sun dragged itself over the eastern wall. The air was cool, damp with the faint promise of spring, and smelled of wet stone and horses. Her dress was still a shapeless gray thing that hung from her shoulders like a sack. Her hair, which Liora hacked off every few months with the same careless efficiency, barely brushed her jaw.

Grimm's head snaked out of his stall window, lips questing until they found the rough wool of her sleeve. He tugged once, insistent. "All right, greedy," she said, "I know what that means." She ducked inside and found the little sack of apples she always kept hidden behind a bale of straw. The only person who pretended not to know it was there was the stablemaster, who had long ago given up trying to be strict with the king's daughter in disguise. "You're my only friend, you know that?" she murmured to Grimm as she poured a meager handful into her palm and offered it. He lipped them up with gentle enthusiasm, tickling her skin. *The books*, she thought, *and you. That's it.* The mare in the next stall whinnied, begging for an apple.

Her days had settled into a dull rhythm since her mother's new rules took hold. Mornings in the stables, grooming or riding Grimm around the castle courtyard. Afternoons, if she was lucky, in the corner of the library, losing herself in stories of far-off lands and forbidden love. Evenings, always in the queen's sight—at meals, in the suffocating quiet of the tower, nothing to see, nothing to do, no one to talk to. Only the stables felt like a remnant of the life she'd had before. Only Grimm remembered the girl who had flown over snow-blanketed fields instead of walking circles within stone walls.

"Do you think I'm foolish?" she asked him now, brushing his neck in slow strokes. "To still dream about...all of it? About someone seeing me and not just seeing her shadow?" Sometimes she knew it was silly to talk to her horse as though he could answer, but Grimm shook his mane and munched on his hay. It was not an answer, but it wasn't a no. Snow White smiled.

She had read about family, friendship, and most especially love in the stolen hours on the library floor. Pages that smelled of dust and ink had shown her princes who crossed oceans for their beloveds, warriors who laid down their swords at a single glance, girls with hearts so bright they melted curses. None of those heroines wore rags or had their mirrors taken away. Sometimes she pressed her hand to her chest and wondered what it would be like to feel that sort of burn there. To have someone look at her as if she were the whole story, not just a character in her mother's.

As she pondered, she heard a name she hadn't heard in years that turned her world sideways again. She was walking through the courtyard back to her quarters when a whisper rippled through the servants crowding near the gate. The guards parted for a rider on a dark, mud-spattered horse. The man swung down heavily and pushed back his hood.

"Captain Hunter!" someone exclaimed. "By the saints, it's really him."

Snow White almost dropped her bundle. Hunter's return was like seeing a ghost. He looked older, mid-twenties now, and stronger. The lines at the corners of his eyes were deeper, his jaw more sharply cut, his hair a darker shade of brown. But his shoulders were as straight as ever, his stance the same blend of readiness and ease. She had always considered Hunter a friend, since he was only around ten when she was born, they had sort of grown up together. Hunter taught her everything about horse care and riding. She was devastated when he left, losing her father and friend all at once.

He had disappeared the night her father died. One moment he'd been everywhere—on the walls, in the training yard, at Wilhelm's right hand. The next, he was gone. Some said he'd ridden out in pursuit of the assassin who'd slipped in through the king's window; others muttered that grief had driven him to the borderlands.

No one knew for certain. Liora had ordered that his name not be spoken in the halls. She had wept and raged and then, very pointedly, not asked anyone to find him. And yet here he was, eight years later, riding through her gates as if nothing had happened.

Snow White ducked behind a pillar, heart racing, and watched as her mother swept down the stairs like a storm. "Hunter," Liora said, her voice an odd blend of cool and something that might have been relief, or calculation. "You took your time."

He bowed low. "I came as soon as I received your summons, Majesty."

Snow White hadn't heard what else they said; a sharp word from the steward sent her hurrying on. But later that day, she found herself crossing the training yard more slowly than usual, intrigued by this young man who had returned to her life.

Hunter was there, as if no time had passed at all, barking orders at a line of young guards with swords in their hands and fear in their eyes. "Again," he said. "You're not peeling potatoes; you're defending a gate. Stance—good. Now swing with your whole body, not just your arm." She felt her cheeks flush as she noticed his hair had gotten longer and the brown curls sat flat against his face from the sweat on his brow.

Snow White tried to slip past the edge of the field unseen. She had almost made it.

"Princess," Hunter said, turning at just the wrong moment.

The title hit her like a forgotten song. Very few people still used it to her face. She stopped, clutching the book she'd been on her way to return to the library. "Captain," she said, suddenly aware of the mud on her hem and the way her hacked hair refused to lie flat. Her cheeks blushed and she could smell dust and sweat as he approached. He took a step toward her, then another, dismissing the recruits with a jerk of his chin. Up close, she could see the new scars tracing pale lines along his knuckles. She had missed him so much.

"You've grown," he said. It was such a foolish, obvious thing to say that she almost laughed, but something in his gaze stole the humor from it. His eyes, once she had thought them steady as stone. "Do you remember me?" he asked.

"Of course," she said. "How I've missed you," she murmured as she threw her arms around him. He wasn't the young soldier she remembered. He was solid; he was a man. She was so happy he had returned that she didn't want to let him go.

He smiled at her genuine warmth. Then his gaze dipped down, lingering just a fraction of a second too long at the curve of her chest where the rough fabric pulled against her.

The back of Snow White's neck tingled. Something about the look was different from all the casual glances she'd collected in the corridors since she had flowered into womanhood. Those had been curious, admiring, sometimes clumsy. This felt heavier, like a hand. She shifted her weight, hugging the book closer to her chest, covering herself. "I'm glad you're home," she said. "Maybe you can take me for a ride sometime. Outside the castle walls?"

"Home," he echoed, as if tasting the word. "Yes. We'll see. My job is to keep you safe for now, Princess. Your mother's orders."

He smiled again then, but this time Snow White saw it for what it was—a man trying to reassure, even as something darker swirled behind his eyes. She told herself she was imagining things.

Still, in the weeks since his return, she caught Hunter watching her more than once. In the yard, from the far end of the great hall, from the shadow of a staircase. Always he looked away when she caught him. Always a fire brewed low in her core afterwards.

• • • • • • • • • • •

"COME ON," SNOW WHITE said to Grimm, patting his neck. "Before the day grows long."

She led him out into the castle yard, past a pair of kitchen lads hauling sacks of grain and a pair of guards who pretended not to notice that the ragged girl with the horse walked like she owned the stone beneath her feet.

Liora's edict still held: Snow White was not to leave the castle walls without explicit permission. Today, that permission had been grudgingly given—she was to exercise Grimm "within sight of the gate" and nowhere near the village. Snow White smiled, knowing it was likely Hunter's doing that allowed her finally outside the castle perimeter.

She swung herself into the saddle with practiced ease. The leather creaked, familiar as a sigh. She settled her weight, gathered the reins, and nudged Grimm into a trot.

They rode straight for the main gate, weaving between piles of firewood and a cart of barrels. Snow White let him stretch his legs a little more along the outer wall, the cobbles ringing under his hooves. From the parapets above, guards watched, some with wary eyes, some with thinly hidden admiration. She didn't notice any of them. "Not too fast," she pleaded, though her whole body wanted to push him into a gallop. "Not until we get outside."

He flicked an ear back, then complied, settling into a steady rhythm that pulled a sigh of pleasure from her. They approached the main gate. Beyond it, she could see the tops of trees, the faint line of the hills. They were finally going to be reunited with the vast meadows of green grass. Each rise and fall as they got closer soothed something inside her.

She was almost there when trumpets blared from the gate tower. Grimm snorted, ears jerking forward, and he half-turned to run back to the safety of the stables. Snow White reined him in, turning him back towards their freedom. The heavy gates were opening. A company of riders came into view beyond the portcullis: men in rich cloaks and polished armor, their horses' tack glinting with metal. At their head rode a man draped in dark fur, his crown a heavy band of gold around his brow. A visiting king.

This was not the first intrusion they'd seen—in fact, since Wilhelm died many lords and princes and kings had visited Queen Liora, likely attempting to win her over and request a partnership in marriage.

But something about this time felt different. Snow White had noticed Liora had been making plans. The throne room had been polished with care that morning.

The great stone floor gleamed. Tapestries depicting conquests and alliances—each one embellished since Wilhelm's time to give Liora a more prominent place in the stitchwork—hung proudly on the walls. Candles blazed in iron chandeliers, making the air shimmer. Servants poured from castle gateways to line the approach, heads bowed. The steward scuttled forward, wringing his hands. Somewhere above, Snow White knew Liora would be watching from a window, calculating.

Grimm danced under her. She patted his neck, exhaling, "Easy, boy," even as her own curiosity sparked. She guided him to the edge of the yard, out of the main path, and watched the procession enter. The visiting king sat on his horse like a man very aware of his own importance. His mouth was thin, his eyes sharp, his cloak lined with something that looked uncomfortably like ermine. She always thought wearing fur seemed cruel, not regal.

Behind him rode a handful of knights and attendants. One of them caught Snow White's eye without meaning to—a young man with hair the color of ripe wheat and eyes so clear a blue they seemed almost unreal. Her breath held. The young man's gaze brushed past her, lingering just long enough for her to feel it. His brows drew together slightly, as if something about the sight of a ragged girl on a fine black stallion had puzzled him. Then the procession moved on, swallowed by the grand doors.

Snow White took a deep breath. "Did you see that?" she asked Grimm. She shook her head, trying to dislodge the image of those eyes.

· · ● ● ●· ● ● ● ·· ·

O N THE THRONE AT the far end of the hall sat Queen
Liora, dressed in a gown of deep red velvet that
hugged her curves and spilled like blood over the steps. The
hue of her dress matched her perfectly lined red lips and
accentuated the cream of her skin. Her crown, adorned
with diamonds from the local mines, caught every scrap of
light from the candles. Her ladies-in-waiting stood arrayed
behind her like a jeweled fan. She had chosen this throne,
these colors, this tableau with care. She knew what story she
wanted the visiting king to carry back to his own land.

"Announcing His Majesty King—" the herald began,
rattling off a string of titles. Liora let the words wash over
her. She watched the man himself: the way he moved, the
way he held his shoulders, the set of his jaw. Strength, yes.
Pride. A touch of vanity, judging by the glittering rings on
his fingers. Good.

He strode down the carpeted aisle toward her, cloak
swinging. At the base of the steps, he bowed. Not deeply
enough for Liora's taste, but more than some had. "Your
Majesty," he said. His voice was rich, practiced. "It is an
honor to stand before you at last."

She smiled, slow and warm. "The honor is mine," she
lied. "I have heard much of your kingdom's strength. Your
armies are said to be unmatched in the north."

"They are," he said, with the easy arrogance of a man
not used to being contradicted.

"Then I am doubly pleased you have come in peace,"
she said. "We value strong neighbors." Her fingers trailed

along the carved arm of the throne, drawing his eye to her hand, to the flash of gems there. She knew men watched what sparkled. Next she drew her hand back to her chest, adorned with a golden necklace feathered with sapphire gems quarried from her own lands. The necklace lay strategically just above the line of her low-cut dress, revealing ample cleavage. As she fingered the jewels she flashed her eyes back up at the king through heavily painted eyelashes which she batted a few times as if she needed more allure.

"Ahem," the king spoke, clearing his throat. "I value strong alliances," he replied. "Especially with those who know how to wield both the sword and subtler weapons." His gaze traveled over her, appreciation clear. She let it.

"Come." She rose gracefully, descending the steps to stand before him. "Walk with me, and tell me of your lands." She laid her hand lightly on his forearm. The touch was chaste by court standards, but the way she did it—thumb resting just so, fingers curling with calculated intimacy—made it feel like more. They walked the length of the hall, talking of roads and trade and border skirmishes. Liora listened, but she also watched: the way his pupils dilated when she laughed, the way his stance opened when she leaned in to whisper a question. By the time they reached the high windows overlooking the courtyard, she knew two things: he was not as clever as he believed, and he was exactly vain enough to be led.

This was the first partnership Queen Liora had truly considered. Sure, other princes and kings from far-away lands had proposed, but the queen was very cunning in the choices she made. She knew this king was from a neighboring lordship to the far west, and a partnership between the two of them would give her power and control over the biggest contiguous area in all the land. She knew this was her chance to really have it all. The only piece left in this puzzle was whether or not she would be able to control this man as she had so many others. The prospect looked good, almost too easy.

"Your men ride well," she said, letting her gaze drift to the yard below. From here she could see a small dark figure on a black horse galloping in the meadow beyond the castle. Even at this distance, she could see the chopped hair and rags.

The visiting king followed her gaze. "Yes, my heir among them," he said. "A fine rider, if not yet as seasoned as I would like. He has never tasted battle. His heart is too soft."

Liora noted the faint impatience in his tone. Fathers always wanted their sons to be more, faster. "He looks strong," she said.

"He will make a good match," the king said. "In time."

Liora smiled. "As will we all, if the fates are kind." She let her hand slip from his arm, fingers brushing the front of his tunic. "You must be tired from your journey," she said. "Shall we retire to a more comfortable room to continue our ... discussions?"

He caught her meaning. "Gladly." She led him to a side chamber off the throne room—a smaller, more intimate space with a lower ceiling and a generous hearth. Intricately adorned stained-glass windows lined one inner wall, and maps of all the nearby kingdoms lay rolled up on the table in the corner. Once the door closed behind them, she dismissed all but one of her ladies with a wave. Even that one she sent to the far side of the room to busy herself with a ledger.

Then she turned her full attention to the king. "Tell me," she said, moving closer, "what you seek from this visit." He spoke of trade, of shared borders, of bandits in the passes. She listened, nodding, adjusting her posture so that each time he looked at her, his gaze would find a new line to admire: the angle of her neck, the dip of her waist, the swell of her hip beneath velvet.

At one point, as she stepped past him to pour wine, she let her hand trail—just so—across the front of his breeches. His breath skipped. "Careful, Your Majesty," he said, an edge of amusement in his voice. "Your servants might talk."

"They talk no matter what I do," Liora said lightly, handing him a goblet. Her fingers brushed his as he took it. "I've learned to give them something worth whispering about." She leaned in to whisper something in his ear—something about the long winter nights and how easily two kingdoms might keep each other warm. The exact words mattered less than the warmth of her breath, the scent of her perfume luring his nose closer. His free hand settled on her waist, then slid a fraction lower.

Across the hall, in the doorway of the throne room, Hunter paused. He had been on his way to report a minor skirmish on the eastern road. The steward had told him the queen was with the visiting king and he'd almost turned back, not wanting to interrupt political business. But a movement in the corner of his eye had caught his attention. Liora's gown, a flicker of the visiting king's fur cloak, their proximity by the stained-glass window. He stood in the shadow of the arch, half-concealed by a pillar, and watched. Watched Liora laugh and tilt her head back so that her throat was exposed in that way he remembered. Watched her hand sweep casually down the front of the foreign king's tunic, lingering over the bulge that had not been there a moment before. Watched the king's fingers flex on her waist.

Rage rose in him so fast it made his vision narrow. It was not that he believed she owed him fidelity. Years and miles and blood lay between the day he'd slit Wilhelm's throat and this moment. He had no illusions anymore about what Liora was capable of, or what she wanted. But some stubborn, painful part of him had still clung to the idea that what they had shared—that tangled mix of lust and loyalty and misplaced worship—had been real. That she had not simply replaced him with the next man who could bring her more soldiers, more gold, more land. He had been a fool. His hand clenched into a fist at his side.

In the side chamber, Liora's laughter floated faintly through the half-open door, bright and practiced. Hunter could not hear the words, but he had heard that tone often enough to imagine them. He did not barge in. He did not make a scene. For all his turmoil, he was still a soldier, and soldiers knew how to withdraw. He turned on his heel and stalked away down the corridor, boots ringing on stone.

Chapter Five

Blue Eyes and Beating Hearts

H UNTER'S THOUGHTS CHURNED AS he went—memories of her body under his, of her lustrous hair sweeping his bare chest, her bountiful breasts in his hands, of the sweet taste of her lips on his. Virility in his body rose and intertwined with rage as those memories of love were quickly followed by memories of the blood on her skin, of the way she had sent him away like discarded armor, of his new realization that she never felt the same about him. And here she was again, using the same tactics, the same arch of the spine, the same tilt of the mouth, on another man. By the time he pushed open the side door that led to the stables, his jaw ached from clenching it.

He crossed the straw-strewn floor in long strides, heading for his horse's stall. His horse, a plain brown gelding with a white star on its forehead, tossed its head and shifted restlessly in the stall as Hunter approached. Animals always seemed to sense when their riders carried lightning under their skin. The animal lifted its head, sensing his agitation. "Easy," Hunter demanded. "Easy, I said, goddammit."

His hands shook as he reached for the bridle. With each heartbeat, the image of Liora's fingers on that man's lap grew sharper. The idea of her lying under someone else, arching and gasping and whispering those same words—his vision went red around the edges. He yanked the bridle too hard. His horse tossed its head, whites of its eyes showing, hooves clattering on the planks.

"Stand still, you stupid beast!" Hunter snapped, slamming a palm against the horse's shoulder. The horse jigged sideways, bumping the stall wall, knocking Hunter back. His temper flared.

From outside the stables, Grimm approached, Snow White astride. They had finished stretching their legs for the day and she was ready to retire to the library when she noticed commotion inside the stables.

Then she saw the way Hunter drew his arm back, hand open, yelling, as if to strike again, this time on the frightened horse's face.

"No!" Snow White cried with a sudden gulp of air.

At that very moment a knight appeared—the boy from the king's processional—he jumped towards Hunter, grabbing his wrist from behind to stop the attack.

The young knight was dressed plainly—white riding coat, metal armor—but everything about him marked rank: the quality of the fabric, the shine of his armor, the easy balance in his stature, the way he'd moved without hesitation into the path of Hunter's anger.

"Unhand me," Hunter growled, low and dangerous.

The boy didn't flinch. "Gladly," he said, "so long as you leave this stable at once."

For a heartbeat, silence. Hunter's ears burned. He yanked his arm free more roughly than strictly necessary and stepped back from the gelding, who seized the opportunity to plant all four hooves as far from both men as possible.

Hunter reached for his sword. Before he could summon a cutting reply, he became aware of Snow White watching them from Grimm's back. He froze, his hand stinging from the impact. He couldn't look at the horse. He couldn't look at the girl. Shame, hot and acidic, flooded his throat, and he turned on his heel.

But her eyes were wide, not with disgust now but with something like fascination. The young man must have felt her gaze as well, because he turned. For a moment, the world in the stable seemed to narrow to the space between them.

He lifted his hand slightly, palm open, in a gesture halfway between greeting and reassurance. "Apologies," he said to her, as if this were his mess to atone for. "We came in loud."

Snow White swallowed. Her heart, which had been beating fast with worry for the gelding, stuttered for an entirely different reason now. Up close, she could see wheat-blonde hair and clear blue eyes that seemed, in that moment, to see only her and nothing else. His mouth was strong and soft at the same time—a mouth that would, she realized with a kind of dizzy horror, be very easy to imagine on hers.

"I..." she began, then stopped because the words in her chest were all tangled. "Thank you," she managed at last, nodding toward the brown horse. "For... for that."

He smiled, and it hit her like a physical thing. Not a practiced smirk, not an oily grin, but something open and a little embarrassed, as if he didn't quite know what to do with his own face. "Couldn't just stand by," he said. "He wasn't doing anything wrong." He nodded at the gelding. "Only feeding off of his rider's energy."

Snow White's lips twitched. "People shouldn't hurt animals," she said quietly.

"I agree," he replied, and something in the way he said it made her feel as if they'd just discovered a secret language. "We have to be their voice, since they cannot speak for themselves."

For a second, the sounds of the stable faded—the stamping horses, the distant wind—leaving only the drum of her own pulse. It wasn't just that he was handsome; she had seen handsome lords before, parading through the great hall. It was the way he looked *at* her, not *through* her. Most people looked at her and saw a problem, an object, or a ghost of the queen. He looked at her and saw... a girl. A girl who liked horses.

"Are you all right?" the young man asked, brows raised as he looked up at her. "He didn't scare your horse?"

"Grimm's seen worse," she said, patting the stallion's neck to steady her own trembling hand. "He only gets nervous when I do."

"Smart," the stranger said. "Knows to trust good judgment."

When he said that, her stomach flipped. She tried to convince herself this was only gratitude, only the relief of someone stepping between anger and an innocent creature. But as she really looked at him—at the way the light from the stable door softened the line of his jaw, at the way a dimple creased his cheek when he smiled again—another feeling bloomed, bright and frightening and sweet.

Is this...? she thought, half breathless. *Is this what those books meant?* Her heart seemed to be everywhere at once: in her throat, in her ears, in her fingers gripping the reins.

She became suddenly self-conscious—of her crooked hair, of the smell of manure on the bottom of her boots, of the smear of dust on her cheek she hadn't wiped off properly that morning. She fought the wild urge to smooth her rags, to tuck her hair behind her ears, to make herself look like the princess she was.

"May I?" he asked, gesturing toward Grimm's shoulder.

It took her a second to realize he was asking permission to come closer. That he thought he needed it. "Yes," she said quickly. "Of course."

He stepped in, hand out, letting Grimm sniff his fingers before stroking the stallion's neck. "He's beautiful," the young man said. "Strong. Proud." He glanced up at her. "Like someone else I just met."

Heat rushed to Snow White's face. She was glad, for once, of the stable's dimmer light. "I'm not—" she began automatically, then stopped, not wanting to argue herself out of a compliment from the first person who had looked at her in years. She slid one leg over Grimm's back to dismount, then hesitated. The ground seemed further away than usual. Or perhaps it was simply that the idea of being on the same level as this boy, face to face, made her more nervous than any high saddle.

"Here, let me help you," he offered, seeing her pause.

She didn't need help. She'd been slipping off Grimm's back like a cat since she was eight. But there was something in his earnest expression that made her nod. "All right," she said.

He moved to her side, hands lifting, careful not to touch her until the last possible moment. As she swung her leg over and slid down, his palms settled lightly at her waist.

The contact shocked her.

His hands were warm and strong through the rough wool, fingers spanning her easily. Her own hands, which had been gripping the saddle, fluttered awkwardly for balance, then landed for a second on his shoulders, which were more muscular than she expected. For that heartbeat, their bodies and breaths aligned. She felt the rise and fall of his chest under her fingertips, the faint rasp of fabric under her palms, the steady strength in his grip. She began to feel like the floor was spinning.

Her boots hit the straw. He did not let go at once. "Steady," he murmured.

"I am," she said, then quickly unsure if he was talking to her or Grimm. "Steady, I mean."

He smiled again, and this time there was a hint of shyness in it, as if he was as startled by their nearness as she was. They were standing very close now, barely an arm's length apart. She could see the deep blue ring around his irises, the tiny freckle at the corner of his mouth, the way a lock of hair refused to lie flat over his forehead. No one had ever told her about love or what it felt like. She didn't know that falling in love could feel like stepping off the edge of a cliff. It was as if every book she'd ever read had gathered itself into a synchronized chorus of *this—this is what we meant.*

"Thank you," she said again, softer now, the words carrying more than one meaning.

"You're welcome," he replied, his own voice lower than before. "Any decent person would have done the same."

But she knew, and somehow he seemed to know too, that what had just passed between them was not something "any decent person" did every day. Grimm snorted, as if to reclaim her attention. Snow White startled slightly, then, desperate to do something with her hands, reached past the young man to the cloth bag hanging from a peg on the wall. It knocked lightly against his shoulder as she fumbled with the ties.

He stepped forward half a pace, misreading the movement. His eyes flickered down to her mouth. For the barest instant, he leaned forward, like a man drawn by gravity.

She felt the air change between them, warmer and tighter. Her own body, responding before her mind could catch up, tipped forward a fraction.

Time stretched.

He closed his eyes, just a little, as if bracing for impact.

Snow White's hand found an apple in the sack. Her fingers curled around it like a lifeline.

She turned her head, reaching past his temple, and the moment shattered.

She lifted the fruit over his shoulder.

"Here," she said brightly—to Grimm, to herself, to the entire awkward universe. "Someone's earned a treat." The stallion nickered. Glad for something safe to do, Snow White pressed the apple to his muzzle. Grimm's strong teeth crunched through the skin. Juice ran over her fingers.

The young man blinked, realization and mortification

chasing each other across his face. "I, ah—" He cleared his throat, stepping back fully now. "Of course. The apple. For the horse. Naturally."

Heat climbed Snow White's neck. "Obviously," she managed. "What else would it be for?" They both laughed then, a touch too loud, a touch too quickly, the sound covering everything neither quite dared to say.

To salvage what little dignity he could, the young man reached for the sack as well. "May I?"

"Be my guest," she said.

He pulled out another apple, this one a little smaller, and turned toward the brown gelding. The horse eyed him with suspicion, then, tempted by the scent of fruit, inched closer. The young man held out the apple flat on his palm, making soft, soothing noises. "There," he said under his breath. "See? We're friends. No one's going to hurt you today."

Snow White watched him, something tender unfolding in her chest. There was an ease in the way he moved around the animals, a patience that matched her own. When the gelding finally snatched the apple, their hands brushed as she steadied the bag. Just a graze of skin against skin. It was enough. A spark shot up Snow White's arm. Her cheeks burned. She was shockingly aware of every place her body existed in space—her fingertips, her toes, the hollow at the base of her throat where her pulse fluttered wildly.

He looked up at her, eyes wide for a half second as if he'd felt the same jolt. Then he ducked his head, smiling into his collar in an attempt at nonchalance.

Above them, unseen, a curtain in the tower window

shifted. Queen Liora, watching from on high, saw only enough to know everything she needed: her daughter on a magnificent black horse, a handsome young prince closer than any man had been allowed to stand in years, the air between them crackling with something new.

Her hand clenched on the windowsill. "Interesting," she murmured, and the word was anything but pleased.

Chapter Six

The Queen's Fury

L IORA DID NOT BELIEVE in coincidence. She believed in timing. In patterns. In threats. The moment she saw the way Snow White and the visiting prince looked at each other in the stable yard, a cold, familiar fear slid into her gut. Not again, it whispered. We will not do this again. She had carved her path to the throne with her beauty. She had learned every way it could be used—for her, against her, over her. She had seen how easily men's loyalties shifted when a younger, fresher face appeared. Now her own daughter—her mirror's ghost—was starting to draw glances the way Liora once had. This could not be allowed. She turned from the window before the scene below could fully play out and swept back into the throne room, skirts swirling behind her like spilled wine.

The visiting king sat in the high-backed chair to her right, a goblet in hand. He was speaking to one of his advisors, gesturing to a map laid across the nearby table. His knights lounged further down the hall, trading quiet jests.

Liora did not smile as she approached. The mask she wore now was colder, sharper.

"Majesty?" the visiting king said, looking up at her change in air.

"Our discussions are concluded," Liora said. "You will

leave at once!"

The table went still. A drop of wine slid down the outside of the king's goblet. "I beg your pardon?" he said slowly.

"Now!" she repeated. Was it anger, jealousy, or fear behind her perfectly painted eyes?

A flush crept up his neck. "We had an understanding. A ball tomorrow night. Time to deepen our alliance—"

"Our alliance," she said, "no longer interests me." In truth, it did. His armies were strong. His coffers full. A union between their kingdoms could have paved a swath of influence across half the continent.

But none of that mattered if her throne—her *mirror*—was threatened.

The king was a man of pride and didn't need to hear another word. He inclined his head—too sharp to be called a bow—and gestured to his men. "We ride," he said. "Make haste."

Chairs scraped. Boots thundered. In moments, the grand hall that had been prepared for feasting and dancing felt more like the mouth of a cave disgorging an angry beast. As they swept past her, the king's entourage split around Liora like water around a stone. She did not move. Her eyes were not on them.

"Hunter!" she called.

He had been lingering near the side entrance, jaw tight from the scene in the stables, anger barely leashed. At her call, he straightened, masking his turmoil under duty. "Yes, Majesty," he said, stepping into her path.

"Bring me Snow White," she said. Her tone could have etched frost onto the tapestries. "At once."

• • • ● ● • ● ● • •

Down in the stables, Snow White was trying to find her courage. She wanted to ask the knight's name. Before she could speak, a commotion rose from the direction of the courtyard. Shouts. The sharp tone of the steward trying to make his voice heard over the clatter of boots. The young man's head snapped up. The shouts grew louder. Someone called for him down the corridor. "Your Highness!"

He winced. "That would be my cue."

Your Highness? Her chest froze, the words rearranging everything she thought she knew about him. He was a prince. Before she could speak again, his attendants appeared in the stable doorway, faces tight.

"Your Highness," one said, catching his breath. "We have to go immediately. Your father is already halfway out the gate."

The prince took a half step toward her, then stopped, clearly torn between impulse and decorum. In a moment of reckless gallantry, he caught her hand in his and raised it gently to his lips. His mouth brushed the back of her knuckles. The warmth of that brief touch seared into her skin. Her heart thundered so loudly she was sure Grimm could hear it.

At that moment, two of the king's men, frustrated by the prince's hesitation as they were being hurried out, grabbed the prince by each arm in a big commotion and started to pull him. Something near the prince's chest went *snap* as the men grabbed him. In three strides he was at the door, his attendants falling in around him. In six, he was swallowed by the corridor shadows. A small object slid free unnoticed by everyone—a simple silver token on a cord from around his neck, oval and worn from years of handling, stamped with the image of a falcon in flight.

Snow White stood very still, the stable suddenly too quiet. From the yard, hoofbeats pounded on stone as the visiting company was rushed toward the gate. "They're leaving," she whispered to Grimm. "He's leaving." Her chest ached in a way that felt wholly new and yet eerily familiar, like a tune she'd heard only once but could hum by heart. She moved to the stable door, drawn as if by a string, and peered out. She dropped her head in sadness or in anguish from the chance to almost have something, and lose it before she even learned his name.

As she stared at the ground something caught her eye. A silver token. She swallowed. Her fingers closed around the token almost without her permission. The metal was warm from his skin. She closed her fingers over it, pressing the metal hard enough to sting. She retied the necklace and slipped the cord over her own head, tucking the token under her dress, where it lay cool and solid against her skin, just above her heart. All she thought of was the feel of his hands at her waist, the look in his eyes when he'd said *let me help you*, the weight of silver between her collarbones.

And somehow, impossibly, it felt like she had just lost something vital. "Fool," she whispered to herself, cheeks damp. "You are a fool." But she didn't believe herself.

The stables were not empty for long. The relative quiet shattered as the side door banged open with force enough to make the hinges protest. Snow White straightened instinctively, hand falling from her chest. Hunter filled the doorway, shoulders nearly brushing the frame. His expression dragged the temperature in the room down ten degrees.

"Princess," he said, and the old endearment sounded wrong in his mouth now. "The queen wants you." His hand shot out and closed around her wrist before she could reply. Pain shot up her arm. His grip was hard, fingers digging into her skin, the opposite of the careful steadiness she'd felt only minutes before.

"Ow," she said, trying to twist free. "Hunter, you're hurting me."

They passed a pair of servants in the corridor. The maids pressed themselves flat against the wall, eyes down, as Hunter dragged Snow White between them. One of them glanced up just long enough to register the redness already blooming on the girl's wrist.

"Could you at least loosen your grip?" Snow White hissed when they turned a corner and the hall emptied. "You're not hauling a sack of grain."

"I'm sorry," he said. His tone had slid into something low and almost... ashamed. "The queen is very upset." Hunter noticed that the girl in his grip moved like Liora, smelled like Liora, and even her voice sounded like Liora's.

"I did nothing wrong," she protested through gritted teeth as the doors to the throne room loomed ahead. Her pulse roared in her ears. The token under her dress felt suddenly heavy, as if pressing her heart further down into her ribs.

"Your queen will be the judge of that," Hunter replied.

He stopped before the great carved doors, shoving them open with more force than was strictly necessary. "Majesty," he called into the echoing hall. "I've brought her."

His hand loosened at last, and Snow White stumbled forward into the cold light of her mother's gaze, the memory of a knight in a white riding coat and silver armor still echoing in her heart.

Chapter Seven

Beauty is Pain

B Y THE TIME SNOW White turned eighteen, the castle had completely forgotten how to glitter. But it remembered—for one night.

For the first time in a long while, the great hall thrummed with preparation. Servants scurried up and down ladders to hang fresh banners. Chandeliers were lowered on creaking ropes so maids could polish each candle cup until it shone. Musicians tested strings and reeds in a corner, their hesitant notes echoing off the vaulted ceiling. She often listened to servants and maids as they gossiped about the guest list, hoping she would hear of a king and his son, of a prince, any clues she could gather. She wanted to ask her mother, but was never able to muster the courage.

From the narrow window of her tower room, Snow White watched the courtyard bloom with color: lords and ladies arriving in carriages, their cloaks flashing jewel tones against the cobbles; grooms leading unfamiliar horses to the stables; guards in dress livery relieving the weary men from the walls.

"Look at them, Grimm," she said, pressing her forehead against the glass. Her breath fogged a circle through which the world appeared softer, dreamlike. "It's like the old days. Before." Down below, she could just make out the black shape of her stallion's back as he paced his stall, unsettled by the influx of strange horses. "I miss you," she whispered.

Two years ago was the best and worst day of Snow White's life. She had met the boy of her dreams. His hair, his eyes, his touch, everything about him made her swoon, yet their encounter was so brief. Liora had chastised Snow White for the meeting, claiming the boy was a stranger and she could have been hurt. "You're too naive," "think of your father," "how can I keep you safe?" and other declarations hurled at her by her mother, while Snow White tried unsuccessfully to tell her mother of the prince and their instant connection. Liora's mind had already been made up. Under the guise of protection, Liora told Snow White she was no longer allowed to leave her tower. That meant no roaming the castle, no rides outside with Hunter's permission, no rides at all. She wasn't allowed in the stables at all. Snow White cried and begged her mother, tugging at her dress as she wept on the floor like a child, but it was no use. She hadn't seen Grimm, except in stolen glances from her window, in two long years.

Her heartbreak was immense that day. She wondered if heartbreak was all she would ever know. Each time she felt content it was met with a shattering of herself, of a loss so unimaginable. The last two years were full of isolation—she had no friends, and no means to visit them even if she had. Besides brief lectures from her mother at meals or short exchanges with Hunter as she passed in the hallway on the way to the library at the very top of the tower, she rarely interacted with another being at all. She was desperate for some attention, for someone to talk to, for someone to be near. She had all but forgotten what it felt like to have the warmth of her father's love surround her in a blanket of security.

But tonight was the ball. Tonight things were different. Snow White was elated at the thought of all the guests. *I can't wait to talk to someone, anyone. I'll sway to the music, I'll laugh, and maybe someone will ask me to dance.* With still hours before the ball, she was eager to get ready and put on a dress instead of the simple rags she'd become so accustomed to.

She caught sight of herself in her broken wall mirror—one of the few that had escaped Liora's purge because it was so broken it barely reflected. Her chopped hair, grown out now to just brush the tops of her shoulders, framed her face in uneven layers. No amount of smoothing ever tamed it. Still, even in the distorted glass, anyone could see what the mirror in Liora's chamber had known for some time: whatever the queen tried, Snow White's beauty was ripening.

She thought of a ball she'd read about in one of her favorite stories: a girl in a dress made from her dead mother's curtain dancing under a crystal chandelier, the prince besotted at first sight. "Ridiculous," she told her reflection, even as her heart whispered, *maybe.*

Her fingers went to the cord around her neck as if by habit. The falcon pendant lay warm against her sternum where it always rested, hidden under her clothes. She closed her hand around it and, just for a heartbeat, let herself imagine what it would be like if he walked through the great doors tonight. It had been two years. Two long, gray years of chores and curfews and the constant, haunting knowledge of her mother's gaze. Two years of tracing the edge of the token whenever she felt too small, too invisible, reminding herself that once, someone had seen her. "Fool," she whispered, though without heat. "You're still a fool."

· · · · ● · ● ● · · ·

"MIRROR, SOUL OF SILVER and glass, who in this land shall I never surpass?" Entranced, Liora repeated her ritual. As she stood naked and oiled in front of her mirror, she noticed an odd sensation—nerves? She had seen her daughter's beauty growing and noticed her changing body over the past few years. When Snow White smiled Liora felt a pang of jealousy wash over her.

The mirror morphed with a familiar ripple, and for the first time since she'd acquired it from an old peddler in her mother's village, did not show Liora her reflection. Instead, it showed the image of Snow White—naked in the bath, skin silky and firm, black hair stringy and wet, breasts perky and sudsy with soap, nipples resting just below the surface of the water, cheeks flushed with warmth, and lips a natural deep crimson.

Liora was taken aback at the sight. Almost in horror. She thought it must be a mistake. She asked the mirror again, and again the mirror showed her daughter getting ready for the ball. Liora suddenly regretted everything—regretted telling her she could attend the ball, regretted allowing her to the stables the day the king and prince visited, regretted allowing any freedoms, regretted having a daughter at all. Liora was jealous, not only of her daughter's beauty, but of her purity. Snow White was an effortless, innocent beauty, but Liora had taken a more twisted path to the throne. Each time Liora's power was threatened she refocused and did what was necessary to maintain her superiority, and each time, over time, she had allowed Snow White's kindness and charm soften her again.

But not this time. The betrayal of her mirror was the most jarring moment Liora had ever experienced. Never again. Never again will anyone, anything threaten Liora's beauty, her power. She knew what must be done.

$$\bullet \ \cdot \ \bullet \cdot \bullet \ \bullet \cdot \bullet \ \bullet \cdot \bullet \cdot \ \cdot$$

A knock sounded at her chamber door.

"Snow White," came Liora's voice.

"Yes, Mother," she called. "Come in."

The queen swept in without waiting for permission. She wore amethyst tonight. Not the deep crimson of her throne room gown, but a deeper shade, like the evening sky just before the dawn. The fabric clung to her like water pouring over her curves. Her hair was piled high, adorned with a crown of diamonds and gold. Her face was a work of art—thick black lashes, lips painted bright apple-red.

Beside the queen, Snow White felt more like a girl playing dress-up. She was almost giddy with excitement, readying herself many hours too early for the evening's agenda.

Liora's gaze made a slow, measuring sweep down her daughter's form. "Well," she said at last, "let's find you something sensible to wear tonight, without holes." She moved toward the wardrobe, snatching a corset and slamming the door. "Hurry up," she insisted. "You move like the slow drip of honey."

Snow White obeyed, stepping into the undergarment.

Liora said. "Turn around."

Snow White hesitated. Something in her mother's tone had an edge she didn't recognize.

"Now," Liora snapped.

Snow White turned, offering Liora her back.

The queen's fingers closed around the laces at once. For a moment, the sensation was almost comforting—a faint echo of childhood mornings when Liora had brushed her hair and hummed while she plaited it.

"Lift your arms," Liora said.

Snow White did. The corset shifted, sliding slightly lower as the queen tugged.

"At least you have posture," Liora scoffed. "All that riding did something besides ruin your shoes." She gave the laces a firm pull.

Snow White felt that same nauseated feeling when her mother first cut her hair. The corset bit her ribs. She winced. "That's... tight," she said.

"Corsets are meant to be tight," Liora replied. "Beauty is pain." She tugged again, harder this time. The whalebone dug into Snow White's sides. Air fled her lungs.

"Mother," Snow White gasped. "Wait—just—a little—"

"You want to look perfect tonight, don't you?" Liora said, her voice smooth as cream. "All those noble eyes. All those fluttering hearts. You wouldn't want to disappoint them."

The laces pressed into Snow White's torso as she grabbed at the doorframe for balance. "I don't—" she tried. "I just want—"

"What you want," Liora said, "is irrelevant. What you are is a reflection. A reflection of me. A reflection of the kingdom. You must act properly, like a lady, like a princess. Strong, proud. No nonsense tonight."

She jerked the laces again. Snow White felt the world tilt. Dots of light danced at the edges of her vision.

"Stop," she whispered. "Please. It's too—"

"Too what?" Liora asked. "Too much like work? Too much like something you didn't choose?" Her tone was pleasant, her hands, merciless.

Snow White's chest burned. Her lungs felt bound, unable to draw in more than a sip of air at a time. The edges of the room blurred. "Mother," she croaked.

Liora leaned in, lips near her ear. "You begged to be allowed at this ball," she said softly. "You've pestered me for weeks. 'Please, Mother, just this once. Let me have a dress, let me hear the music, let me be there with you.'"

Snow White's fingers slipped on the frame. "I—just—wanted—"

"You wanted." Liora repeated, as if tasting the word. "And wanting is dangerous. For you. For me." Her hands moved faster, tugging the laces until the corset felt less like clothing and more like a cage.

Snow White's knees buckled. She tried to suck in air; her chest refused to expand. Panic flared. Her heart hammered against the unyielding bone, desperate. "Mama," she whispered, the word barely a sound.

Liora didn't stop. "You think this ball is about finding me a husband," she said. "You think some foreign king will win my affection and renew something in my life. You think I will soften, because he will take some of the burden from my shoulders."

Snow White's vision tunneled. The room shrank to the feeling of her mother's hands at her back and the roaring in her ears.

"I will tell you a secret, my little snow-thing," Liora spat. "Husbands are not saviors. They are dogs waiting to be commanded and are lured by the simplest bone."

The words barely registered. Snow White's fingers slipped from the doorframe. She staggered forward. Liora gave the laces one final, brutal yank. Something in Snow White's chest screamed, then went eerily silent. Her head spun. The floor rushed up to meet her. She was vaguely cognizant of falling sideways onto the narrow bed. The last thing she thought before darkness swallowed her was of her father's comforting arms.

Liora stood over her, heart beating only a little faster than usual. She watched the shallow rise and fall of Snow White's chest, counting. Satisfied that the girl still drew breath, she turned at once. Her face, in the shattered reflection of the little mirror, was calm. Not a hair out of place. She turned to the door. The key in the outside lock glinted faintly. Liora stepped out and turned it with a decisive click. "There," she said to the empty corridor. "Safe and sound." Safe from the visiting dukes and lords. Safe from the mirror. Safe from any wandering, treacherous hearts she might catch. Liora's own heart did not ache at all as she walked away.

Chapter Eight

A Mother's Gift

S NOW WHITE DREAMED OF drowning. In the dream, she was at the bottom of the castle well, looking up at a round slice of sky. Her corset was made of stone. She clawed at it with numb fingers, nails tearing, but it would not loosen. Water rose around her, cold and relentless. When she opened her mouth to scream, no sound came out—only bubbles that drifted toward the unreachable opening above.

"Snow White." Her name floated down from the circle of light. Liora's voice. It echoed oddly off the stone. "Poor thing," it cooed. "Always wanting air." The water closed over her head.

She woke with a gasp that turned into a wheeze as pain shot through her side. Her ribs felt like they were on fire. For a moment she didn't know where she was. The room around her swam in and out of focus: familiar stone walls, the narrow window with a slice of daylight showing, the rough wool blanket twisted around her legs.

"Snow White?" The voice came from closer this time—from just inside the room.

Snow White turned her head slowly. The movement made the world sway. "Mother?" she croaked.

Liora stood near the foot of the bed, dressed in a

morning gown the color of cream. Her hair was loose down her back, unadorned. To anyone else she might have looked almost soft. "My poor girl," she said, bringing a hand to her chest in an artful gesture of concern. "You slept through the entire ball."

Snow White's mind scrambled to catch up. "The—ball?" she echoed. The corset shifted under her as she moved. It dug into her still-tender ribs, a vicious reminder. "Wait, what... happened?"

"You must have fainted," Liora said. "The excitement, no doubt. When I came to fetch you, you were already asleep. You barely stirred when we tried to wake you."

"We?" Snow White echoed, trying to remember any touch but her mother's hands on the laces.

"The maid and I," Liora said smoothly. "Don't you recall? No, of course not. You poor thing. You looked so pale. I thought it kinder to let you rest."

Guilt flickered across Snow White's face. "I—I'm sorry," she said automatically. "I didn't mean to cause trouble."

"Nonsense," Liora said. "It's my fault for not realizing how delicate you still are. You need so much protection, my little snow-thing."

Snow White almost laughed at that. Delicate. The girl who'd hauled buckets and mucked stalls for years. The girl whose hands bore calluses where other noble girls had rings. Her ribs throbbed. She winced, hand flying to her side.

Liora's gaze sharpened. "Pain?" she asked.

"Just... sore," Snow White said through gritted teeth. "I think the laces were tight."

Liora's lips curved in a sympathetic smile that never

reached her eyes. "Yes, beauty is pain," she said.

At that, Snow White had a faint recollection.

"But I have something that might make you feel better," Liora interrupted. She stepped closer, reaching into the pocket of her morning gown.

"I thought missing the ball might sting less if you had a little present," she said. "It's been so long since I gave you anything. That was neglectful of me. A mother ought to spoil her only daughter now and then."

Snow White blinked. The bruises on her ribs gave a sharp throb, a warning she couldn't ignore. Suspicion won out over trust. "I don't want it," she said, pulling back against the pillows. "Please, Mother. I just want to sleep."

Liora's smile didn't waver, but the temperature in the room seemed to drop. "Don't be difficult, my little snow-thing," she said, her voice a steely purr. "I went to such trouble." She stepped closer, withdrawing the object from her pocket. It was a comb, gleaming with bone and garnets that looked like drops of frozen blood. It seemed to catch the light and hold the glare, like the jewels were pulsing with a faint, hypnotic rhythm. Snow White stared at them, feeling a sudden, strange lethargy seep into her limbs. She tried to look away, to scramble off the bed, but her body felt heavy, pinned by the Queen's gaze.

"No," Snow White whispered, the word barely forming on her lips. Something about the comb felt sinister.

"Hush," Liora commanded. She moved with a speed that was terrifyingly graceful, sitting on the edge of the bed and gripping Snow White's shoulder. Her fingers were like iron bands. "You used to love when I brushed your hair.

You used to be such a good girl."

"Mother don't—" Snow White gasped, raising a weak hand to push her away.

Liora caught her wrist easily, pinning it to the mattress. "Beauty is obedience," she murmured. She raised the comb, her eyes flashing with a dark, silent power that froze the air in Snow White's lungs. "Let me make you perfect."

Before Snow White could scream, Liora drove the comb into the hair at her temple. As soon as the first point scraped across her scalp, a strange sensation washed through her. It was not like the brief, sharp sting of a snag. It was a spreading, numbing cold, then a rush of heat that made her vision flicker. Her hand spasmed. The comb's teeth bit fully into her skin.

"Oh," she said faintly.

"Beautiful, isn't it?" Liora said. Her tone had shifted. There was a hungry, almost eager edge to it now. "Here, let me." The queen grabbed the comb and brushed a second time, raking the teeth across her daughter's scalp.

Snow White tried to push the comb away. Her fingers wouldn't obey. They felt heavy, distant. A dizzy wave surged up from her feet to her head. The room tilted. "Mother?" she whispered. "I feel—" Sleepy, she meant to say, but her tongue felt thick. The word tangled somewhere between her mouth and her mind. Her knees buckled. This time, when she fell, there was no bed to catch her. She hit the floor with a dull thump, the sound muffled by the rug. The comb remained tangled in her hair, its venom—magic or something darker—already pulling her under.

"I will finally be rid of you now," Liora confessed,

watching her daughter's body slacken. One hand twitched once, then lay still.

For a moment, the queen simply stood there. Then she smiled. Not the brittle mask she wore in the hall. Not the charming curve she used for suitors. A small, private, satisfied smile. She looked down at the girl—so young, so foolish, so trusting. "Good girl," Liora mocked. She stepped forward and toed Snow White's shoulder lightly with her slipper, as if checking whether she might startle awake. Nothing.

Footsteps sounded in the corridor—light, like a maid's. Liora glanced around. She wasn't expecting to be interrupted. Satisfied that the girl was dead, she opened the door a crack and peered out into the hallway. Two maids scurried by, towels in hand. The queen quietly stepped out into the hallway, closed the door, and darted towards her room.

Chapter Nine

Into the Woods

Night fell heavily on the castle. Clouds smothered the stars. Moonlight seeped only faintly through the narrow tower windows, turning stone to silver and shadow. On the floor, Snow White lay like the dead. Her breathing was shallow but steady, her limbs slack. Time dripped past in thick, dreamless drops. At some point, the comb slipped from her hair and clattered to the floor. No one was there to hear it. An hour passed. Two. The castle quieted. Then, somewhere deep inside Snow White's slumber, something stirred. A memory of fingers at her ribs, of the corset's merciless grip. A flash of blue eyes in a stable. The feel of Grimm's warm breath on her cheek.

Her lungs spasmed. She sucked in a ragged breath that turned into a cough. Her body convulsed once, twice. Her eyes flew open. For a moment, she had no idea where she was. The room loomed around her, familiar and wrong at the same time. Her sides throbbed. Her head felt full of cotton. The comb lay a foot away on the rug, its delicate vines suddenly sinister. She stared at it.

The memory of sliding its teeth into her scalp came back in a sickening rush. The cold. The tilt. The way her mother's voice had sounded just before the world went black. Her hand went to her ribs, fingers tracing the deep, tender bruises left by the corset laces. Her mother's hands. Her mother's voice saying, "Beauty is pain."

The tightness in her chest was not only physical now. It was something else pushing outward: a dawning, terrifying realization. "She did this," Snow White whispered into the dark. "She did this. Again." The rags, the hair, the imprisonment, the corset, the comb. All of it clicked into place. "She's trying to..." The word stuck. She forced it out. "Kill me?" Saying it out loud made it real. Tears formed at the corners of her eyes. Not the hot, helpless kind she'd cried into Grimm's mane when her father died. These were sharp, cold, like ice splinters. *Why?* Her heart wanted to ask. *Why? I'm your daughter. Your daughter! The princess! Father would never have... I loved you, even when you were cruel. I excused you, even when you hurt me. I blamed... How can you... Your own daughter! Why—?*

Snow White pushed herself upright, swaying. The room spun for a moment, then steadied. Her head pounded. Her legs trembled when she swung them over the side of the bed. She stood anyway. She crossed to the window and pressed her hands to the cold stone frame. Outside, the night waited. The courtyard was mostly empty now. Torches burned low along the walls. A few guards paced the parapets, dark shapes against a darker sky. Far below, in the shadow of the outer wall, she could see the stable roof. "Grimm," she whispered. The name was both a plea and a promise. Her mind skittered over the possibilities.

She could stay. She could confront Liora, demand answers, throw the comb at her feet and say *I know what you did*. Her bruised ribs throbbed in response. No. If she stayed, she would die. Maybe not tonight. Maybe not tomorrow. But eventually, when Liora found a poison that lingered longer than this one, a trap that didn't leave room for waking.

She was eighteen, with no money, no allies, no map of the world beyond the castle walls. She had no friends, no skills, no protection. She had been coddled all her life and hidden away from the world. She had only what she could carry and what she knew of the woods from glimpses through barred gates.

And yet. She had a horse. She had a body that, for all its bruises and aches, was strong. She had lived half a life in the stables and halls; she knew how to move quietly, how to make herself unseen. Most of all, she had a desperate, clawing need to stay alive.

"Once upon a time," she said, "a princess ran away."

She didn't allow herself time to think further. Thinking meant doubt. Doubt meant paralysis. She moved. She grabbed the plainest cloak she owned—a rough brown thing more patch than fabric—and swung it over her chemise, not bothering with a proper dress. She snatched a small sack from under her bed and shoved into it what little she had that might be useful: a heel of bread, a waterskin, a stub of candle, flint, and a knife left from the kitchens.

Her fingers closed around the falcon token beneath her shift. She hesitated, then tucked it safely back against her skin. Leaving that behind would be like leaving a piece of herself. She crossed to the door and put her ear to it. Silence. The key still sat in the lock on the other side. Snow White smiled without humor. Liora had always been so careful about keeping her in. She had never thought to guard the window.

Snow White pushed the small casement open. Night air clawed at her skin. The drop to the ground below was dizzying. But just below the window, half buried in shadow, a stone ledge jutted out—the ornamental lip of the tower. From there, she could see the faint outline of the jutting stones that led down to a lower roof. She'd climbed these walls as a child, before the rules tightened. Little princess fingers had found holds where grown men's hands would have slipped. Her palms were calloused now. That might help.

She took one deep breath, tasting fear and old dust and something like hope. Then she swung a leg out the window. The stone was cold under her bare hands. The wind was vicious; it snatched at her hair and bit through her thin cloak, threatening to peel her off the wall like a dead leaf. She made the mistake of glancing down. The courtyard was a swimming abyss of shadow, the cobblestones so far away they looked like pebbles. Vertigo washed over her, a sickly swooping sensation in her gut.

Her warm bed was right behind her. The cage was safe. The cage didn't require her to dangle over nothingness. "Move," she commanded her frozen limbs. Her fingers gripped the sill until her knuckles went white. "Don't look down," she muttered. "Just don't look down." She eased herself out, belly scraping the rough edge, until she hung for a moment by her hands alone, legs dangling over nothing. Then she let go.

Her feet found the ledge. She wobbled, arms pinwheeling, then pressed herself flat against the wall, cheek scraping mortar. "Good," she whispered, breathless. "Good girl." She moved sideways, inch by inch, feeling for each foothold before she shifted her weight. Once, a bit of crumbling stone broke away under her toes, sending pebbles skittering down into the dark. She froze, heart ramming against her ribs, listening for shouts.

None came. She kept going. By the time she reached the lower roof—a sloping stretch of slate tiles above the kitchen wing—her fingers ached and her arms trembled. Sweat slicked her palms. She slid down the roof as quietly as she could, boots scraping, and caught the gutter before she toppled over the edge. From there it was a shorter drop to the packed dirt of the inner courtyard. She let go.

The impact jarred her already tender ribs. She muffled a cry, biting her lip until she tasted blood. For a second she crouched there in the pool of shadow, panting, forcing herself not to crumple. Desperation rose inside of her. She straightened and ran.

She hugged the walls, slipping from darkness to darkness, pausing only when a guard crossed her path. Twice she flattened herself behind stacks of firewood; once she dove under a wagon, dust clogging her throat as boots passed inches from her face. At last, shaking and out of breath, she reached the familiar sight of the stables.

"Please," she whispered, fumbling with the latch. "Please, please, please." The door creaked. She winced at the sound and slipped inside. The smell of horses wrapped around her like an embrace. "Grimm," she hissed. "Grimm, it's me."

He answered with a low nicker that made her throat tighten. When she reached his stall, he was already at the door, ears pricked, eyes bright. Snow White could barely see him through the tears in her eyes. He recognized her immediately even though he hadn't seen her for almost two years. Her love for Grimm grew deeper in an instant. "We're going," she said, pressing her forehead to his. "We have to go. I need you," she choked out between tears. He snorted, as if to say that she had nothing to worry about anymore.

She worked quickly, hands moving by muscle memory despite their shaking. Saddle, then bridle. She grabbed a blanket and tied her little sack to the strap. She led Grimm out through the far door, the one that opened onto the section of wall where the guards rarely glanced down. The main gate loomed ahead, the portcullis down, its iron teeth biting into the stone. Torches flared in the gatehouse above. There was no way out there—not without wings. "No," she breathed. "We can't..."

Grimm shifted his weight, his hoof striking the cobblestones with a sharp *clack*. Snow White froze, glancing up at the battlements. A guard's helmet glinted as he turned. She pulled Grimm deeper into the shadows of the stable overhang, her mind racing. *Think,* she commanded herself. *You know this castle better than the queen. You know the dirt, not just the gold.*

Her eyes darted to the far corner of the stable yard, obscured by a pile of rotting hay and old barrels. The Midden Gate. It was a narrow, low archway used only by the stable hands to cart manure out to the compost fields beyond the moat. It was never guarded because no one in their right mind would use it—it was filthy, forgotten, and half-overgrown with nettles on the other side.

"This way," she whispered, tugging on Grimm's reins.

She didn't mount; the arch was too low. They crept through the darkness together on foot. The smell near the gate was sharp and pungent, but to Snow White, it smelled like hope. She reached the heavy wooden door, iron-bound and ancient. There was no lock, only a rusted drop-bar on the inside. Her hands, slick with sweat, slipped on the cold iron. She gritted her teeth and shoved upward. The bar groaned—a sound like a dying animal in the quiet night. *Scrape. Screech.*

"Who goes there?" a voice called from the wall above. Snow White froze, heart hammering against her ribs like a trapped bird. She pressed her face into Grimm's neck, praying he wouldn't snort. A pause. "Probably just rats," another voice muttered. "Wind's picking up."

She waited five heartbeats, then ten. When no alarm sounded, she wrapped her cloak around the bar to muffle the sound and heaved again. With a shudder of rust, it gave way. She pushed the door. It stuck in the mud, then swung outward just enough to create a gap. "Come on," she urged softly.

She slipped through first, mud soaking her boots immediately. Grimm followed, dipping his head low, his sides scraping the stone frame. He hesitated at the narrowness, the darkness beyond. "Trust me," she whispered, tugging gently. "Please." He stepped through. As soon as his hindquarters cleared the arch, Snow White pushed the door shut behind them as best she could.

On the outer side of the wall, tall wild grass brushed Snow White's ankles. The forest hunched in the distance, dark and waiting. She pulled the reins over his head, letting them rest on his mane, and reached her left toe up to the stirrup. In one quick, quiet motion she jumped and swung herself up onto his back. "Now go," she whispered. "Please." He moved quietly across the blackness of the open field until they reached the edge of the forest.

They plunged into the trees, branches clawing at her cloak, leaves whipping her cheeks. The moon, when it broke through the clouds, painted everything in stark silver and deep black. Grimm picked his way through roots and stones, sure-footed even in the dark. Snow White clung to him; despite the cold her body was quickly slick with sweat—not from effort but from nerves. Every scrape of a branch against her bare legs as her ragged chemise tore made her flinch. Her clothes, already thin, shredded further—fabric catching and ripping, baring skin to the night air. She tried to wrap the cloak tighter around her core. Wind knifed her thighs. Twigs scratched her calves. A bramble caught her arm and left a line of stinging fire along her skin.

She didn't dare stop. Behind them, far away now but still too close, the castle loomed in her mind's eye like a crouching beast. Above, clouds shifted. A sliver of moonlight speared through the treetops, glinting on Grimm's black coat, on Snow White's pale knees where the cloth had given way. The forest pressed in on all sides. Trees stood like sentinels, branches woven into a canopy that let only scraps of light through. An owl called, a low, mournful note. Something small scurried in the underbrush.

Snow White's ribs ached with every inhale. Her throat burned. The taste of fear and adrenaline and something like exhilaration coated her tongue. She was cold. She was half-naked. Her hair whipped her face. Her thighs burned from gripping the saddle. She had never felt more alive. The rawness of the night mirrored the rawness inside her. All her illusions had been stripped away as thoroughly as her dress. What was left was a girl on a horse in the dark, fleeing the woman who had given her life and then tried to snuff it out. She had no map. She had no plan. She only knew that the danger in the forest was preferable to the danger in her mother's smile.

• • • ● • ● • ● • • •

Back in the castle, Liora woke to an odd stillness. The morning bells had not yet rung, but some instinct tugged her from sleep. She lay in the dimness for a moment, listening. She slipped from bed and pulled a robe around herself. The braziers from the night before had burned low, embers winking faintly. She crossed the room to the window and peered out. The courtyard lay quiet. No unusual movement. No smoke. No sign of an attack. Her unease didn't ease. She left her chamber and padded barefoot down the corridor toward Snow White's room.

From down the hall she could see the key still in the closed door. She remembered the feel of it in her hand, the small satisfaction of the click. She turned it and pushed the door open. She was shocked to find the room was empty. The bed was rumpled but unoccupied. The comb lay on the floor where it had fallen, its carved vines unremarkable now. The little window stood open, curtain stirring in the cold air. Liora stepped closer. She looked out. The drop to the courtyard below stretched, dizzying. On the stone lip just beneath the sill, faint scuffs marked where a foot had slipped, then found its hold. Farther down, on the lower roof, a tile lay cracked.

Liora's lips peeled back from her teeth. "Hunter!" she shouted, the name snapping from her throat like a whip.

He appeared in the corridor a moment later, sword belt slung hastily over his nightshirt, hair disheveled. "Majesty?"

"She's gone," Liora said. "Snow White."

He blinked, sleep clearing from his eyes. "Gone?"

She pointed at the open window.

He moved to the casement, peering down. The set of his shoulders shifted as he understood. "You want her found," he said quietly.

"I want her dead!" Liora said. The words came out cold and steady. If Snow White was snow, Liora was all ice. "I want her gone from my story once and for all."

"What do you mean?" Hunter asked slowly. "Kill her?" he asked, half jokingly.

Liora laughed, a brittle sound. "Don't grow a conscience now, Hunter. Not after everything you've done."

He flinched. "Snow White is..." He hesitated. "She grew up under my watch. I taught her to ride. She is—"

"Like family?" Liora finished, mocking. "Spare me. Family is whatever we say it is. Today, she is a threat. You will hunt threats. That is what I keep you for."

He opened his mouth, then closed it. The memory of Snow White's face when he'd dragged her down these halls last, the fear and stubbornness in her eyes, flickered across his mind. Killing enemies on the field had never troubled him. This felt different. "Majesty," he said carefully. "There are other ways. We could bring her back. Lock her away. Send her to a convent—"

Liora's expression hardened. "Do you think I am a fool? I already tried to kill her, and she escaped! As long as she breathes, she is a knife pointed at my back."

"What did you do?" He swallowed.

"You know what I've been growing in the gardens. All my vials, herbs. I made a poison, but it must not have been strong enough," she lamented. "I just want it done the old-fashioned way—the easier way. Oh, if only I were a man and were taught to wield a sword. The only weapon I've ever had is my body."

He swallowed. "My queen, I... I don't know if I can—"

She stepped closer, eyes narrowing. "Can't?" she repeated softly. "Or won't?"

He held her gaze for a long, taut moment. "I won't," he said at last. The word tasted like treason.

Liora watched him, something old and ugly twisting in her chest. "Funny," she said. "I remember a time when you would have done anything I asked. Steal, cheat, lie, murder, fuck. For me."

He said nothing.

"Have I grown so little in your estimation?" she asked. "Or has the girl grown so much?"

"Neither," he said, but he heard the lie in his own voice.

Liora's mouth curved. "Very well," she said. "If words

won't move you…"

She loosened the belt of her robe and let it slide from her shoulders. The garment fell in a soft rush to the floor, pooling around her bare feet.

Chapter Ten

Prey

HUNTER'S HEART SKIPPED. YEARS had not dulled her. If anything, time had honed her beauty into something sharper, more dangerous. Her skin glowed in the early daylight. The curves he remembered—had tried, and failed, to forget—were still there, perhaps a fraction softer, perhaps more human. "Majesty," he said, looking away.

"Look at me," she commanded.

His eyes were dragged back of their own accord. Liora, naked before him, slowly crossed the room. She used every inch of herself the way a swordsman uses his blade: deliberate, controlled, knowing exactly where to cut. The sway of her hips, the length of her stride, the tilt of her chin—each movement was a calculated strike against his resolve. She stopped when there was only the width of a breath between them. "You remember," she sighed, pressing the length of her body against his fully clothed front. His nightshirt did little to dull the heat of her skin. "How you once worshiped me?"

God, he did. The memory was a physical ache in his chest. He remembered the nights he'd spent guarding her door, listening to her breathe, wishing he were the silk sheets against her skin. He remembered the way she'd looked at him earlier—like he was a tool to be discarded—and how much it had shattered him. But now? Now she was looking at him like he was the only man in the world.

Her hands slid up his chest, over the scars and the hard planes of muscle... He should push her away. He should remember the girl he'd promised to protect. But Liora smelled like sin and salvation, and his body was betraying him, hardening with a traitorous, desperate need. He trembled, caught between instinct and conscience. "Liora," he said, voice barely a whisper. "I won't..."

"Won't what?" she asked, letting her lips brush his jaw without quite becoming a kiss. "Won't kiss me? Won't fuck me?" She rocked her hips against him, just enough pressure to make him suck in a breath, but not enough to give him relief. "You will. You will find her," she said, her words a soft rasp against his ear. "You will kill her, and you will leave her bones in the woods. And when you return..." She let her hand slide lower, palm cupping him through the cloth, squeezing just enough to make his knees weaken. "...then," she continued, "I will give myself to you fully. No more stolen moments. No more half-measures. You and I, together, on this throne. A king at my side, at last."

"King," he echoed, dazed. The word hit some deep, gnawing hunger in him that had nothing to do with sex and everything to do with the way he had always stood just outside the circle of true power. He had never really considered it before. He only wanted Liora. But this new thought woke something deep inside of him that he didn't know was there.

"Say it," she urged, drawing back a fraction so she

could see his face. "Tell me I'm beautiful."

He swallowed, Adam's apple bobbing. "You're... beautiful," he said, the word coming out strangled.

"Again," she said.

"You're beautiful," he repeated, breathless. His hands, which had been hovering uselessly at his sides, rose of their own accord to rest on her waist.

"Tell me," she said, grinding her hips against him in a slow, tantalizing rhythm, "that there is no one more powerful than I am."

"There is no one more powerful than you," he said, the confession ripped from him like a prayer. "No one."

She smiled, eyes half-lidded. Praise always did more for her than any caress. "Good," she said, and rewarded him by rolling her body once more along his, enough to make him bite back a groan.

He was trembling now with the effort of not grabbing her, not taking, not begging. He wanted to sink into her, to lose himself, to forget that he'd said *no* a moment ago.

She could feel his restraint fraying. She pulled away.

The sudden absence of her warmth made him stagger a fraction, like a man leaning on a wall that was no longer there. "Majesty—" he began, reaching for her.

She stepped back, out of reach, lips curving in a small, cruel smile. "No," she said. "Not yet."

He stared, pupils blown wide. "You said—"

"I said when Snow White is dead," she corrected. "Then you will have me. Then we will speak of marriage, of crowns, of you sitting beside me as king. Until then..." Her gaze flicked meaningfully downward. "...you may keep yourself hungry," she finished. "Hunger makes men do such... impressive things."

He stood there, chest rising and falling, straining against his own skin. The ache between his legs pulsed in time with the ache in his chest. "You are a cruel woman," he said thickly.

"You like it," she replied. "You always have." She bent to pick up her robe, taking her time, knowing his eyes were on every inch of bare flesh as she straightened and shrugged back into the silk. "Go, Hunter," she said, her voice more cool and queenly now that the bait was set. "Follow the trail. She cannot have gotten far on that horse, not if the poison still drags at her limbs. Bring me proof when it's done."

He swallowed hard. His body screamed to stay, to push her back against the wall, to take what she had dangled in front of him like a treat before a starving dog. But the part of him she had always known how to use—the part that craved her approval, her touch, her promise—won out. "I'll ride at once," he said, voice rough.

"Good man," she purred. "Don't keep me waiting."

He left her chambers turned on, frustrated, and utterly controlled by her promise, heart twisted by unrequited love and the hope—always just out of reach—of finally claiming his reward.

• • • • • • • • • • •

B Y THE TIME SNOW White slid from Grimm's back, her legs felt like they belonged to someone else. They had been riding for what felt like days, but in truth it had scarcely been two hours since she'd thrown herself out of the tower window and into the forest. The poison from the comb still clung to her nerves, a fog that made her limbs heavy and her thoughts hazy. Every few minutes her vision blurred; every few steps her knees trembled. "We have to stop," she whispered, stroking Grimm's damp neck. "Just for a little. Just until my head stops spinning." He snorted softly, his sides heaving with exertion. They had run hard to put distance between themselves and the castle. Snow White knew it was unfair to ask more of him for the moment; neither of them was physically fit enough for such a grand adventure.

They had come to a small clearing where the trees parted enough to show a strip of sky. The grass here was patchy but soft. A fallen log, half-swallowed by moss, lay near the edge of the clearing. Beyond, the forest pressed in again, dark and dense. Snow White slid down, boots squelching slightly in the damp earth. Her muscles protested. Her ribs still ached with every breath, the bruises from the corset laces lighting whenever she twisted. She led Grimm to a low-hanging branch and looped his reins over it, giving him enough slack to lower his head and graze on the sparse grass. She patted his neck. "Don't go far," she sighed. "I won't be long."

In truth, she intended only to sit for a moment. Just long enough to let her heart stop galloping and her legs remember how to stand. She sank down with her back against the tree, cloak pulling around her. The bark was rough through the thin fabric. The ground was cool and damp. It felt solid, at least—more solid than anything had since the comb's teeth had bitten her scalp. Her eyes drifted closed. "I'll just... rest," she told herself. "Only until the sky lightens a bit. Then we'll go."

But sleep pulled her in as her eyelids turned heavy. She didn't feel herself slide fully onto her side. She didn't notice the way her cloak fell open, baring a pale length of leg where her chemise had torn on a branch. She didn't see the way the moon, slipping between clouds, painted her skin in soft silver.

She didn't hear the hoofbeats. Hunter had ridden hard from the castle, following what traces he could: broken twigs, disturbed underbrush, the faint, almost invisible marks of a horse's passage. Snow and rain had since softened some tracks, but Grimm's large hoofprints were easy enough for a trained hunter to spot.

His body still ached with longing. Liora's touch burned on his skin; the press of her hips, the promise in her voice, the way she'd pulled away just as he'd been ready to break. His arousal, denied and then harnessed, throbbed faintly with every stride of his horse. He told himself he was here because of duty, because of the oath he'd taken, because of the bargain her words had fashioned. He did not dwell on the part of him that still felt loyal to King Wilhelm's memory. The trees thinned. He pulled his horse back to a walk as they neared the edge of a small clearing. The early morning sky was still dark, the horizon only just beginning to gray. Mist clung to the undergrowth. He saw the stallion first—Grimm's dark shape, head down, ears flicking as he tore at the sparse grass.

Then he saw her. Snow White lay curled at the base of a tree, cloak fallen open. Her knees were half drawn up, one bare calf streaked with dirt and a faint line of blood where a bramble had caught her. Her nightdress—if it could still be called that—was torn in several places, gaping enough at the neckline that the swell of one breast was visible, the cloak doing little to conceal it. Her hair, spread around her head in a dark sway against the bark. In sleep, the tension she'd carried in the castle was gone. Her lips, chapped from the wind and cold, were deep red and parted.

Hunter almost startled at her sight. For a moment, standing at the edge of the clearing, he saw not Snow White but Liora as she had been years ago—lying half-covered on sheets in a darkened room, hair spread on pillows, chest rising and falling with post-coital breaths. His body responded to the memory with humiliating eagerness. He dismounted slowly, every motion deliberate. His knees felt stiff; his hand shook slightly as he looped his horse's reins over a branch. He stood and looked at her. He told himself he was gauging how deeply she slept, whether the poison still dragged at her. He told himself he was deciding where best to strike: a quick cut to the throat, perhaps, or a thrust to the heart.

But his gaze did not linger on vulnerable arteries or vital organs. It lingered on the pale curve of her thigh where the cloak had ridden up. On the shadow between her breasts where the torn dress gaped. On the smooth line of her throat, the flutter of her pulse visible just beneath the skin. He swallowed hard. *You grew up with her,* part of him hissed. *She's your king's daughter. Your—*

But she was a woman now. Had Liora ever arranged

for her marriage, Snow White would likely be caring for a young infant by the age of eighteen. She so looked like Liora. The same black hair. The same full, red mouth. The same complexion that seemed to glow even in poor light. Liora, younger and softer, without the hard edges power had carved into her.

His hand slid to the knife at his belt. "Get it over with," he whispered to himself. "Before you start thinking." He drew the blade. The metal gleamed in the faint moonlight, a thin line of silver promise. Promise of a throne and a kingdom, promise of Liora's body and her sex, and a promise of her love? He stepped into the clearing. The grass muffled his steps, but Grimm's head came up at once, ears pricked. The stallion snorted, eyes rolling slightly. Hunter muttered a low reassurance, keeping his tone even, the way he did with skittish horses and green recruits. "Easy," he said. "Easy, boy. I'm not here for you." Grimm stamped once, then, reassured by his familiar voice and presence, lowered his head again.

Snow White did not stir. Hunter came to stand over her. Up close, the resemblance to Liora was even more uncanny. Only the innocence in her expression, the faint smile on her lips even in her sleep, differentiated them. He could see now, in a way he never had when she'd been a ragged girl in the stables, why Liora's eyes had hardened every time they'd walked side by side. Snow White was truly a masterpiece.

He tightened his grip on the knife. He raised it.

Snow White's eyes snapped open. For a moment they were unfocused, fogged with the remnants of poison and sleep. Then they cleared—and fixed on the blade above her. She jerked, instinctively raising an arm. The movement knocked his wrist slightly sideways. The knife skimmed the trunk of the tree instead of descending into her flesh. Steel rang faintly as it glanced off bark.

"What—?" she gasped, scrambling up against the tree. Her cloak tangled around her legs; she half fell, catching herself on one hand, her other arm coming up defensively. She looked up at the shadow looming over her. "H–Hunter?" she stammered.

His name on her lips hit him like a fist. He'd expected fear, perhaps curses. He had not expected the raw, bewildered hurt in her voice.

"What are you doing?" she demanded, breath coming fast. "Why are you—? Why are you here?"

He could have lied. He could have said he was tracking bandits, that he'd stumbled upon her by accident, that he'd come to help. But something about the way she stared at the knife in his hand made the lies shrivel on his tongue. "The queen sent me," he said, the words heavy as lead. "She wants you dead."

Snow White's face went still. There it was—the last shard of doubt, the last childlike belief that maybe this had all been some terrible misunderstanding, shattered. "My mother," she said slowly, "sent you. To kill me."

"Yes," he said.

She pushed herself fully upright, leaning back against the tree. Her knees were still weak, but she held her chin high. "And you came," she remarked. "You always come when she calls."

"I had no choice."

"There's always a choice. You, of all people, should

know that."

His grip tightened on the knife. "Turn around," he said roughly. "I can't... I can't do it looking at your face."

She laughed then, a small, broken sound. "You think that's better?" she asked. "To have my back turned when you kill me? You can't look me in the eye?"

They stared at each other. The forest held its breath. Snow White spat in his direction, narrowly missing his face. Hunter, virility rising inside, grabbed the defiant target and spun her facing away from him, hand curled on her own back.

The warmth of her body soaked through his clothes before he even raised the knife. She smelled of sweat and dirt and pine, a far cry from Liora's juniper and mint—but under it all, something familiar: the faint, clean scent of Snow White herself, something he couldn't have named but recognized all the same.

He lifted the blade, pressing its edge gently—almost tenderly—against the delicate skin of her throat. His other hand settled on her shoulder, trying to steady both of them.

"Breathe," he muttered. "It will be quick."

She laughed again, bitter and soft. "That's what she said about the corset."

The words slipped under his armor like a knife. He thought of the bruises he'd glimpsed on her side. He imagined Liora's hands on laces, her calm voice asking about dessert while her daughter gasped for air. He thought of Liora's hands on him, just hours ago, stroking and promising and withholding. Her naked body before him, her naked promises of the throne. His body responded to that last memory with cruel timing. Hunger flared in his blood. The position—they, here, pressed together, blade at her throat—was wrong in every way, and yet his flesh did not care. He could feel her pulse under the knife. He could feel the rise and fall of her back against his chest. He could see the soft weight of her breast shifting under the torn dress as she breathed.

He took a deep breath, trying to clear his head. He inhaled her. The smell of her sweat. The faint, sharp tang from between her legs, where fear and flight and the confusing flush of womanly desire had mixed.

His hand on her shoulder slid, almost of its own accord, down along her upper arm. The skin there was smooth, warm. Goosebumps rose under his palm.

Snow White took a deep breath—nerves and something else. "What are you doing?" she whispered, not quite a question, not quite a protest.

He swallowed hard. Liora's voice floated through his mind: *You will find her. You will kill her. You will come back to me, and then...* Then she had pressed herself against him, naked and gleaming, and left him throbbing and desperate.

Chapter Eleven

The Knife's Edge

S NOW WHITE SHIFTED, UNINTENTIONALLY pressing her hips back against him. Hunter's restraint shredded another inch. The knife's edge still lay against her throat, a cold, thin reminder of what he was supposed to be doing. His other hand drifted over the curve of her shoulder, the dip of her collarbone, to the torn edge of her bodice. Her clothing had been pulled and ripped in the flight through the forest. One strap had snapped entirely, leaving the rough fabric gaping. The upper swell of her breast was exposed, skin pale and vulnerable. His fingers brushed there.

Snow White froze. The sensation was like nothing she'd ever felt. This was heavy and deliberate and charged with something that made her stomach flip. Fear. Maybe. But something else too. Something that felt like standing too close to a fire—hot, dangerous, but impossible not to reach for. She felt comfortable with Hunter. She had known him all her life. He was almost like an uncle to her in many ways, a young, brave, strong... "Hunter," she said, her voice thinner now. "What—"

"Don't speak," he muttered. "Just... don't move." His thumb grazed the curve of her breast, tentative at first, then bolder when she did not flinch away. The rough pad of his finger caught on the sensitive skin of her nipple where it strained against the torn cloth.

A sound—small, unbidden—escaped her throat. The smell between her legs thickened, slick heat spreading low in her belly. Her knees went weaker for an entirely different reason than they had just hours ago. Confusion roared through her. This man had been her closest peer once, her friend, the one who'd lifted her into the saddle and called her "princess" in a tone that hadn't felt mocking. Now he held a knife to her throat with one hand and cupped her breast with the other, his breath hot against her ear. Old trust warred with new excitement. Somewhere between the two, something wild stirred. Right now, she was shocked to discover that her body felt open, felt excited, and even felt like it truly yearned for his touch to continue.

He doesn't want to do this, she realized. The thought struck her with the force of a blow. *He's not a killer. He's a man in thrall.* And she knew, with a sudden, sharp instinct she hadn't thought she possessed, that there was only one power greater than Liora's command. "Hunter," she whispered. She didn't pull away. Instead, she leaned *into* him. The movement was so unexpected that his hand jerked back, pulling the knife a fraction away from her skin. "You're shaking."

"Stop," he rasped. "Don't make this harder. You're confusing me." At that, the threat of death vanished from her mind, replaced by a thick, suffocating tension. Snow White knew she should run. She should push him and flee; she knew he wouldn't chase after her. But his body was against her, heavy and warm, and her body—betraying her, twisting her feelings—didn't want to run. She had spent years being invisible. Here, now, under his gaze, she was the center of the universe.

Hunter's mind flickered like a broken lantern between two images: Liora under him in a darkened room, lips parted as she rode him; Snow White, here and now, in his arms, her body echoing the queen's at a younger pitch. He called himself every name he could think of in his head. Pervert. Traitor. Beast. But his hand did not stop. The knife stayed at her throat, but its pressure slackened mostly as his grip on reality slipped. He knew he should move it away, apologize, run. "You look so much like her," he rasped, lips close to her ear. "Do you know that? Her face, her smell. I've loved her for so long."

Snow White's heart lurched. Of course. Of course, this was about her mother, even now. The tickle of his warm breath on her ear sent a signal to the warmth between her legs. Her yearning grew stronger. "Is that what you see?" she asked, voice shaking. "Her? Not me?"

"Sometimes," he said honestly. "Sometimes I can't tell where one ends and the other begins." His hand slid ever so slowly over her breast, fingers spreading to touch as much of her as he could. The rough, calloused palm scraped her nipple through the torn gown, sending a jolt of pleasure straight down her spine. She made another sound.

Her moan made him harden more against her back. She became acutely aware of the difference between them: his size, his strength, the fact that if he chose to, he could snap her like a twig. And yet, in this tangled moment, she realized she had one tiny sliver of power he did not. He wanted her. Badly enough that his hand shook with desire. Badly enough that the knife at her throat wobbled. And she wanted him, too. If she could turn that wanting... If she could bend it away from her death and toward something—anything—else... She swallowed, throat moving against the cold flat of the blade. "Hunter," she whispered. "You don't have to kill me."

He laughed once, harshly. "You think I don't know that? You think I haven't told myself that ten times since I left the castle?" His hand tightened on her breast. "But she—she'll know. She always knows."

"She promised you something. Didn't she?"

The tremor that went through him had nothing to do with the morning chill. "She promised," he admitted, voice rough, "to marry me. To make me king. To give me—" He cut himself off.

"To give you what?" Snow White pressed.

His silence was answer enough. She closed her eyes. Typical. Typical Liora dangling herself like a bone in front of him. Typical that she'd tied his leash to her own body. Jealousy. Anger. Fire. All of it moved through Snow White at once. And under it all, that insistent, traitorous throbbing where his hand moved and his hardness pressed.

This was madness. But madness, she thought suddenly, might be the only thing that she wanted. She reached behind her back, nervously. Her fingers closed over the bulge in his trousers.

He swore softly, the word breaking open on his tongue. "Snow White," he breathed. "Don't—"

"If you kill me," she said quietly, fingers squeezing, "she'll have you for one night. Maybe two. Maybe until she gets bored again. And then what? Another errand boy. Another blade. Another toy."

He made a low, animal sound as her hand moved again, uncertain but determined.

"If you let me go," she went on, emboldened by the way he shuddered, "I promise I'll never return. And you'll have me. Here. Now."

He closed his eyes—his mind in turmoil. Torn between love and duty, kindness and lust, allegiance and mercy. In the dim light, with the fear and the adrenaline mixing in his blood, the lines between mother and daughter were blurring. "You just look... so much like her," he groaned.

"Then pretend," she whispered.

She arched her back slightly, pressing herself more firmly against him. His hand on her breast had nowhere to go but tighter, needier. She had never felt the electricity of foreign fingers on her nipple, and in this moment she thought she'd do anything to have more. His hands found the tears in her dress, widening them with a rough urgency that made her gasp—not in pain, but in a sudden, sharp intake of pleasure. When his calloused palm finally cupped her bare breast, the sensation was so intense she nearly buckled. It wasn't the gentle romance of her books. It was raw. It was real. And god help her, she wanted more.

"You're—" he began, then stopped, as she stroked him once more. His hips jerked forward involuntarily, pushing into her palm. The knife slid another fraction of an inch away from her throat. He was unraveling. She could feel it in the way his breath hitched, the way his fingers dug into her breast, the way his body strained against her touch. "If you really want to do this, turn around," he said, but this time his voice was different. Hungry.

Slowly, she obeyed. "Show me," she said, looking up at him with wide eyes. "Show me what you wanted from her."

Hunter made a low, animal sound. The knife dropped from his hand, thudding harmlessly into the grass. In the next breath, his hands were on her—not violent, but desperate. He pulled her against him, burying his face in the curve of her neck.

"Hunter," she moaned, her head falling back.

"Liora," he whispered back, his eyes squeezed shut.

The name hit her like a slap. "I'm not her!" she said.

His gaze flicked to her face, focusing for the first time. "No," he agreed hoarsely, feeling his erection grow strong. "You're... not." For a heartbeat, something almost like sanity hovered between them. In the next breath he had his hands on her shoulders, pushing her back against the tree, mouth crashing down onto hers in a kiss that was part apology, part hunger, part something uglier.

She gasped, the sound swallowed by his tongue. Her first kiss—if this could be called that—was nothing like the chaste, soft touches in her books. It was rough, desperate, edged with the memory of steel at her throat. Heat flared through her all the same. For a moment she was unsure what to do. *Should I undress? Should I undress him? What will it look like? What will it feel like? Will it hurt?* But as her arousal grew the worries faded and instinct took over.

Hunter's strong hands ripped the other sleeve of her dress, fully exposing both breasts. "Oh, princess," he whimpered, unable to look away.

She had always been sort of annoyed by her large chest. It tended to get in the way during riding and other things. Now, seeing how much her breasts pleased Hunter, she was grateful. She had never been desired by anyone before, and right now, as he looked at her chest, she felt alive. It was more than thrilling, more than exciting. She felt a sort of ecstasy in the notion that her body had this kind of importance. It was intoxicating and his words of admiration about her body had awoken something primal inside her. Those brief moments while he just stared, but his hands were not on her body, felt like an eternity and she wanted—needed that electricity back. "Touch me," she commanded.

Without hesitation Hunter kissed her again, both hands desperately groping her breasts now. His kiss was deep and passionate as his thumbs grazed her nipples over and over, matching the swirl of his tongue in her mouth. Then he bent down and brought her nipple to his lips, almost teasing her for a moment while he focused on unbuckling his belt and lowering his trousers.

Snow White's back arched and her head tilted looking at the sky, pushing her breasts further towards his mouth. The sky was growing lighter with a pinkish hue as the sun started to rise. Hunter's lips closed around her nipple, and he slowly swirled his tongue in circles. The warmth of his mouth on her nipple ignited her body, despite the chill in the early morning air. "Ohhh," Snow White moaned, aching for more.

"Gods," he muttered against her skin. "I can't... I can't stop."

"Don't stop," she breathed.

When his mouth crashed onto hers it was the kiss of a man who had been denied for too long. And Snow

White, who had expected to feel only fear or revulsion, felt a shockwave of heat tear through her. It was a revelation. The friction of his stubble, the crushing weight of his arms, the taste of him—it woke something dormant in her blood. She trusted him—he was a friend, but she feared him all the same.

This is living, a voice in her head screamed. *This is fire.*

She kissed him back, clumsy but fierce, her hands pulling at his hair with urgency. She wasn't just surviving anymore. She was taking.

With that, Hunter lifted her up, spread her legs around his torso, pushed her back against the tree and slowly pushed his erection inside her. She felt pain at first, and gripped his arms tightly, leaning forward over his shoulder. He moved at a slow, steady rhythm, in and out. With each thrust she relaxed her legs and allowed him in further. The air was awake with the sounds of morning doves and the smell of pine entangled with the sounds and smells of sex. He felt her thighs widen and he grunted as he pushed in more fully. She felt secure in his arms and his muscles bulged under her grip as he held her up in the air against the tree as if she were weightless.

The slight pain didn't subside but it was matched by the feeling of pleasure. *What am I doing? Why am I doing this? Why do I like this so much? Why do I feel so good, so right? I feel like I was made for this. I want his mouth on my nipple again. It felt so good.* Her thoughts were interrupted by Hunter's breathing turning increasingly heavy. The exhilaration of doing something that felt so wrong and so right swelled inside her chest. Snow White arched her head back, looking up at the sky again and subtly pushing herself further onto his hard cock. As she leaned back her bare breasts pushed forward and tilted up towards his face. His gaze instantly drawn to them as if he'd never seen anything more spectacular. She saw his eyes roll in his head as he groaned loudly, "Ohhh."

Hunter started pumping faster and her wetness allowed him to slide in and out with quick ease. Snow White thought she noticed him suddenly grow even bigger inside her as he gave one last strong shove. "Oh, Liora," he moaned, eyes closed. In that same moment he stopped moving completely and held her tightly pressed onto his center, throbbing in steady pulses, releasing himself inside of her. Snow White felt the sting. *Was he thinking of her the whole time?*

Moments later he pulled away and lowered her legs to the ground. She was confused: she was a little relieved, but a little disappointed—like something new was now alive inside of her. She felt an odd sense of pride in herself, in her body, and somewhat of a sense of accomplishment. The yearning she had for his touch was still there. She wanted his hands on her breasts, his tongue on hers.

Hunter slumped against her for a moment, forehead pressed to her shoulder, breath sawing in and out. The forest seemed to shrink in around them; the world narrowed to the ragged sound of his breathing and the wild drum of her heart. He grabbed her in a sort-of bear hug and leaned them both back against the tree, her back against his chest, their legs curled together. "Liora..." he said again, burying his head in her hair, as he faded off to sleep.

Snow White stared up at the paling sky, teeth sunk into her lower lip hard enough to taste blood. Her mind slowly returned back to reality. She had not died. She had not died. She had changed, but she had not died. She was not sure yet what she had sacrificed in its place. *Did he really think I was her? Did he want her, or me? His body felt so...amazing, but also so wrong. I feel ashamed, almost dirty—like I've done something wrong. But it felt so good to be desired. The way he looked at my chest—like he worshipped the view. Oh god. Oh, what have I done?*

Within moments, he was snoring softly, arm flung over his face, knife glinting forgotten in the grass beside him.

Snow White slowly rose, dress torn, skin marked where his hands had held her. She looked down at him. Part of her wanted to kick him. Part of her wanted to curl up with him and sleep for a week. Part of her wanted to scrub the memory from her skin. Part of her wanted him to take her again.

She gathered her cloak around her, wincing at the soreness in her legs, her ribs, and now her groin. She grabbed the knife from the ground, considering for a long, tense moment the ease with which she could now press it to *his* throat. She didn't. "Not you," she whispered. "Not like this."

She felt something roll down her inner thigh as she put the knife in her boot and turned towards Grimm. She wiped it away with the inside of her nightdress which was barely hanging on at this point. She clumsily tied the shoulder strap through a hole on the front of the dress, hoping it would hold. The stallion blew softly at her, as if asking where she'd been. "Far away," she said. "Too far. We're leaving, old friend. We need to go far from here." It took some effort to haul herself back into the saddle, every muscle in her protesting.

She cast one last look back at the man sprawled against the bark, the knife's empty scabbard on his belt. "Good-bye, Hunter," she said softly. Then she nudged Grimm into motion and rode away, deeper into the forest, farther away from the only life she'd ever known.

Behind her, Hunter slept on, ignorant of how many lines he had just crossed and how little he could ever tell the queen.

Chapter Twelve

Hunger and Lies

H UNTER WOKE WITH THE sun in his eyes and grit in his teeth. For a few blessed seconds, he didn't remember where he was or why his body felt like it had been dragged behind a cart. He only knew that the ground beneath him was hard, his back ached, and his mouth tasted like stale fear. Then the memories crashed in.

Liora's promise. Snow White's throat under his knife. Her voluptuous breast in his hand. Her body against his. His own, traitorous release inside of her. He groaned and rolled onto his side, one arm flung over his eyes.

"Oh gods," he said to the sky. "What have I done?"

He pushed himself up to sitting, joints popping. The clearing looked different in daylight: less like a secret world, more like a patch of ordinary forest. Birds flitted in the branches overhead. Somewhere nearby, water trickled.

Snow White was gone. So was Grimm. And his knife? Only the trampled grass and a few torn threads of cloth on the rough bark of the tree bore witness that she had ever been there.

He should have felt relief that she'd run. That he wouldn't have to look at her cooling body and tell himself it had been necessary. Instead, a different dread settled in the pit of his stomach. Liora. "She'll know," he whispered.

"She always knows."

He pressed his palms to his eyes, hard enough to see bursts of color. He could not tell her what had really happened. Not the failure, not the weakness, not the way he had turned a murder into something fouler in its own right. The queen had no idea how far he'd gone. If he lied—if he said he'd done the kill quickly, cleanly, as ordered—how would she ever prove otherwise?

He could chase her. Try to cover his sin with belated duty. Or he could turn back and weave the neatest, safest lie he could manage. He stared at the faint hoofprints leading deeper into the woods, then at the direction of the castle, where Liora's promise waited like a glinting hook. In the end, he did what he always did: he turned his horse toward the queen.

The ride back felt shorter than the ride out, though his muscles complained with every step. He rehearsed the story in his head with each hoofbeat. Found her. Did as ordered. No, there's no body—the forest took it, or wolves, or the river. Yes, I'm sure. No, Majesty, I would not lie to you. As a soldier, he hated himself for his traitorous act. As a man, he understood. All he ever wanted was Liora. He eased his guilt by renewing his devotion to his queen as he fled the scene of sin.

He imagined Liora's gratefulness. Thanking him with her body nightly. Appreciating him with her warm mouth. His pants felt suddenly tighter. He questioned his own thoughts. Would she follow through this time? He cared less of the kingdom she promised, and more of herself. He pleaded with his own mind. He wanted her devotion more than the throne.

By the time the castle's gray walls rose between the trees, the lie he conjured had worn grooves in his tongue. The guards on the gate towered above him as he approached, squinting down. "Captain!" one called, surprised. "We'd not expected you back so soon."

He forced an innocent smile. "Duty doesn't wait," he said.

They saluted, chains clanked, and the gate lifted. Inside the courtyard, the usual clatter of morning had begun: buckets sloshing, boots on stone, the murmur of servants exchanging gossip. A few heads turned as he rode in, noting the mud on his cloak, the weariness in his posture.

He dismounted stiffly and tossed his reins to a waiting boy.

"See to him," he said. "Rub him down well."

"Yes, Captain."

He took the stairs to Liora's chambers two at a time, ignoring the protest in his knees. Outside her door, he paused for half a breath. Then he knocked once and entered without waiting for an answer.

She was already awake, of course. She sat by the window in a loose robe, hair unbound, face bare of paint. Even like this—especially like this—she radiated a dangerous sort of beauty. The kind that drew blades as easily as it drew men.

Her eyes flicked up as he entered. "Well?" she asked. One word, razor-sharp.

He bowed, more deeply than usual. "It is done," he said. "She won't trouble you again."

Silence pulsed between them. "Show me," Liora said.

His mind scrabbled for purchase. "Majesty—"

"You know," she cut in. "You've led men long enough to understand what proof looks like. Where is it? A lock of hair? A scrap of dress? A finger?"

Revulsion coiled in his gut. He wished, absurdly, that he had thought to cut some prize from the girl while she lay unconscious under his knife. "I—" he began. "She fell into the ravine," he blurted, the lie tumbling out. "When I cornered her. We struggled. She lost her footing. The river... took her."

It wasn't what he rehearsed. It wasn't even a good lie. But once started, he had to finish it. "The current was too strong to go after her," he added. "The rocks—" He spread his hands. "There would have been no body left to find." He braced himself for her fury.

Instead, she stared at him for a long moment, eyes flat, unreadable. Then, slowly, she smiled. "You always did have a way with... messy tasks," she said.

Relief, sharp and bitter, flooded him.

"To be clear," she went on, rising from her chair with liquid grace, "you're certain she's dead?"

"Yes," he said. The word scraped his throat. "Majesty, I swear it."

"The horse?" she asked.

"Gone," he said. "He leapt after her. Or ran. I didn't see. But he didn't come back up."

She tilted her head, studying his face, weighing every short breath, every twitch of muscle.

Hunter forced himself to hold her gaze. Bitter experience had taught him that looking away only made her suspicion bloom.

After a long, taut silence, she nodded. "Good," she said. "Very good, Captain."

Relief sagged his shoulders. "Majesty, I—"

"You look tired," she observed, crossing the space between them. "Come closer. Let me see what my loyal hound dragged himself through for me."

He obeyed.

Her hand slid up his chest, palm warm through his shirt. Her fingernails grazed the line of his jaw.

"Blood?" she asked softly.

"No," he said. "The river took everything."

"Even so," she murmured. "You did what was necessary. You have my gratitude." The words—a rare currency from her—lit something in him he wished he could kill.

"And my reward?" he said before he could stop himself. The need in his voice embarrassed him.

Her smile sharpened. "So eager," she said. "Have you been thinking of nothing else?"

He didn't answer. He didn't need to.

She laughed quietly. "Men," she said. "Always so sure they are the hunters."

She leaned in, lips brushing his cheek, the ghost of a kiss.

"We have time," she said. "Time to plan. Time to arrange... everything."

He stiffened. "You promised—"

"You will get what you're owed," she whispered, lips brushing his earlobe. She grabbed his jaw with her hand and turned it towards her lips, kissing him with one deep motion. She walked back toward the mirror, her robe trailing. "Go," she said over her shoulder. "Wash. Sleep. You smell like death."

He ground his teeth, torn between anger and guilt, hope and desire. In the end, he bowed. "As you wish," he said. He turned and left, the lie he'd told her sitting heavy on his tongue.

• • • ● • ● ● • •

For Snow White, the world was Grimm's back, the endless rhythm of hooves, and the darkness of the forest. After leaving Hunter in the clearing, she pushed Grimm as far as she dared, moving quickly when they could, and moving slowly when they couldn't. Fear and shame and fury snapping at her heels like wolves. The adrenaline that had fueled her escape eventually ebbed, leaving only exhaustion and a nagging ache everywhere his hands had been.

She did not have the luxury of stopping for more than snatches of sleep. Every time she closed her eyes, she saw Liora's face, the glitter of the comb, the flash of steel. Every crack of a twig behind her made her whip around, half expecting to see Hunter's shadow. But nothing followed.

Days blurred. She rode through rolling meadows where wildflowers nodded in the wind, their bright heads bobbing like gossiping courtiers. She slipped between stands of fir trees that made their own dark cathedrals, the air beneath them cool and sharp with resin. She forded shallow streams, cold water numbing her toes, watching as curious fish scattered when Grimm drank. More than once, she caught herself thinking that the moment would all have been beautiful—if not for the bruises, the soreness, and the fear. She kept believing that right after that next ridge she'd see a village, or just around this path's bend she'd come across a farm—any kind of civilization—people to help her, a place to live, a place to start her new life.

At night, she rested under low-branched trees, cloak wrapped tight, Grimm standing watch nearby. Dreams came in a tangle: her father's laugh, her mother's hands, blue eyes in a stable, rough hands on her body, the press of a knife. But what she thought about most was the way she felt when Hunter looked at her body. *With shock? With amazement? With hunger? With greed?* She didn't know exactly, but she knew it felt powerful.

Food was whatever she could find: berries along the path, water from streams. She wished she was a horse and could sustain herself on grass and water. She wasn't good at survival in the forest. She didn't know which mushrooms or roots she could eat. She didn't know how to find safety from bears or snakes or how to keep warm at night. She didn't know how to ensure she wasn't riding for days in circles. She had never had to survive. She had never had to struggle. She had never had to worry much at all. She just assumed there must be neighboring villages nearby, but in truth, she didn't know. *How much longer until I find someone—somewhere? How much longer could I survive, starving and cold? How much longer before the wolves closed in?* She was thankful to have Grimm. Without him, she would have certainly given up.

Her mind circled the same questions over and over. *What had I become in that clearing? What did it mean that I had used my body like that, as a bargaining chip, a distraction, a shield? Was I now more like my mother than ever?* Sometimes she gripped the falcon pendant at her throat and thought of the prince. Of the way he'd looked at her without calculation. Of the gentleness of his hands and the kindness in his eyes. "Would you still see me the same?" she whispered once into the dark. "If you knew?" The trees did not answer.

On the fourth day, as the sun sank low and her stomach growled in protest, she saw it.

At first she thought it was a trick of the light—a darker patch among the trees. Then Grimm flicked his ears forward, and Snow White, squinting, realized it was a roof. A cottage. It sat in a small hollow by a sparkling stream, its walls of rough-hewn logs gone gray with age. Smoke rose lazily from a stone chimney. A small patch of ground nearby had been turned into a vegetable plot, currently just neat rows of dark earth waiting for planting.

Snow White's heart leapt. A dwelling meant people. People meant food. Perhaps shelter, if she begged hard enough and kept her story vague. "Please," she pleaded to Grimm. "Just a little luck, for once." She urged him downhill.

The cottage door was shut. No one moved in the yard. "Hello?" she called, sliding from Grimm's back on legs that trembled. Her head was spinning. "Is anyone—" Her voice cracked. Her throat was too dry. She cleared it and tried again. "Hello?" No answer. She staggered to the door and knocked. The wood was solid under her knuckles. Silence.

Her head swam. The long days of too little food and too much fear pressed in.

If no one's here, she thought, dizzy, then at least there might be bread. The thought shamed her, but not enough to stop her hand from testing the latch. It gave. She pushed the door open and stepped into the dim interior. The air smelled of stale smoke, sweat, and old stew. Dust motes danced in the thin shaft of light that sneaked in through the small, dirty window. Her eyes adjusted slowly.

A rough table with mismatched chairs. Hooks on the wall hung with coats and belts and tools. Heavy pickaxes leaned against the dark wood like silent sentinels, their iron heads caked with the glitter of false hope and gray stone. A shelf sagging under the weight of dented tin plates and chipped mugs. In one corner, a small stove, its coals dead but the ashes still faintly warm. On the table, a loaf of bread sat under a cloth. Next to it, a wedge of cheese and a crock of something that might be stew. Snow White's stomach cramped. "I'll leave something," she whispered to the empty room, as if someone might be listening. "I'll... sweep. Or wash. Or just... be gone before you return home."

She stumbled to the table and tore a hunk from the bread. It was coarse but fresh enough. She bit in, barely chewing before swallowing. The cheese followed. Then a few cold, greasy bites from the crock, the flavors so intense after days of foraged berries that she almost wept.

When the worst of the pangs eased, her body remembered other needs. Her legs buckled. The floor seemed suddenly much closer. There were a few rooms down a short hall. She peeked in the first one and saw a large unmade bed in the far corner topped with a pile of rough wool blankets. It might as well have been a royal canopy bed for how inviting it looked.

"I'll just lie down," she told herself, staggering toward the bed. "Just for a minute. Then I'll think what to do." She reached the edge of the mattress, fell forward, and was asleep before she hit it.

Chapter Thirteen

The Bargain

SNOW WHITE DREAMED OF those blue eyes again. In the dream, she was back in the stable, standing between Grimm's warm side and the boy with the wheat-blonde hair. He held out his hand, the silver token glinting between his fingers, and when she reached for it, their hands slipped together instead. He laughed softly and tugged her closer. "You can't run forever," he said in the dream. "But you don't have to keep running alone." His mouth brushed hers—gently, not like the rough clash in the clearing—and something unknotted in her chest.

Voices floated in from outside the dream, singing some work song she couldn't quite make out the words to. Deep, rough voices. Male. The dream shifted.

She was still in the stable, but the walls around her had changed—rougher, darker. The air smelled less of straw and more of earth and sweat and something metallic, like iron dust. The boy's face blurred, then faded.

The singing grew louder. Snow White's dream dissipated. Her lashes fluttered. The cottage door creaked open.

Six men trudged into the back door of their home, voices trailing off as they wiped sweat and dust from their faces. They were solid men, broad-shouldered, their hair and beards streaked with grime from the mines. Their clothes bore the indelible stains of coal and earth. Boots clumped on the floorboards.

"Long day," one muttered.

"Aren't they all?" another replied.

They stopped short when they saw the horse through the small window—a black stallion tied out front, peacefully grazing.

"Whose beast is that?" Gage asked, frowning.

"Don't know," Dax said, the automatic leader's wariness sharpening his gaze.

They exchanged looks.

"Someone's in our house," Gage said, hand going instinctively to the knife at his belt.

Drew didn't say anything at all. He rarely did. But his eyes were alert as he stepped just behind Dax's shoulder.

They moved through their home warily, boots softening on the old boards. At first, they saw only the usual disarray: mugs left in the sink, a shirt draped over a chair, the stew crock on the table with a hunk of bread missing. Then their boots followed the trail of discarded crumbs into the nearest room. Toward the largest bed. A small figure lay sprawled across the mattress, cloak half on the floor, hair a dark tangle on the rough pillow, blankets twisted around her thighs.

"Saints preserve us," Bennett whispered.

"Not saints," Harry joked. "Something with a sense of humor."

She looked nothing like the dainty heroines of court tales. Her face was smudged with travel grime. A strand of hair clung to the corner of her mouth. One arm lay flung above her head, revealing the dark bruise of sore ribs where the dress gaped. Her chest rose and fell with the slow, deep rhythm of true exhaustion.

Gage's eyes traveled over every inch of her—lingering, unabashed. He was aroused before he even realized it, the sight of a real woman, soft and breathing and right here, hitting his starved senses like a blow.

"Who is she?" Bennett whispered, more to himself than anyone, cheeks reddening as he realized how intently he was staring.

"An intruder," Gage said, though the word came out rough. "Or a gift."

"We don't get gifts," Dax said, but his voice lacked conviction.

It had been a long time since any of them had even seen a woman up close, let alone had one asleep in their bed. Years of isolation and underground shifts had honed their edges, starved their softer parts.

Silas tilted his head, studying her like a puzzle. "She's pretty," he said in his slow drawl. "Even like that."

"Especially like that," Harry amended with a grin.

"Shut it," Gage said again, though his own gaze was glued to the flash of cleavage where her bodice had slipped.

Drew shifted, hands flexing unconsciously.

Silas, standing slightly behind the others, sneezed. A sudden, unmistakable, echoing *achoo* that startled everyone—including the sleeping girl.

Snow White's eyes flew open. For a moment she had no idea where she was. The low ceiling, the unfamiliar shadows, the weight of several blankets over her—all of it hit at once. She sat bolt upright with a little gasp.

"Oh," she said. Because there, at the foot and sides of the bed, stood six men. Tall. Wide. Handsome. Dirty. Staring at her as if she'd dropped from heaven. For a heartbeat, none of them moved.

From Snow White's perspective, they were a wall of muscle and stubble and stunned expressions. One—Dax—had a calculating, almost clinical gaze, his eyes sweeping over her as if taking stock of goods for trade. Gage's expression was a scowl half-melted by the unmistakable bulge in his trousers. Harry's grin was already beginning to tug at his lips. Silas blinked slowly, a little out of sync with the rest. Bennett went scarlet and dropped his eyes to the floor, then dragged them back up in guilty little darting looks. Silas wiped his nose on his sleeve, trying to pretend his sneeze had not just happened. Drew simply watched, eyes wide and bright, hands twitching as if he wanted to reach out and touch, but didn't dare.

Snow White snapped into anxiety. Her dress had ridden low during sleep; the rough neckline exposed more of her breasts than she'd ever let show on purpose. Her legs, tangled in the blankets, were bare from mid-thigh down, smudged with dirt, a bruise shadowing one shin. She was dirty, she smelled bad, she was half-naked. Heat rushed to her face. "I—" she stammered, fumbling at the blanket to cover herself. "I'm sorry. I didn't—I was just—"

Dax's voice cut through, clipped and steady. "Who are you..." he asked, "and what are you doing in our house?" The authority in his tone steadied her a fraction. Authority she could answer to. She'd been doing that her whole life.

"My name is Snow White," she said, clutching the blanket to her chest. "I—" Her throat closed for a second on the urge to say *Princess Shay*. That title felt like a joke now, somewhere between tragic and obscene. If they knew who she was, would they help her or throw her out in the cold? The nickname felt safer. "I was riding through the woods. I got lost. I hadn't eaten in days. I saw your cottage and…" She looked guilty. "There was bread. On the table. I thought I'd leave something in return, but I was so tired and I—I just sat down for a moment, and I must have fallen asleep."

Silas huffed. "That's a fairly honest confession for a thief. Snow White, what kind of name is that? Sounds funny!"

"I'm not a thief," she protested. "I mean—I suppose I am, but not usually. I'll work to repay you, I swear it. I'll clean, or cook, or—" She floundered. "Something."

Dax's gaze moved from her face to the torn state of her clothes, to the calluses on her hands, to the way she held herself, hunched as if she expected a blow. "All alone?" he asked. "No one with you?"

"No," she said. "It's just me. And my horse." She nodded vaguely toward the window where Grimm's hindquarters were visible.

Harry interjected sarcastically, "Oh, we need to stable a horse, too? Make yourself at home, apparently." He added with a half-smile and a half-chuckle.

Gage snorted. "Pretty girl," he muttered. "Pretty story."

Snow White's stomach twisted. "It's the truth," she said. "I have nowhere else to go."

Silas yawned. "She looks tired enough, Dax. If she's lying, she's very committed to it."

Bennett's hands twisted in the hem of his shirt. "Let her stay," he blurted, then went redder when five heads turned toward him. "I mean—just for the night. We can decide in the morning. She looks like she needs help."

Gage's scowl deepened. "We don't even know who she is. For all we know, she's bait for some bandit gang. We bring one pretty stray in and wake up with our throats cut."

Harry shrugged. "Then at least we'll die smiling."

Dax shot him a look, but there was a glimmer of amusement in his eyes.

Snow White clutched the blanket tighter. Her heart hammered. She could feel their gazes on her: hot, curious, hungry. Not like the look Liora gave her, cold and weighing. These were raw. Honest. Unvarnished. Did she feel frightened or excited? Something about these men made her feel safe.

"Please. I'll do anything," she said, the words spilling out. She was so desperate for human interaction, somewhere to go, somewhere to belong, "Truly. I can sweep, or chop wood, or tend the garden. I grew up…" She swallowed the word *in a castle*. "…with people who worked. I can learn how to scrub floors and—"

"Cook?" Harry cut in hopefully.

She hesitated. "No," she admitted. "I can't cook."

"Clean?" Silas asked lazily.

"I can try," she said. "I can learn."

Gage looked unconvinced. "What kind of woman doesn't know how to cook or clean? What are you—some kind of princess?" he said sarcastically.

Dax exhaled slowly, rubbing a hand over his jaw. The men exchanged a series of looks that spoke of years spent together, their conversations long since distilled into small gestures. Some said *why not*. Some said *this is trouble*. Some said *trouble might be better than the way things are*. "We don't have room or need for charity cases," Dax said finally, voice firm. "We work hard. We've made a life here. We don't need anything to change."

Snow White's throat closed. "I won't be a burden," she said. "I'll earn my place. I'll sleep on the floor. I'll do anything you need around here. Please. I'm—" She hated the tremor in her voice, but couldn't stop it. "I'm desperate. And I'm alone. And I have nowhere else to go."

Silence.

Harry, always the first to speak—tilted his head, considering her. "Awh, let her stay," he said. "She can learn to cook and clean." Snow White opened her mouth to protest—she really, truly couldn't cook—but before she could, he added, "Or at least stand in the kitchen and look pretty while someone else does." A couple of them chuckled.

"I don't know how to cook," she said honestly. "Isn't there anything else I can do for you?"

There it was. The opening. Gage stepped closer to Dax, lowering his voice to a whisper, though Snow White, with ears honed in castle corridors, still caught some of it. "Let her earn her keep. We provide the hearth and home; she provides the ...warmth." His gaze slid back to Snow White's partially exposed chest. "Seems fair."

Dax's jaw tightened. "Have you lost your honor?" He whispered back.

"How many years since any of us has seen a woman?" Gage shot back under his breath. "We're not saints, Dax.

We're miners. We break our backs all day and sleep in the dirt. This is the first soft thing to walk through that door, ever. Think of it as a morale booster for the men."

Dax's eyes flicked to Snow White again. She met his gaze, seeing the calculation there. The muscle in his cheek ticked. Dax looked at Gage, then at the leaves blowing by outside the window. They couldn't feed a useless mouth. But the way Gage was looking at her, the way the air in the room had shifted, they were starving men — and she was a feast. He exhaled. "All right," he said aloud, turning fully toward her. "We have an offer."

Snow White's stomach churned. "An offer," she repeated carefully. "Oh thank you."

"We aren't a charity," Dax said bluntly. "We're not unkind, but we're not fools. Food, a roof, a bed—those are worth something. We don't need another pair of hands enough to justify the risk of bringing a stranger into our home. Especially hands as unskilled as yours seem to be."

Her fingers tightened on the blanket. "So, what do you need?" she asked.

The other men looked at each other, wondering if they were all starting to realize the same thing.

Dax's eyes did another quick sweep of her, more clinical than Gage's but no less aware. "We're men," he said. "We spend long days underground and longer nights alone in our beds. It's been... a very long time since any of us have had the company of a woman."

Bennett coughed, face flaming. Harry grinned outright. Gage's eyes darkened with open hunger. Silas just looked faintly amused. Drew's gaze skittered away, then back, curious and uncertain.

"There is a price," Dax went on, voice even, almost businesslike, "We are six men alone in the woods. We have needs, unfulfilled needs. If you want our care and protection, you provide our comfort. All of it. Whenever we ask."

He held her gaze. Her cheeks burned. He could see in her eyes she understood more than he expected.

Bluntly, Dax laid out, "You let us have your body. For pleasure. When we need. How we need."

The words were crude in their honesty, but there was something... clean about it, too. No pretense. No hidden blades in compliments. No poisoned combs disguised as gifts.

"You mean—" She swallowed. "All of you?"

"Yes," Dax said. "All of us."

Her heart pounded. "Whenever you want?"

"When we want," he agreed. "But you will be fed, clothed, and kept warm. We'll make sure you don't come to harm. No one here will hit you or starve you or lock you in a room. If you say no to something, we listen. No one will force you. You'll be... ours. But we'll be yours, too. In our own way."

"A pact." Silas blurted.

"We'll be respectful," Bennett promised.

It was twisted and imperfect, and yet more straightforward than anything she'd ever been offered in the castle. "And if not?" she asked quietly.

"Then you eat the bread you already took," Dax said, "and we'll point you toward the nearest road. You and your horse can take your chances out there. No ill will."

Silas nodded lazily. "Everyone's free, one way or

another."

Snow White's mind raced. She thought of the forest: the cold, the hunger, the unknown. She thought of Liora's hands and Hunter's knife and the way danger seemed to seep from every stone of the life she'd fled. She thought of Grimm outside, alone except for her. She thought of the way these men looked at her—not as a rival, not as a pawn, but as something they wanted unabashedly. Something they were willing to name their price for, openly, instead of pretending it was something else. Were they cruel? Were they kind? She wasn't yet sure.

Her stomach knotted. Her thighs still ached faintly from the clearing. Her ribs hurt when she breathed. Her heart felt like a bruised fruit. She could leave. Ride until she dropped. Keep trying to find a village where they'd take pity on a ragged girl with a good horse. But maybe not. Maybe she'd die a slow death of starvation in the woods before she ever got where she was going. Or maybe the wolves would eat her alive. Maybe Grimm would get hurt. Where *was* she really going anyway?

She could stay. Trade her body—already used, already claimed—for safety, food, a kind of belonging. The choice would be hers. No one would push her into a corset so tight she fainted. No one would dress poison up as love. She let herself sit with that for a long heartbeat.

"I don't know how to please six men," she said finally, voice steady despite the blush burning her skin. "I barely know how to please one."

Harry chuckled. "Oh, beautiful — we're not picky!"

"We haven't seen a woman in a long time," Silas said.

Or ever, young Drew thought, though he didn't say it

aloud.

"And I think I've never seen a lady as beautiful as you before," Bennett blushed.

Dax's gaze softened by a fraction. "You don't have to know everything now," he said. "You will learn. We will teach. You have the right to walk away anytime if you decide it's too much. No one chains you here—" Dax shoots a sharp look at Gage.

"No one," Gage echoed, though there was a challenge in his smirk.

Snow White looked at each of them in turn. She saw their desire. She saw their loneliness. She saw a kind of rough, battered honesty that felt almost like kindness. Her mind went a hundred miles a minute: *I feel almost sorry for them, all alone without a woman's touch. But am I willing to be their play-thing? Is that what I was looking for when I left the castle? Why am I feeling like I want to say yes? Why am I feeling a pulse in between my legs? Why am I feeling intrigued? I wonder what they'll do to me. I wonder how it will feel. The way Hunter looked at me made me feel so alive. They're looking at me like that right now.* The idea of being touched and desired on her own terms, of not being cold and alone anymore, tempted her more than it frightened her. And for the first time in a very long time, she felt something in herself reply to all of that with a word she hadn't expected to think again: *yes.*

She took a shaky breath. "All right," she said. "I agree." Her heart hammered. "I'll... do it. On those terms. Food, shelter, protection—for my body. Whenever you want, however you want." She was nervous, but spoke with a sort of inspiration.

Gage's grin turned feral. Bennett's eyes went wide. Harry whooped once, then clapped a hand over his own mouth, suddenly aware of the gravity of the moment. Dax nodded slowly. "Then we have an agreement," he said. "You can rest today. Eat. Get your strength back. Tonight..." His eyes flicked briefly to the bed. "We'll talk again."

Silas smiled, "I'll warm the sheets for you," as he approached the bed ready for a nap.

Gage, never one for waiting or following orders, had other ideas. He stepped forward, fingers already reaching for his belt, the bulge at the front of his trousers straining the worn fabric. "Or," he said, voice low and hungry, "we can start right now." His hand went to his fly. He tugged it down.

Snow White's eyes widened as he freed himself. The sight stole her breath for a beat—not only because of the unexpected size and blunt maleness of him, but because there was no shame, no apology in the way he stood there, aroused and firm, letting her see exactly what she'd agreed to.

Her heart kicked against her ribs. Her mouth went dry. Her thighs pressed together under the blanket, a confusing mix of fear and anticipation and something she refused to name yet spiraling low in her belly. The hunger in the room sharpened, but it did not feel like Liora's cruelty. It felt like six starving men handed the first real feast they'd seen in years. For the first time in her life, Snow White felt herself seen not as a weapon, or a threat, or a reflection. But as a woman. It terrified her. It thrilled her. And, on her own battered, complicated terms, she chose it.

Chapter Fourteen

Earning Sanctuary

S HE MOVED TOWARD HIM, a little unsure of what to do. With Hunter, he had taken charge and she had let her body do the rest. Now there was no map to guide her, no ancient law to follow—only the bargain she had agreed to, and six pairs of eyes waiting to see if she would honor it.

"Come closer," Gage said, voice low, rough around the edges. There was defiance in every syllable, like he expected her to bolt but dared her to try. "You think you want this? Prove it." He stepped forward first, as he always did. The hardened loner with scars etched deeper than any mine shaft, shoved in front of the others, his broad frame blocking them out. He had already stripped down, his trousers tangled around his ankles as he gripped the base of himself—thick, heavy, the dark head flushed and slick with a shining bead that caught the lantern light.

Snow White's arms trembled as she crawled toward him on the bed. Her breath came in shallow bursts, her heart pounding hard enough to hurt. Up close, the sheer size of him made her throat tighten. He was thicker than her wrist, veins standing out along the length, the blunt head glistening with heat. She hesitated just a second, unsure what to do. She looked up at him and he stepped even closer, pointing himself right at her face. Slowly, she leaned in, lips parting as her tongue flicked out to taste that first tentative drop. A shiver ran through her. The flavor was strange—salty, musky, undeniably male—but not as shocking as she'd imagined. The reality of it, the warmth, the weight, the way he twitched to her touch, all anchored her to the moment. This was the price she had named. She could give this.

Gage didn't wait for finesse. His fingers slid into her hair, not cruel but not gentle either, a man ready to grab and hold. He tightened his grip and drew her forward until her mouth stretched around him. She gasped around the intrusion, jaw burning with the unfamiliar stretch, but she forced herself to relax, to breathe through her nose, to hollow her cheeks and seal her lips around him.

She let her tongue trace along the underside of him, clumsy at first, then bolder as she felt him respond. He began to move, short, hungry thrusts that pushed him deeper with each pulse. "That's it," he muttered, voice gone hoarse. "Just like that, aghh—," he grunted a low moan.

The others didn't need more invitation than that. Clothes hit the floor in a hurried rustle, belts clinking as they were unbuckled, boots kicked aside. The air seemed to thicken with heat and breath and male bodies suddenly freed from layers of rough work-clothes. The sharp, cold scent of rain and wet wool that had clung to them began to evaporate, replaced by the heavier, muskier scent of men suddenly stripped of their defenses.

Light glanced off bare skin—shoulders, chests, stomachs, each man shaped by hard labor and lean living. The sight ignited a fever in her blood she hadn't known she possessed. She looked at the circle of men. In the castle, she was a princess who had to hide. Here, she was a queen holding court, and they were her subjects, waiting for her time. They closed in, a half circle of warm flesh and rough hands, breaths ragged with anticipation. The thought of these men all wanting her, all desiring her, all about to have their way with her, made the warmth between her legs begin to throb. She longed to be touched.

Harry, the easygoing thrill-seeker with a grin that could light a room, chuckled low as he circled to her side, tugging his shirt over his head to reveal a broad chest dusted with dark hair. "Look at her go," he said, awe threaded through the teasing. "Eager little thing, aren't you?" His own arousal jutted from his open trousers, curved slightly and bobbing gently as he moved, the tip flushed.

Snow White's cheeks burned, but something inside her loosened at their reactions. None of them were pretending they weren't affected. None of them even tried pretending she wasn't the center of this.

Gage braced his knees on the mattress, thighs framing her face as he guided himself into her mouth again, deeper this time. Tears pricked her eyes when his release hit the back of her throat, but she swallowed against the reflex, one hand bracing on his thigh, the other holding lightly around the base of him to steady her rhythm. "Swallow it down, girl—earn your keep," he ground out, the words rough but not mocking. She gagged softly at the flood, but it wasn't as horrible as she'd feared. When he pulled back, panting, his hand lingered in her hair for a heartbeat, almost like a silent, grudging 'thank you', before he stepped away, tucking himself back into his trousers.

Harry slid in immediately to take his place with an

almost boyish eagerness, his laughter bubbling even as hunger thickened his voice. "Room for one more in that pretty mouth?" he asked, eyes crinkling at the corners. He didn't force it, just nudged gently against her lips, giving her the chance to lean away. She didn't. Her jaw ached, but she opened for him anyway, tasting the sharper tang of his desire, different from Gage's. His hand cupped her cheek with surprising care, thumb stroking her skin as he eased forward.

"Good girl," Harry breathed. "Look up at me." He set a slower pace than Gage, rolling his hips rather than driving, watching her carefully. When she glanced up at him through damp lashes, his expression shifted—heat flaring, yes, but something like tenderness too. That look, the way he saw her even with his body this undone, almost undid her more than the act itself. "Saints, you're beautiful," Harry whispered, and cum followed the words like an exhale, his body shuddering as he spilled into her mouth. His other hand smoothed her hair back from her face as if she hadn't already seen every filthy thing about him.

Dax's voice cut through the swell of panting and low curses like a whip. "Ok," he said with the same tone he used to call men to order in the mine. "Get her on her back. Spread her out."

Strong arms moved at once—Drew's careful grip at her waist, Silas's slightly shaky hold under her arms—lifting her as if she weighed nothing. Her world tilted, then her back hit the bed with a soft thud, the mattress dipping under her.

Her filthy nightdress was already hiked high; now

it was shoved further, cool air kissing her thighs and the damp, untouched heat between them. She hadn't realized how wet she'd become, how her own arousal had grown quietly in the background of everything she was doing. Now the air on her slick skin made her incredibly aware of it. Embarrassment flared. So did a hot, swirling need.

They descended around her like a storm breaking—hands, mouths, bodies. Silas grabbed the scraps of what was her dress and ripped it open, exposing her completely with a wide smile on his face. Lying naked and exposed on the bed, she felt terrified. But as she looked around she saw a familiar sight. The men looked at her the way Hunter had—with adoration, with overwhelm, with need. She allowed that foreign feeling of confidence to rise in her chest, growing stronger with each adoring look from the men. Her body—hers, herself—was powerful. At that moment she felt she could negotiate any deal she wanted, but she chose to say nothing.

Dax stepped between her parted legs, his presence steady and unyielding. Up close, there was nothing soft about him: all deliberate lines and controlled strength. He met her gaze for a brief second, then looked away as he guided himself to her entrance. The blunt, rigid head of him brushed her, parting her folds. She sucked in a breath, fingers curling in the blankets. There was no teasing, but there was no violence either—just a firm pressure as he pushed into her. The stretch was sharp, a sting blooming into an overwhelming fullness that made her toes curl. She'd had Hunter inside her, yes, but this was different. Dax was larger, more precise; his control made every inch count. Her body fought him for a heartbeat, clenching, then yielded, muscles loosening with a helpless gasp.

Above her, Silas slid onto the bed to her side, his movements unhurried even now, as if they had all the time in the world. He caught her gasp with his mouth, kissing her deeply, lazily, as Dax pressed in until his hips met her thighs. Her cry was swallowed against Silas's lips, turning into a muffled, shocked moan. The dual sensation of a slow, thorough kiss and Dax stretching her from below made her spine arch off the mattress.

"I'm so glad you've chosen to stay," Silas said between kisses as he nuzzled into her neck, curled up by her side. He guided her free hand down, wrapping her fingers around the weight of him—heavy and warm, pulsing with a lazier urgency. "Just... hold me," he whispered, eyes half-closed. "Slow and tight." She curled her hand around him, thumb accidentally skimming the sensitive ridge beneath the head. He let out a quiet moan. Encouraged, she stroked him in strong, unhurried pulls, matching the dreamy pace of his kisses, almost forgetting Dax was working her inside.

Dax set a rhythm that was almost clinical in its precision—deep, even, smooth strokes that sought out the end of her, grinding against places she didn't know she had. Each movement nudged her higher, the sting fading into a thick, aching fullness that made her hips lift to meet him without conscious thought.

Bennett hovered at the edge, his usual shyness battling with the heat flushing his cheeks. His eyes were softer than the others', filled with something close to awe as they drank in every shiver and caught breath. "You're so beautiful," he managed, the words tumbling out before he could stop them. He reached to brush a stray lock of hair from her damp forehead, fingers feather-light, as if afraid she might break.

She whimpered into Silas's mouth, body overwhelmed by the storm of sensation: Dax's controlled thrusts, Silas's slow kiss and steady pulse under her palm, Bennett's gaze over her sweat-slicked body. It should have been too much. Instead, some part of her woke up, recognizing this strange, overwhelming abundance as something it had always been denied.

Dax's pace sharpened, his composure fraying. The measured rhythm broke into something harder, more urgent, his jaw tight as he chased his own edge. With a low groan he pulled out abruptly, chest heaving, and wrapped his fingers around himself. Hot spurts spilled across her inner thighs and mound, marking her in messy, glistening lines. She gasped at the sudden coolness where he'd been, at the strange sensation of his release painting her skin. He stepped aside with a curt nod, wiping his hand on a discarded rag. There was no apology on his face, but there was no cruelty either. Simply a man who had taken what he needed and, for now, was done.

Drew, the youngest of them all, lingered back for a long moment, his wide eyes taking everything in. A faint blush crept up his neck to the tips of his ears. He looked almost boyish still, but he was standing stiff and straight, untouched, hand hovering uncertainly at his side.

"Come on," Harry coaxed him with a crooked grin. "You'll regret it if you don't."

Drew swallowed and edged closer, the heel of his hand brushing Snow White's calf. Tentatively, he traced a shape on her skin—a circle, then another—before daring to slide his palm higher, over her knee, to rest on her thigh. The contact was gentle, almost questioning.

Bennett moved in like a shadow, quiet and apologetic even as he shed the last of his clothes. Everything about him felt different from Gage and Dax—softer, more tentative.

"May I, Miss Snow?" Bennett asked, and the simple question eased something in her chest.

She nodded.

He guided himself into her with care, one hand fanning over her hip in a grounding touch. When he slipped inside, he did it slowly, inch by careful inch, watching her face for any flicker of pain. He murmured nonsense under his breath—soft reassurances and half-formed praises—as if he were soothing a skittish colt. The angle was different this time. His hips rolled in small circles rather than driving straight in, each pass brushing a sensitive spot inside her that made her toes curl and a low sound catch in her throat.

Her body, already opened and slick, welcomed him more easily. Her hips lifted, meeting him in a small, answering rhythm that surprised her. For the first time that night, a spark of something like pleasure rose from within her, not just on her skin.

Silas, worked by her slow, steady hand, finally let his façade crack. "Mmm," he hummed, voice deepening. "Yes, just like that. Please don't stop." His hips jerked, thrusts growing shorter, breath catching. With a drawn-out groan that sounded almost like relief, he spilled into her hand. He sagged against her shoulder, pressing lazy kisses to her skin in thanks as she blinked at the sticky evidence of his undoing.

Drew, emboldened by the sight of the others losing control, stroked the inside of her thigh with more confidence now, fingertips drawing idle patterns in the mix of arousal and release that slicked her skin. The room had become a tangle of limbs and heat, but within the chaos, small pockets of gentleness bloomed—Bennett's thumb rubbing circles on her mound, Harry brushing hair away from her eyes, Silas's weight a comforting presence cuddled against her side.

Bennett's pace faltered, his face tightening. "Snow," he rasped, the half-formed nickname slipping out. "You are... you have no idea...you..." His hips buried deep with a final, shuddering thrust, warmth pulsing inside her. He groaned softly, forehead dropping to her shoulder, his free hand braced beside her head.

She exhaled, not quite satisfied but humming with a strange, full arousal. The men had all finished rather quickly. She didn't want it to end.

Drew took his place last, almost reverent as he slid into the space Bennett left behind. They were all slick now—her, them, the bed. It should have felt too much, but somehow his careful entry was a new kind of shock, gentler and curious. He climbed on top of her so they were face-to-face. His movements were light, exploratory—shallow dips that tested her response, then deeper, steady thrusts as he found a rhythm that worked for his inexperienced body. His hands roamed with unfiltered curiosity, tracing the line of her waist, the curve of her hip, the gentle slope of her ribs.

Snow White inhaled with a sharp neediness. The contrasts—the roughness of Gage, the eagerness of Harry, the precision of Dax, the tenderness of Bennett, the laziness of Silas, the boyish awe of Drew—wove together inside her, leaving her buzzing, over-stimulated, and yet oddly... grounded. "Oh, oh, ohhh..." Drew moaned. His quiet gasps built into little whimpers, his slender frame tensing as he finally tipped over, pouring himself into her with a surprised, breathless sound. He stilled, chest heaving, then slowly pulled back, eyes wide and dazed.

Bennett, still pressed against her side, shifted to press soft kisses along her arm, her shoulder, her temple. Little words spilled from him—"beautiful," "brave," "thank you"—half-whispered into her skin.

Around them, the others settled, the first wild edge of hunger worn off. Harry gave her a playful squeeze on the calf before rolling away to the foot of the bed. Gage had retreated to the other room, perhaps unsettled by how quickly his anger had turned to need, how deeply this bargain had lodged under his skin.

Snow White lay sprawled among them, limbs loose, body glistening with sweat and the evidence of all she'd given them. Her core throbbed with a low, insistent ache—arousal left hanging. The cottage echoed with heavy breaths and the faint creak of cooling wood. Outside, the world carried on: the stream burbled, a night bird called, the forest shifted restlessly.

Inside, everything had changed. She waited for shame to crash over her, for the sense of being used and ruined to crush her chest. It didn't. She was vulnerable, yes—stripped open, known in a way she had never been before. But beneath that, something else stirred: a fragile, tentative sense of safety. No one here was mocking her. No one was calling her names. No one was trying to hide her away because of how she looked. They had been greedy and selfish. They had not asked how to pleasure her, only how to spend themselves. But they had been honest about it. They had named their price and given her, for the first time in years, a choice. For now, that was enough.

As she drifted toward sleep, tangled amid their exhausted bodies, Snow White realized with a strange, quiet certainty, that she didn't feel hollow. She felt... claimed, yes. Marked. But also anchored. This was her new world: raw, unpolished, at times overwhelmingly intense. But it was one she had stepped into with her eyes open. It would not always be kind, but it would be hers to navigate.

Chapter Fifteen

The Softest Thing

B Y THE TIME THE fall faded into winter, Snow White's life in the cottage had begun to feel less like a bargain and more like a strange kind of rhythm. They had given her some space, made room for her, an extra chair at the table, things kept tidier. They had built a small shed for Grimm to seek respite from the autumn winds and the coming winter cold, and would often pick up hay from a farm on their way home from the mines. Days blurred into one another: mornings of clattering bowls and sleepy grumbles, afternoons of silence while the men were underground, evenings of heat and laughter and the creak of the big bed under too many bodies.

She slept with them now as if there had never been a time she didn't. It was easier that way; there were a few rooms and many beds in the cottage, but they often argued about who got to have her next to them at night; she was the softest thing in the house. She often woke pinned between two heavy forms, a thigh slung over her hip, a hand resting across her waist, the deep, even breathing of exhausted miners around her.

In the first weeks, she had startled at each touch. Now she recognized them by weight alone. Silas's arm, heavy and lax, draped over her ribs like a warm blanket. Drew's tentative knee nudging the back of her calf, as if he were afraid to take up space even in his sleep. Bennett's fingers intertwined with hers, their palms sweat-slicked even in the cold.

The sex, which had seemed like everything that first night, became only one thread in the weave of their days. They still used her. They still pushed into her mouth and hands and body with a needfulness that sometimes left her head spinning. There were nights she had two of them filling her at once, or woke to Silas already moving gently behind her, his breath warm against her neck. But between those moments, there were hundreds of others that were quieter, softer, almost ordinary.

She learned, slowly, how to cook more than porridge. At first, the kitchen intimidated her more than the big bed. Pots and pans and herbs and sacks of flour seemed like another language she hadn't been taught. Her first attempts were disasters—thick, burned stews that even the men, desperate as they were, had trouble swallowing.

Harry was the first to help. "Here," he said one afternoon, rolling up his sleeves as he stood beside her at the rough-hewn table. "You're murdering those onions."

She looked at the pale, uneven cubes under her knife. "Are they supposed to be smaller?"

"They're supposed to be less... sad," he said, bumping her shoulder with his. "Watch." His big hands moved with surprising deftness, fingers curling under as he sliced, knife ticking neatly against the board. The pieces fell uniform and finely chopped.

"You cook?" she asked, surprised.

"Ma worked in a tavern," he said with a shrug. "She

said no son of hers was going to burn water and starve his wife." He grinned. "Haven't got a wife yet, but the rest took."

He didn't push her aside, didn't take over. He handed the knife back, wrapped his arms around her from behind, guiding her grip, and adjusting the angle of her wrist. "Rock the blade, not your whole arm," he said. "You're not swinging a sword."

Her back instinctively arched as she pushed herself into his groin and her chest protruded further. She laughed under her breath and tried again. Her next attempt was better. Not perfect, but better.

"See?" he said. "You'll have us all fat and lazy in a month." He took her body language as an invitation and fondled her breasts while she continued cooking.

She doubted that. No amount of stew could undo ten hours a day underground. But each small success—bread that rose instead of collapsing, a rabbit stew that didn't taste like ashes, porridge dressed with honey and dried berries—felt like a kind of magic.

During the days while they worked, the cottage was hers. She swept soot from the hearth, beat dust from blankets, patched worn shirts with careful stitches. She learned to scrub stubborn stains from miners' trousers, dirt so ground in it seemed a part of the fabric. She hauled water from the stream, arms trembling the first few days and then growing stronger, the slosh of the buckets becoming familiar music. Sometimes she took their shirts down to the stream to wash, kneeling on the damp grass as the water numbed her fingers. She would spread the wet fabric over rocks to dry, watching the current tug at fallen leaves.

Always, Grimm grazed nearby, his dark shape a steady reassurance. "Are you happy?" she asked him once, running a brush down his side as he leaned into the pressure, eyes half-closed. He flicked an ear and nudged her shoulder with his nose, snuffling at her hair until it stood on end.

"I'll take that as a yes," she said, smiling.

He was leaner now, his muscles defined from days of small, careful rides along the deer tracks she'd found. She didn't push him hard; they'd both had more than enough running for their lives. Instead, they wandered happily: through stands of birch that glittered like silver in the low light, along the ridge where the land dropped away into a patchwork of trees. The men were kind to Grimm and tended to him as needed. Some even slipped him some carrots from the garden or let him lick the bottom of their bowls of oatmeal.

Above the neckline of her simple dress, under the rough fabric, the prince's token always lay warm against her skin. Sometimes, when she sat on a rock to catch her breath, she would slip her hand under the dress and squeeze her fingers around it. It had warmed to her body, the once-cool silver, familiar now. She would thumb the worn edge, the tiny engraved falcon, and remember the way his fingers had pressed into her waist as he helped her down from the saddle. "It's foolish," she told Grimm. "Two years and more, and I still think of a boy I knew for less than an hour." Grimm flicked his tail, uninterested in human folly.

"I have men who hold me every night," she went on, looking at the river far below. "Who feed me, keep me warm, make me feel wanted. And still..." Still, at night, when the cottage had gone dark and the men's breathing had deepened around her, her thoughts drifted elsewhere. There were moments when a hand brushing her hair off her face or lips grazing her neck made her wonder how that nameless prince might have touched her. Whether he'd have been more like Bennett—soft and careful—or more like Gage—rough and unflinching. Or something entirely different from them all. "Maybe I'm greedy," she whispered once to the dark. "Wanting all this and still wanting... more." The cottage gave her a kind of freedom she'd never had in the castle. The bargain was blunt, etched into the fabric of her days, but there was a crucial difference: she could leave.

Once, over breakfast, she set down her spoon and said casually, "What would you do if I decided to go? If I said I wanted to see what's beyond the next valley?"

Dax looked up from his cup, brow raising faintly. "We'd tell you which road not to take," he said. "The one with the sinkhole. And we'd pack you food. Why?"

She shrugged, heart tight. "Just wondering."

Silas added, "We'd tell you to head west. There is a castle not too far from here. The king is a wise and good man. I've heard stories of his son, Prince Jacob. His people adore him. You would be safe there."

Harry, across the table, reached out to steal a slice of bread from her bowl. "We'd miss you," he said, waggling his eyebrows to soften the admission. "Who else is going to burn the porridge exactly the way I like it?"

Bennett's eyes dropped, hurt flickering too quickly to hide. Drew's hand, resting on the bench beside hers, curled subtly closer.

Gage snorted. "Don't put ideas in her head," he

muttered, jabbing at a bit of sausage with unnecessary force. "She'll try it just to spite you."

"That sounded suspiciously like you'd care," Harry observed.

Gage shot him a look. "I care about having a woman around here," he said. "I care about myself."

Silas yawned from his end of the bench. "If she goes," he drawled, "I'm going with her. I'm too old to learn my own laundry now."

"Time to go," Dax muttered, "we're late," shouldering his pickaxe and rope as the dawn grayed the window.

Harry groaned, wiping the breakfast from his chin, "Another day in the dark. Lookin' for jewels. When we have the most precious gem of all at home." He teased, "Try not to miss us too much while we're gone, Snow."

They laughed, the tension dissolving. But Snow White filed the answers away. None of them had said they would stop her. None had hinted at locking the door. The choice sat in her chest like a stone and a feather both. Most days, she stayed because leaving would have meant walking back into a world where she was either hunted or utterly alone. Some nights, as she lay between Silas and Drew, or with Bennett curled at her side and Harry's foot occasionally nudging her calf, she realized she also stayed because she wanted to see what it meant to be wanted without it turning instantly to danger.

Each man, over the months, carved his own pattern against her life. Dax always came to her with a certain distance. He used her quietly, a few times a week, often when the others were asleep or already drifting toward it. He would whisper her name at the edge of the bed, and she'd feel the mattress dip as he slid in behind her. His hands were always careful—never bruising, never grabbing. But he never looked at her face. He would guide himself into her from behind, one arm sliding under her neck to pull her back against his chest, the other bracing beside her head. His movements were steady, controlled, as if he were measuring out his pleasure by the inch. Sometimes, when she risked a glance over her shoulder, she saw his eyes squeezed tightly shut, his jaw tense enough to crack. Her instinct was to tease him once, to make him meet her eyes when he was inside her, to see what it would do. But when the moment came, when she felt him above her, breath hot against her ear, she kept her gaze on the wooden beam overhead. So she shut her eyes and let him touch her as carefully as a man handling something that didn't belong to him.

Gage was the opposite. He never came to her alone. He joined her when there were already hands on her, when her body was already readied by someone else's touch. He'd slip into the edge of the frenzy with a low, frustrated growl, his contributions all sharp angles and blunt need. He never spoke softly. He didn't kiss; he bit. His hands were rough, his thrusts quick and heavy, the sounds he made primal and unpretty. She always felt used when he left her, breathless and panting, chest heaving as he rolled away. And yet, even there, something shifted over time. He never left a mark. If anyone else's hands strayed somewhere she clearly didn't like, his voice would be the first, surprisingly, to cut in with a curt "Leave it" that snapped them back. He growled the most when she laughed with someone else.

Once, Harry had coaxed a rare giggle from her by

getting flour all over his beard while "helping" with the bread. The sound had filled the cottage, light and unguarded. Gage, walking past on his way to the washbasin, had scowled so hard the room cooled by several degrees.

"What's so funny?" he demanded.

"Your face will be if you don't unclench," Harry shot back, smearing a bit of dough on Gage's arm.

Gage had cursed him out, but there was something tight and tangled in his gaze when it slid over Snow White's smiling mouth. Later that night, his thrusts into her had carried a certain extra sharpness, as if he were trying to scrub the memory of her laughter from both their bodies.

Harry was, unexpectedly, the first to make her feel... cherished. He teased, yes. Filthy jokes, dramatic moans, theatrical compliments. But under the playfulness was a core of warmth that never seemed to dim. He was the one who brought her a dress. He barged in one evening with a bundle under his arm, eyes alight. "Found it," he announced, tossing it onto the bed where she sat folding socks. "In a trader's pack headed for the next town. Had to win three rounds of cards to keep it from some tavern girl—you're welcome."

She unfolded the dress carefully. It was simple—a soft, faded green cloth that had seen better days—but someone had taken care to keep it mended. The neckline was modest, the sleeves tight to the wrist, the waist nipped in just enough to hint at curves without shouting them.

"It's beautiful," she said, running her fingers over the fabric. "Harry, I can't—"

"You can," he said. "And you should. You deserve to feel like yourself sometimes, not just like..." He gestured vaguely at the pile of gray and brown she usually wore. "Besides, nobody else around here is gonna wear it!"

He wasn't wrong. The first time she put it on, the men went quiet in a way that startled her more than any catcall would have.

"You look..." Bennett began, then seemed to lose his words entirely, blushing down to his collar.

"Like some lady in a painting," Silas finished for him. "Or one of those storybook princesses you read about." The word made her shoulders tense. She forced a laugh to cover her uneasiness.

Harry stepped closer, tipping her chin up with one knuckle. "You look like you," he said simply. "And that's more than enough."

He kissed her then, not with the urgency of the others but with a slowly building heat that curled her toes. His hands mapped her curves through the fabric, reverent and playful by turns.

With Harry, sex began to feel less like a debt and more like a shared adventure. He made her laugh in bed as often as he made her gasp, always attuned to her responses, always willing to change pace or try something different if she tensed. "You good?" he'd murmur sometimes, lips at her ear as he moved inside her. "Too much? Not enough? Tell me, Snow." No one had ever cared, in bed, whether she was "good" in any way but accommodating.

Silas became her constant. He was the one she most often woke up beside, his breath slow and deep against the back of her neck. His brand of intimacy was unhurried, half-dreamed, like everything important in life could be tasted best in the quiet spaces between. On countless nights, she would stir to find his body pressed along hers, his front warm against her back, his hand resting low on her belly. Sometimes he would shift closer, the unmistakable evidence of his desire nudging her gently. "Shh," he'd murmur when she rolled in surprise. "Go back to sleep." Then he'd rock into her slowly, almost languidly, filling her with careful movements that barely woke the bed. There was no grabbing, no growling, just the steady slide of bodies already so familiar with each other's shapes that they fit without fuss. It was easy, with Silas, to forget the bargain entirely and just feel.

Bennett's attachment grew quickest. He hovered near her in small, earnest ways: always the first to hand her a cup of water when she finished hauling buckets, the one who quietly took over beating rugs when he saw her arms shaking, the one who slipped the best piece of meat from his own plate to hers, thinking she didn't notice. He rarely initiated sex himself, too shy to be the first to reach. But when the others did, he was nearly always there at the periphery, not pushing forward so much as filling in the gaps. If someone's hands were rough on her hips, his would be smoothing over her shoulder blades. If a mouth was on her throat, his would be at her wrist, pressing soft kisses to the thin, fluttering skin there. If she gasped in a way that sounded too much like pain, his eyes would find her face at once, silently asking if she was all right. Bennett was also the one who most consistently cared about her pleasure as well as his own. Sure, the others would rub her nipples from time to time, but Bennett spent more time kissing, rubbing, and touching her body than any of the others.

Drew remained her softest spot. At first, his

inexperience had made him awkward, his hands unsure of where to rest, his movements within her tentative and light. He would look at her with wide, questioning eyes, as if waiting for visible approval before every new touch. He always finished terribly quickly, his inexperience shining through. She found herself guiding him almost without thinking: moving his hand a little higher on her hip, adjusting his angle with a small shift of her own body, advising him quietly. Their moments together felt less like a transaction and more like a lesson taught and learned in secret, both of them discovering what they liked or disliked. With Drew, she felt less like an object to be taken and more like a fellow thief sharing a secret.

As the weeks rolled into months, the sharp edges of her fear dulled. She still startled at sudden noises outside. A snapped twig could send her heart racing, memories of Hunter's knife and Liora's comb flaring bright. Sometimes, hanging damp shirts by the stream, she'd look up thinking she saw a shadow in the trees, only to realize it was only the play of light and leaves.

She never told the men about the queen. About the poisoned comb, the corset, the ordered murder in the forest. When they asked where she was from, she kept her answers vague. "A village far from here," she'd say.

"What's it called?" Dax would ask.

She'd shrug. "It doesn't matter. I'm not going back."

"Family?" Drew pressed once, curious.

She stared at the fire until its afterimage burned behind her eyelids. "I left home," she said. "I don't have much of a family." They didn't push. Or if they wanted to, they respected her silence enough not to. At night, when she lay amid the tangle of limbs and breath, she sometimes imagined what would happen if she told them the truth.

I am Princess Shay, she would say. *My mother is the queen. She tried to kill me, twice. A man you'd probably respect once held a knife to my throat because she told him to. If you keep me here, you're harboring a fugitive.* In her mind, their faces changed: Dax's mouth thinning with worry, Harry's laughter faltering, Gage's scowl deepening. She pictured them bundling her onto Grimm, patting his flank, giving her bread and jerky and careful directions to the nearest border. She wasn't ready to risk that. Not yet.

So she lay there instead, listening to the steady breathing of six men who had slowly, improbably, grown used to her presence. And she told herself that for now, for this season of her life, this was enough.

Chapter Sixteen

Unanswered Questions

BY EARLY SPRING, THE snow had retreated to the highest ridges, leaving the forest floor spongy and green. New leaves unfurled on branches, fragile and bright. Birdsong returned in earnest. In the cottage, a similar softening had taken place. Snow White was comfortable. She would have denied it if anyone had accused her of it out loud. Comfort, to her mind, seemed almost like a sin. But there was no denying that she knew the sounds of the house now as well as she had once known the echo in the castle halls. She knew the creak of the third stair, the one Drew always skipped. She knew the whistle of wind through the chink near the chimney and how to stuff it with old cloth when the wind howled too loudly. She knew which boards squeaked near the bed, which ones were safe to tread on when she needed to slip out to get a glass of water at night. She knew the rhythms of six men's tempers and tendernesses.

And they, whether they knew it or not, had begun to orbit her the way planets orbit a sun. Small gestures gave it away.

Harry, as always, gave his devotion in jubilation. "Look at you," he'd say when she came in from the stream, skirts hitched, hair damp and cheeks flushed from the cold.

"Like some forest spirit. We don't deserve you."

"Stop," she'd say, swatting at him, but she'd be smiling.

When she burned the first batch of bread he'd taught her to knead alone, he didn't tease. He tore off a piece of the darker crust, chewed it thoughtfully, and said, "Could be worse. It's still better than Gage's cooking."

Gage, passing behind them, rolled his eyes. "You've never tasted my cooking."

"There's a reason for that," Harry replied, winking.

In bed, Harry had become less of a frantic grab for release and more of a steady source of warmth. He lingered after, one hand playing absently with her hair, murmuring ridiculous things against her temple.

"If any of us had half a brain," he said once, "we'd be courting you properly. Flowers every week, fancy dinners, the whole lot."

"You can't even manage not to track mud into the house," she pointed out.

"True," he conceded. "But in another life..."

She didn't let him finish that sentence. Another life was a dangerous thought.

Drew developed a habit of taking her hand. It happened first by accident. They were walking back from the stream, she with a basket of damp shirts balanced on her hip, he with an armful of firewood. The path narrowed, muddy on one side, steep on the other. She slipped. "Snow!" he cried. His hand shot out, fingers catching hers, steadying her.

They both froze. "Thank you," she said, breathing a little harder than the stumble warranted.

He nodded, cheeks pink, but didn't let go right away. His fingers were calloused but gentle around hers. After that, it happened more often. Sitting on the bench after dinner, shoulders touching, his hand would creep over to find hers. At first she thought it was only nerves, something for him to fidget with instead of his own sleeves. Then she realized he liked the contact for its own sake. It wasn't sexual, not really. There was no immediate lunge for her body afterward. It was just... closeness. A quiet reassurance that he was there, that she was real, that between the chaos of shifts and shared nights, they existed in the small, calm moments too.

Bennett seemed to worship her. He was always nearby. If she went to fetch water, there was a good chance he'd be in the yard chopping wood. If she mended shirts by the fire, he'd be at the table whittling something, stealing glances at her over the shavings. She caught him more than once halfway across the cottage with his mug, clearly having stood up to refill it and then forgotten his purpose because she'd smiled at something Silas had said.

He never quite found a reason to ask her for more of herself outside the bed. But in small ways, he gave her the kind of attention she had never gotten from anyone but her father. "Are you cold?" he asked one evening, noticing the way she'd rubbed her arms.

"Just a little," she admitted.

The next day, he came back from town with a bundle of wool in his arms. "I thought," he said, almost dropping it in his haste to get the words out, "maybe you could make yourself a shawl. Or I could—no, you probably don't want me knitting—I just thought..."

She laughed softly and took it from him, pressing a kiss to his blushing cheek.

Even Dax softened at the edges. He began to ask her questions at odd times. Not probing ones about her past, but small, practical ones about her. "What do you like to read?" he asked once, catching her with a book in her lap when he came in early from the mine.

She blinked at him, finger marking her place. "Stories," she said. "All kinds, fantasy, romance, stories about characters who are one way at the beginning of the book and entirely different at the end."

"That sounds... complicated," he said.

"It is," she replied. "That's what makes it interesting."

Another day, as she sliced carrots, he nodded toward the pot. "Less salt," he advised. "You always reach for it twice. Once is enough."

She stared at him. "You noticed that?"

He shrugged. "I notice a lot of things. It's my job."

"Not here," she said. "Here you could pretend not to notice if you wanted to."

"You're part of 'here' now," he pointed out. "I don't get to stop noticing you." The words landed heavier in her chest than he'd probably intended.

Silas made no grand declarations of affection. He just drifted over to her wherever she happened to be and leaned. If she sat on the bench, he flopped down beside her, his head finding her lap as naturally as if it had been made for that spot. If she stood at the stove, he wandered by and looped an arm around her waist, resting his chin on her shoulder until she hip-checked him away. If she sat on the floor to mend a tear, he lay down behind her, pillowing his head on her back and sighing like someone who'd carried too much weight for too long. He didn't ask for much with words. But his body spoke clearly: you are safe.

Even Gage, grudgingly, began to show that he cared in his own twisted way. He snapped at her when she made mistakes. "What are you doing with that knife?" he barked once when he caught her trying to pry a stuck lid off a jar with the blade pointed toward her palm. "Trying to lose a thumb?"

"I'm just—"

"Doing it wrong," he cut in. He snatched the knife, turned it, and popped the lid from the other side with a deft twist. "There. Try not to stab yourself before supper."

"Thank you," she said dryly.

He grunted. "Don't thank me. I'm the one who'd have to bandage you."

When he walked in on her and Drew playing some silly hand game Harry had taught them, laughing breathlessly as they tried to see who could tap the other's fingers faster, he stopped in the doorway, jaw tightening. "Don't you two have work to do?" he snapped. "The wood's not going to chop itself."

Drew opened his mouth, clearly about to retort. Snow White squeezed his hand subtly. "We were just going," she said, smoothing the moment. "Come on, Drew."

Later, when she found Gage alone in the shed sharpening tools, she leaned against the doorframe. "You know," she said, "if you're jealous, you could just say so."

His head whipped around. "I'm not jealous," he said at once. "Of what? That fool dropping the basin every time you smile at him?"

Her lips twitched. "So you've noticed I smile."

He scowled harder. "Hard not to. It's loud."

She stepped closer. "It doesn't mean anything," she said softly. "With Drew. Or Harry. Not the way you're thinking."

His jaw worked. "I don't know what it is," he said. "I know I don't like watching you laugh with other men when I haven't finished my shift. That's all."

She considered that. "Well," she said lightly, "you'll just have to get home earlier, then."

He stared at her for a long moment, then huffed, the ghost of a reluctant smile tugging at one corner of his mouth. "You're trouble," he muttered.

"You invited me in," she replied.

He shook his head and went back to his sharpening, but his movements were less harsh now, as if some tension had uncoiled.

None of the men ever said the word "love." Not out loud.

Snow White, for her part, was careful not to examine her feelings too closely. What she felt for them was complicated: affection, gratitude, desire, occasional annoyance, a budding sense of belonging. But this was not what the stories had promised her.

It wasn't that she didn't care. She did. When they came home late, hearts pounding from a near cave-in story, she clung to them harder than she meant to. When one of them scraped a hand or bruised a rib, she fussed with salve and bandages until they squirmed. When they grumbled and bickered over nothing, she smoothed their ruffled tempers like she smoothed sheets. They had become her people—her allies, her family.

And yet, when she closed her eyes at night, the face that floated up first was still the prince's. She would lie there with Silas's arm heavy over her, Dax's back a solid line of warmth at the other side, and her fingers would creep up to the token at her neck. She'd trace the tiny falcon, wondering where he was now. Whether he'd ever married some noble girl. Whether he ever thought about the ragged stable girl who'd bonded with him over their shared love of horses. Part of her scolded herself for such foolishness. "You have what you need," she'd remind herself silently. "You're fed. Safe. Not hunted. Wanted." Another part whispered, *But he saw you when you were no one at all, and he didn't shy away.* She didn't know which part of her would win in the end. For now, there was laundry to scrub and bread to knead and men to send off to work with full bellies and clean shirts.

• • • ● ● • ● ● • •

T HERE WAS A NEW batch of shirts drying on the rocks by the stream one afternoon, so Harry and Bennett decided to join her. She knelt at the water's edge, the stream cold and quick around her bare calves, the men's shirts heavy in her hands as she dunked and scrubbed, dunked and scrubbed. The dirt of the mines leached slowly into the water, turning it cloudy downstream. She didn't mind the work. It gave her something to do with her body while her mind wandered.

Today, unfortunately, her thoughts had wandered back to a blade at her throat. She could feel it as clearly as if it were there again: the cool metal, the warmth of Hunter's body behind her, the way his hand had slid from her shoulder to her breast. She shook her head once, sharply, trying to dislodge the memory.

"Want some help?" a voice called. She looked up, startled.

Harry and Bennett were descending the slight slope from the cottage, each with a bundle over their shoulder.

"We brought the rest," Harry said cheerfully, hoisting his load. "Figured we'd speed this along. Maybe get a swim out of it."

Bennett smiled in a small, apologetic way, his arms full of trousers.

"You don't have to," she began.

"We know," Harry said. "That's why it's fun."

They made a show of rolling up their trousers, then, with a whoop, stepped straight into the water, splashing her in the process. "Hey!" she protested, laughing as the cold hit her.

"Oops," Harry said, utterly unconvincing. "My foot slipped."

Bennett's quieter chuckle joined hers. They helped wash for a while, the three of them falling into an easy rhythm. Harry teased each shirt as if the garment were responsible for the dirt. Bennett hummed while he worked, a half-remembered tune from somewhere far away.

After the last shirt was wrung out and laid on the rocks, Snow White sank back onto her heels, stretching her arms. The sun was warm on her face for the first time in days. The chill water had numbed her feet, but her blood felt pleasantly heated from the work.

She sensed it before she saw it: the weight of their gazes shifting from the laundry to her. She opened her eyes. Harry and Bennett stood side by side in the shallows, water lapping at their calves. Both had paused halfway through whatever they'd been doing, eyes fixed on her with a warmth that made her cheeks flush. "What?" she asked, half-laughing, self-conscious.

"Nothing," Harry said, though the dimple in his cheek gave him away. "Just thinking we're very lucky bastards."

Bennett nodded, his expression softer. "You look happy," he said. "By the water. It suits you." The compliment landed differently than the usual ones. Happiness was not something people often told her she wore well.

On impulse, she stood. Her dress clung to her shins, already damp from splashing. The stream glinted, inviting. The men's smiles were easy, familiar. "Turn around," she said.

Harry raised an eyebrow. "Why?"

"So you won't get an eyeful too early," she said, surprising herself with the boldness in her tone.

They laughed, but they obeyed, facing the bank.

With quick fingers, she unlaced the front of her dress and pulled it over her head. The air kissed her bare skin, raising goosebumps along her arms. She set the dress on a dry rock, then reached back to untie her chemise.

Sliding into the water naked was shocking, cold, and

exhilarating. The current curled around her thighs, then her waist, then—when she ducked lower—her shoulders, washing away soap and sweat and the constant, invisible weight of eyes.

"All right," she called. "You can look now."

They turned. For a heartbeat, no one spoke.

She stood waist-deep in the stream, hair tumbling over her shoulders, water beading on her skin. The sunlight turned the droplets into tiny sparks as they slid down her collarbones, over the rise of her breasts, along the soft curve of her stomach.

She felt vulnerable and wild at once.

Harry let out a low whistle. "Now that," he said, "is a sight to cure a man of mining forever."

Bennett swallowed, color high in his cheeks. "You're so breathtaking," he confessed quietly. "I still can't even believe it."

She met his gaze steadily. "This time I want you both," she started, confidently. "On my terms." That last bit was new, and it rang true in her own ears.

Harry and Bennett exchanged a glance. Then, with twin grins—Harry's shameless, Bennett's still tinged with shyness—they stripped off their clothes and waded toward her.

The water swirled around them, cool on hot skin. Hands found her under the surface—one sliding along her hip, another tracing the line of her spine. Mouths found her shoulders, her throat, the hollow at the base of her neck. She laughed when Harry splashed her, gasped when Bennett's hand cupped her behind.

In the cool water they played, naked, together. Harry

being silly, and Bennett devoted to her—as usual. Harry splashed around and flirted, stealing glances and proposing dares. Bennett kissed her softly, deeply, and then lowered his head to explore her nipples with his tongue, his warmth on her breasts, contrasted with the cold water Harry splashed on them.

"Snow, Bennett wants you to take him in your mouth," Harry said sing-songedly.

Bennett blushed. He had never presented himself for her mouth, thinking it was probably a little demeaning for a woman. But Snow White jumped at the chance.

She took his hand as they waded to shallower water, and she got down on her knees in front of Bennett and looked up at him.

"You don't have to..." he started to say.

But she gripped both hands around his base and slowly guided him into her mouth, eyes fixed on his the whole time. Bennett had never felt anything better. He had never felt more on fire, more in love with a set of eyes.

Harry appeared at Bennett's side, peering over his shoulder. "Isn't it the best? Especially when she looks up at you. Ugh, I want to melt right then every time."

This made Snow White smile and she pulled back and stood up again. Bennett immediately kissed her deeply as if to say thank you, or I love you, or both.

"Okay, now it's your turn, Snow. Let Bennett taste you," Harry challenged Bennett.

Snow White wasn't sure what Harry really meant, but Bennett took her hand and led her to the riverbank. He laid her down on the soft moss with the rush of the stream chanting a rhythm for their coupling. Harry joined them and lay naked by her side. His touches turned more focused, his kisses more sensual. Bennett moved between her legs and spread her thighs with his gentle hands. Snow White wasn't sure what was about to happen. The men had occasionally used their mouths on her body, kisses down her torso, licking her nipples, but none of them had ever kissed her down there.

"Hold on tight, Snow. You're in for it." Harry said, excitedly watching.

Bennett started slowly, kissing her inner thighs and moving to the middle. The sensation was electrifying for Snow White. His lips sent tremors through her body, reminding her of the first time her breasts were ever touched. She felt his warm tongue slowly drawing circles and then slowly licking up and down as if not wanting to miss a spot. She let out a loud moan, and then another, her voice growing stronger.

He continued licking and sucking as Harry watched, kissing her, caressing her breasts, and tugging on himself so as not to interrupt her pleasure, but soon Harry couldn't wait any longer. "Ok, get on all fours, Snow," Harry said. And he positioned himself behind her as she moved.

"Bennett, will you let me finish what I started?" she asked, waving him over to her face. Bennett nodded and moved around to her face, full and throbbing from the enjoyment he derived from the taste of her juice on his lips.

"Okay, let's make this fun. Ready?" Harry said, "One...two...three!" On three both men pushed into her at the same time, gently, but firmly—Harry from behind and Bennett from the front. "Amwh," she screamed, sounds muffled from Bennett's erection in her mouth. The men tried their best to make the moment last. They took what they needed from her mouth, from her breasts, and from the heat between her thighs and finished by pooling a collection on her back.

As they lay in a tangle, catching their breath, Snow White's fingers clenched and unclenched until her knuckles turned white. While the men drifted into a quiet riverside nap, spooning Snow White's body, her own blood still raced with a frantic, static energy. She stared at the sky, jaw clenched, the heat between her legs pulsing with a question that had received no answer. She didn't understand the feeling. She didn't understand why she felt angry. This had been happening more and more. She was like a stallion, ready to run, but caged in a stall. She needed someone to unlock the door.

• • • • • • • • • • •

S PRING TURNED TO SUMMER and summer to fall. One day after lunch Dax pulled Snow White aside. "It's been almost a year since you've been here with us. We've loved having you, but I want to make sure you're happy here, too," he confessed. "I sense that you are, but I wanted to be direct and ask. Is there anything we can do to make you more comfortable?"

They sat down on the front porch bench as they spoke.

"There's nowhere I'd rather be. You have given me a

life, given me a family. Something I haven't had in a very long time," she said. *Should I tell him about my father? My mother? I think I can trust Dax. I know he will know what to do. But he's also the sensible one, the one who makes the decisions for the good of the group. What if he decides I need to leave?*

"Ok. I'm glad you feel comfortable. I want you to know you can tell me anything. I will always look out for you," Dax assured, looking down at her with eyes bright and certain. She smiled, heart twisting.

Over time, their hands had learned her more carefully. What had once been taken without question was now offered with pause, with listening. They learned her body and noticed when she winced or when she smiled, when she pushed closer to them or withdrew. She noticed the difference not in the moments themselves, but also in how she was treated afterwards—as if something unspoken had shifted. For the first time in her life, the attention she received didn't feel like a weapon being used against her—it felt like a choice she'd made. Not a perfect one, not a safe one in every sense, but one that had given her, here in the middle of the woods, something she'd thought she'd lost forever: A home.

Chapter Seventeen

Line Crossed

S NOW WHITE FOUND THAT she liked honest toil and hard work. She enjoyed her time with Grimm at the river washing clothes. She liked cooking, experimenting with new herbs and spices. But she especially liked sweeping. It was strange, maybe, to prefer such a simple task after having grown up among marble floors and servants who materialized at the first speck of dust. But here, in the miners' cottage, sweeping meant she could see her work. She could watch the day's grit and crumbs and stray bits of coal gather into piles she could banish out the door. It was satisfying, this small control over chaos.

The men were at the mine. The cottage was quiet in a way it never was when they were home. The beds lay unmade, the sheets twisted from the tangle of bodies that had slept the night before. The fire was down to embers, giving off a gentle warmth instead of a crackling roar. Sunlight pushed through the small windows in soft bands, carrying dust motes that danced lazily in the air.

Snow White hummed under her breath as she worked. Her hair, grown past her shoulders now, tickled the corners of her jaw when she bent. She'd tied it back with a strip of cloth, but strands still escaped to fall into her eyes. She'd long since given up on keeping it neat.

Her mind drifted as the broom whispered against the floorboards. This was her life now: wood smoke and bread dough under her nails, men's laughter at the table, the creak of the beds at night. The idea of balls and banners and jeweled hairpins seemed like something from a book she might have read once and then forgotten. She wasn't unhappy. She wasn't in love, but she wasn't hurt either. Here, her body was part of the bargain, yes—but each day she felt less and less like a toy and more and more like a partner.

She reached the table and bent to sweep the last few crumbs from beneath it. The door opened. She startled, straightening so quickly her back gave a little twinge. The men weren't due back for hours. For one jolting second, her mind supplied the image of Hunter in the doorway, knife in hand. It wasn't Hunter.

Gage filled the frame, broad shoulders blocking out the light from outside. His beard was dusted with coal, his hair damp with sweat where it curled at his neck. He'd shed his outer layer on the hook by the door; his shirt clung to him, outlining thick arms and a torso built from years of hard work.

"Gage," she said, more breathless than the sight should have warranted. "You're back early."

He shut the door behind him with a heavy thud. The sound seemed to cut the cottage off from the rest of the world. "Dax cleared some of us out," he said shortly. "New tunnel needed shoring; they didn't want too many bodies under it until it's braced." He shrugged, a crack of tension easing, then fixed his gaze on her. There was a gleam in his eyes she wasn't used to seeing there. He always looked intense—scowling, frowning, glaring—but this was different. Bright, almost... excited. A half-smile tugged at one corner of his mouth, not soft, but sharp. Snow White's pulse skipped.

He let his gaze trail slowly down her body, taking in the simple dress hitched up a little at her calves, the bare arms dusted with flour from the bread she'd kneaded earlier, the flush on her cheeks from her work. "I'm going to have you now." No preamble. No question.

Heat shot through her, confusing and immediate. Gage had always gotten under her skin more than the others. His roughness, his bluntness, the way he refused to pretend he didn't want what he wanted—it all irritated and thrilled her in equal measure. Her heart beat faster. She swallowed. "Here?" she asked. "Now?"

He stepped forward, the distance between them shrinking. "You have someplace to be?" he asked. "Something more important than doing what you bargained for?"

The words should have stung. Instead, they sent a low thrum through her belly. Still, she hesitated. "The others—"

"Are down in the dark," he said. "They won't be back for hours." He stopped a pace away, close enough that she had to tilt her head back to hold his gaze.

"I couldn't work," he said simply. "Couldn't get your scent out of my head. Had to leave before I took my temper out on some poor sod's skull." His eyes flicked to her mouth, lingering. "Figured I'd take it out on you instead."

She froze.

He stepped closer again, and she found herself

backing up until her hips bumped the table.

His hand came up, fingers wrapping around her wrist. His hand was enormous. Calloused, rough, but warm. The heat of his touch seared through her skin. Her heart skipped from fast to racing.

She tugged once, out of instinct more than intent to escape. He held on easily. "Gage," she said.

"I want you," he said bluntly. "All to myself. No Harry making jokes, no Bennett sighing like a ballad, no Silas snoring before I'm done. Just you and me. My cock and all of your holes to bury it in." He glanced down and noticed the strip of rope coiled beside the bed—it was always there, used to secure gear when storms rattled the roof.

Her pulse jumped as she followed his gaze. "How rough?"

"Tie you up. Take what I want. Make you beg." His eyes searched hers. "But you need to say yes. Really yes. Not 'I'm afraid to say no' yes."

She swallowed. "And if I say no?"

"Then I go chop wood until I'm too tired to think about it." He stepped closer. "We don't tell any of them about this. Ever. Understand?"

Something in his intensity called to something in her. "What do you want to do?"

Ignoring her question he added, "We need a safe word," glancing at her neck, "Falcon. If you say falcon, I'll stop immediately, no questions asked."

Snow White thought for a moment. "Okay, I understand. What are you going to do to me?"

"I want you," he said, as if that explained everything. His mouth curved further. "Come on," he said. "Drop that broom."

She did as she was told. He tugged her toward the bed, the rope already in his other hand, rough fibers catching on his calluses. She should have said no. She knew that, somewhere under the rush in her veins. But the lump of curiosity in her chest was almost as tight as the knot he was about to tie.

"You're not scared?" he asked suddenly, eyes flicking to her face.

She swallowed. "A little."

He snorted. "You should be," he said. "I'm in a mood." He sat her down on the edge of the bed, then turned and dragged the chair closer, the legs scraping on the floor. He pushed her back into it with firm hands.

Her breath came faster. He lifted her wrists one by one and wrapped the rope around them, binding them to the arms of the chair. The fibers dug into her skin. "That's tight," she said, fingers flexing.

"Good," he replied. "I don't want you running when it gets good." He crouched to tie her ankles to the chair legs as well, his head level with her knees. Her skirt slid up with the movement, baring her calves, then her thighs. The air was cool against the dampness she hadn't realized had already gathered between her legs.

When he stood, she was open. Trapped. Heart thudding, limbs pulled just far enough apart that she couldn't close them. A small, involuntary shiver ran through her.

"Cold?" he asked, though the glint in his eye said he knew it wasn't just that.

"I'm okay," she whispered.

He stepped between her spread knees and cupped the back of her neck, thumb stroking just under her ear. "You have no idea," he mumbled, "what you do to me." Then he let go, undid his belt, and pushed his trousers down.

She couldn't look away. She'd seen him before, of course—a dozen times, more. But somehow this felt different. There was something about being the only one in the room, about his body focused solely on her, that made the sight hit harder. He stood there a second, letting her see the extent of his want. The thick shaft standing out from his body, the flushed head, the heavy weight of him. Her mouth went dry.

His gaze dropped to her lips, then back up again. "Open," he said. Her pulse hammered. She parted her lips.

"That's my pretty girl," he grunted. He stepped closer until he was close enough that she could smell him: sweat and iron and something darker, uniquely his. He braced one hand on the back of the chair, the other threading into her hair. Gently, almost unexpectedly so, he guided her mouth to him.

The first brush of him against her lips pulled a small, involuntary sound from her. Her tongue darted out to taste, to ease the path, and he made a low noise that sounded disturbingly like a groan. "That's it," he said. "Just like that." The praise, crude as it was, warmed her chest.

Then he pushed deeper. Her jaw stretched around him. She managed to relax, remembering what had worked before, breathing through her nose, letting her throat open. But Gage wasn't Harry, with his teasing patience, or Bennett, with his careful gentleness. He was Gage: muscular, driven, a man who lived his life at the sharp end of things. He set a rhythm she barely had time to adjust to, hips rolling forward, withdrawing, then pressing deeper. The back of the chair dug into her spine; the rope scraped her wrists when she instinctively tried to lift her hands and couldn't.

She gagged once when he hit too deep. He slowed and pulled back. "Do you want to say falcon?" he asked, loosening his grip.

"No," she replied, opening her mouth again.

He smiled and his hand tightened in her hair. "Breathe," he said, voice rough. "You can take it. I know you can." She blinked up at him, eyes wet. She felt thrilled at the way his face had gone soft and fierce all at once when he'd said *I know you can*.

His thumb brushed the corner of her mouth. "Look at you," he said, something like awe threaded through the heat. "Most beautiful sight I've seen in years." The words hit her, arousal building. No one had ever told her that her openness, her surrender, could be beautiful.

He thrust again, and she choked around him, but the burn in her jaw blurred with a throbbing heat between her legs. She thought of how exposed she was, how the cool air kissed her damp skin, how the rope bit, how utterly she belonged to this moment and this man's choice. "Look at you taking it deep," he praised as he shoved in further.

Fear crept around the edges of her mind. He was rough. Rougher than any of the others dared to be. She had been just starting to believe she was loved here—valued, at least. Now, with each demanding push into her mouth, she felt that certainty wobble.

What if this was all she was to him? A hole. A bargain.

A thing.

"What are you thinking about?" he panted, noticing the way her gaze had gone distant.

She hummed around him, too full to answer. He pulled back abruptly, leaving her gasping, mouth wet and empty. "I asked you a question," he snapped.

"I—" Her voice came out hoarse. She swallowed. "You're... rougher than the others." She tried to catch her breath. "I didn't think I would like this."

His eyes flashed. "You want me to be gentle?" he asked, mocking and serious at once.

She licked her lips. "No."

"You like it," he said. "Don't lie. I can smell when you're scared and when you're wet. Right now you're both."

Humiliation flooded her cheeks. The worst part was that he wasn't wrong. "I'm not—" she started.

He stepped closer, crowding her again. "If you crave honeyed words and gentle touches, find Bennett. But if you wish to feel the very core of your existence shake? You come to me."

His hand slid between her thighs, fingers grazing the slickness there, and she couldn't bite back the sound that tore from her. "That's what I thought," he said. "Tell me you want my cock, Snow."

She swallowed her fear and let him see her want. "Please," she whispered, hating how needy it sounded.

"Say it louder."

"Please," she said again.

He smiled, slow and wicked. "There you go," he said. "That's what I wanted to hear." He untied her ankles first, fingers quick on the knots. Then he set to work on her wrists. The rope slackened, fell away.

Before she could draw a full breath of freedom, he had her spun around and pushed onto the bed, his hands moving her like she weighed nothing. She landed on her stomach, the blankets soft against her skin. He grabbed her hips and lifted, tucking a pillow under her belly so that her behind was raised, knees sinking into the mattress, arms outstretched above her head.

A moment later, the rope was back, looping around her wrists, securing them to the headboard this time. The new angle left her chest pressed into the mattress, her backside high, thighs parted. She could move even less now. Her heart skittered in her chest. She felt the mattress dip as he shifted behind her. Cool air brushed over the backs of her thighs, then lower, making her shiver. She tensed as his hand skimmed the inside of her knee, sliding up her leg, over the curve where thigh became hip.

His fingers didn't go where she expected. Instead, they parted her gently, baring her in a way that made her face burn even though no one else was there to see. She heard him inhale sharply. "You smell like you've been thinking about this all morning," he said.

She made an inarticulate sound into the mattress.

He chuckled, low. "I told you," he leaned in. "Couldn't get you out of my head."

For a heartbeat she thought he was going to kiss her where she ached most. Her body clenched in anticipation. Instead, his mouth found a different hole, more forbidden.

The first wet, warm swipe of his tongue over the tight ring of muscle made her whole body jerk. It was like being struck by lightning in a place she hadn't even known had nerves. "Gage," she gasped, voice half shock, half warning.

"New, isn't it?" he said, his breath hot against that sensitive skin. "No one's ever touched you here."

She shook her head, too stunned to be ashamed.

"You want me to stop?" he asked.

Honesty warred with modesty. Modesty lost. "No," she whispered.

"That's my pretty girl," he said again, and then his tongue circled her slowly, teasing the edges, making her toes curl into the blanket. The unfamiliar feeling sent strange, shivery waves through her, radiating outward in a way that somehow made the dull ache between her thighs even sharper.

He moved his face lower until his tongue reached her clit. She instinctively repositioned her legs, spreading her thighs so he could get in close. Gage's tongue lapped at her clit, then drew small, torturous patterns that made her moan into the mattress. "Say you want more," he said, voice roughening.

"I... want more," she gasped.

He stilled. "Not good enough," he said, louder. "Beg for it."

She bit the pillow, pride warring with need. "Please," she managed, the word muffled. "Please, Gage. I want more."

He made a satisfied sound. Then he obliged. His tongue continued circling her sensitive nub as his finger slowly traced her back entrance, still wet from his tongue. His fingers pressed more insistently now, tracing and circling. He began to gently suck on her clit, while at the same time finally pressing past the tight resistance of her back entrance. The intrusion was strange and intense and impossibly intimate. For a second, discomfort flared. Then it turned into something else—hot, shocking pleasure that made her vision blur and her fingers clench uselessly against the rope.

She moaned, louder this time, hips bucking without her consent. The sensation of both her front and back being worked at once had her eyes rolling back in her head. He held her steady as his free hand slid up to cup one breast, thumb rolling the nipple through the thin fabric of her dress.

Her body felt like it was on fire. No one had ever dared to touch her like this. It felt like she was with three men at once, but it was only Gage. Every stroke of his tongue, every teasing retreat and plunging return of his finger, every hard pinch of her nipple, rewrote the map of her own body. "Listen to you," he said loudly between licks, his voice vibrating against her. "You're loving this, aren't you?"

"Yes," she choked out. "I—Gage, please."

He moved his tongue back and forth. Moving to her slit briefly, letting her feel his breath against her soaked entrance, then returned to the place that made her toes curl and her vision go white. "Do you want more?" he asked again, as he gave her nipple a hard flick.

"Yes," she cried. "Yes, oh, please—"

"Keep being good for me. You dirty girl," he said, cruel and almost tender all at once.

"Please," she begged. "Please, Gage, I need you. Inside me. Please. I'm so close, I—"

Suddenly he pulled away. She almost sobbed at the

loss.

Cool air rushed in where his tongue had been. The gap felt raw.

She heard him spit into his hand, heard the slick sound of him stroking himself. Then his weight shifted, and she felt the broad, hot head of him nudge against her entrance. He didn't tease now.

He pushed forward in one long, punishing stroke, sinking into her until his hips hit the backs of her thighs. The fullness was almost unbearable, made more intense by the lingering buzz of his tongue's work. She cried out, the sound high and desperate. He groaned, low and deep. "Fuck," he breathed. "You're... you're gripping me like you were made for this." He withdrew partway and slammed back in, hard. The pillow muffled her scream.

He set a brutal rhythm, each thrust driving her higher and higher. Her body, already strung tight, responded helplessly, clenching around him, pleasure coiling low and tight.

"Ahh, I love how you take me. Your ass looks so good from this angle. With me pounding deep into your pussy."

Then, just when she thought she couldn't take more, his hand moved from her hips back down to her backside, a single rough fingertip finding the place he'd just been with his mouth. He pressed there gently, not quite entering, just adding that extra edge of sensation that made her see stars. Her mind dissolved. She had never felt anything like this. Every nerve seemed to be firing at once. The pressure built and built, like a wave drawing back.

"You're doing so good. You're my good fucking girl," his voice growing louder. "You're mine," he boomed.

His words pushed her closer to the edge than she'd ever been. "I'm—" she gasped, words tumbling over themselves. "Gage, please, I'm going to explode, please don't stop!" She managed to twist her head enough to look back at him, hair sticking to her cheeks, eyes wide and wild. He saw her, truly saw her in that moment—disheveled, bound, flushed, on the brink of something she'd never reached before.

And then he made his choice. He pulled out. The sudden emptiness was like being dropped from a great height. "Wait," she cried, voice cracking. "No—no, please, I—"

He was already fisting himself, hand moving in quick, harsh strokes. He stepped to the front of her so that when his release came, hot and sudden, it spilled across her forehead, her eyes, and her ruby lips in warm ropes. "Guahhhh" he roared as he came. She flinched, eyes squeezing shut as the warmth splattered her skin. His breath came in harsh pants. For a moment, he braced one hand on the headboard above her, head hanging, hair falling into his face.

Then he stepped back. The only sound in the cottage was her ragged breathing and the faint drip of his release sliding down her cheek onto the mattress. He stared at her wrists, where the rope had left faint pink tracks, and then at her face covered in his release. A sudden, violent flash of clarity crossed his features—not the satisfaction of a conqueror, but the wide-eyed look of a man who had looked into a mirror and didn't recognize the beast staring back.

His hands shook as he reached for the knots. He

fumbled with the rope at her wrists, his movements frantic. "Gage?" she whispered, confused by the sudden change in temperature.

"I have to go," he rasped, the words catching in his throat. He yanked the last knot free. He didn't look at her. He couldn't. He practically scrambled off the bed, hauling his trousers up and buckling his belt with trembling fingers.

"Gage, wait—"

But he was already at the door. "Gage," she said, voice small, humiliated. "Gage, please—" He flung it open so hard it cracked against the stone wall. He didn't look back at the bed, where she sat up, clutching the blankets to her chest, wiping her face, dazed and unfinished. He bolted into the sunlight, his heart thundering in his chest like a trapped bird.

The door shut behind him with a heavy finality. He didn't get five paces before he slammed into a solid wall of wool and muscle. "Whoa! Gage, where's the fire—" Harry's cheerful greeting died instantly as he gripped Gage's shoulders to steady him. Gage pushed past him and stomped outside.

In the bedroom time stretched. In the few seconds before the men found her a million thoughts flooded her mind. *Oh please, it felt so good—I felt like I was about to explode. Oh no, Oh no. What was that? Why did I enjoy that so much? Nobody has ever touched me there. But I liked it so much. What does that mean? What has Gage done to me? I wish he would come back and just touch me there one more time... I'm sure that's all it would take. I just need it—more of it. Why did he just leave? I feel so dirty. If any of the men find me here like this I will be so embarrassed. I won't be able to stay here anymore. I'll have to go. I'm sure Gage will come back any minute. I'm sure he will. He loves me, doesn't he? Oh, what am I doing here? What have I become? This is so wrong. Is it wrong? How can it be wrong if I like it so much?*

The door opened again. "Snow—" Silas's voice cut off abruptly. He stood there for a heartbeat, then retreated so fast the door banged against the frame. "Dax!" he shouted, voice high and panicked. "Dax! You— you need to come here."

Footsteps thundered. The next time the door opened, it was with authority.

"Where is—" Dax's words died as he saw her. He crossed the room in three strides, jaw clenched so hard the muscle in it jumped.

"Oh, Snow," Harry breathed, moving to her first. He dropped to his knees, his hands hovering, afraid to touch her. "Did he—did you say no?"

She looked at them, her throat working as she tried to find her voice. "I...where did he go?" she whispered, her voice trembling. "Did he leave me?" She looked down at her shaking hands. "We just...he just... he looked at me like I was a monster. And then he ran."

Dax crossed the room in three strides, his face a mask of controlled fury. He didn't look at the bed; he looked at the discarded rope. He picked it up, the fibers rough in his hand.

"Are you hurt?" Bennett asked as he rushed in, voice worried but strong. "Were you scared?" He got her a blanket and wrapped her in his arms.

Dax's eyes darkened. "Where is he?" he asked, the words like stones dropping into a well.

Drew, white-faced in the doorway, pointed vaguely toward the tree line. Dax straightened. "Stay with her," he ordered Bennett. "Don't leave her alone. Not for a second."

Outside, the air was warm and sharp. The tree line loomed at the edge of the clearing; beyond it, the forest stretched. Dax found Gage not far from the cottage, standing with his back to the house, hands braced on a tree trunk as if he were holding it up. His shoulders rose and fell with deep, uneven breaths. "Gage," Dax said.

Gage didn't turn. "If you're here to thank me for coming home early," he said, voice flat, "save your breath."

"I'm here," Dax said evenly, "to tell you that if you ever leave her like that again, I will knock you out cold."

Gage's fingers dug into the bark. "She's fine," he said. "She knew what she was agreeing to. You all seem to have forgotten."

"Fine?" Dax repeated, a dangerous calm in his tone. "There's rope burn on her wrists. She's confused. And you just left her alone like that."

Gage turned then, slowly. His expression was a complicated tangle: anger, shame, defiance. "What did you think this was, Dax?" he demanded. "A courtship? You made the deal. Food, shelter, protection—for her body. I'm just taking what I'm owed."

"We agreed," Dax said, taking a step closer, "that it would be consensual. That she could say no. That we wouldn't treat her like something to be left on a butcher's hook."

"She could have said no," Gage shot back. "She didn't. She begged me for more, begged me not to stop."

Dax's jaw clenched. "You left her like that. That's not

free-use, Gage. That's cruelty."

Gage's eyes flashed. "Oh, and you're innocent?" he sneered. "Creeping into her bed when you think the rest of us are asleep, eyes closed so you feel better about what you're doing? We've all got our sins."

"That's different," Dax snapped.

"How?" Gage barked a laugh, ugly and humorless. "Because you're gentle? Because you turn your head when you shame yourself? At least I don't lie to myself about why she's here."

Footsteps pounded behind them. Harry skidded to a stop, chest heaving, Silas on his heels. Drew hovered further back, wringing his hands.

"She's not a toy you can wind up and walk away from," Harry added, eyes blazing behind his usually mild expression.

Silas leaned lazily against a tree, but his gaze was sharp. "You broke the spell," he said softly. "That wasn't part of the game."

Gage's shoulders hunched, every line of him defensive. "You all act like saints," he snarled. "You forget who brought her here, who laid out the terms! We're not her princes in shining armor. We're miners. Men. We take what we're given!"

"You don't get to hide behind that," Silas shot back. "You wanted her. Fine! We all do. But you don't get to... to hurt her because you're angry at yourself or at the world!"

"She wasn't hurt," Gage insisted. "Did she bleed? Did I break a bone? No. She liked it! She wanted more!"

"Until you decided she should be humiliated," Harry cut in. "Until you decided your pleasure was the only one that mattered!"

Gage snorted. "When did you grow a spine, Harry?"

"When she started trusting us enough to fall asleep between us," Harry said. "Maybe try not to make her regret that."

Dax lifted a hand. "Enough!"

They all fell quiet, breathing hard.

"We are not going to stand here and pretend there isn't darkness in what we're doing," he said. "We made a bargain that sits on the edge of a cliff. If we push it, she falls. If we respect it, maybe we all get what we need."

He stepped closer to Gage until they were chest to chest.

"You crossed the line today," he said quietly. "I won't have it happen again. Not in my house."

Gage held his gaze, something like guilt flickering under the anger. "And if it does?" he asked. "What then, Dax? You going to throw me out? March me down to town and tell the people I was too rough with the woman we all use?"

"If you keep treating her like this," Dax said, voice low, "you throw yourself out because she'll leave. Maybe not today, maybe not tomorrow. But she will. And where will that leave us? Back where we started. Six men in cold beds. No one laughing in the kitchen. No one making this place feel like a home."

The word hung there. Home. Harry's jaw worked. Drew looked away, throat bobbing. Even Silas's lazy posture tightened.

Gage's gaze slid past Dax to the cottage, to where he left her. Something in him shifted, only a fraction. "I'm not apologizing," he said finally, though the words rang less sure. "I did what we agreed."

"We agreed she's not just payment," Harry said quietly. "She's... ours. And we're hers. That means we don't walk away like that."

Silence fell again.

Gage scrubbed a hand over his face, dragging down his beard. "I need to think," he said.

"Good," Dax said. "Do it away from her for a while."

Without another word, Gage turned and stalked into the trees, his broad back soon swallowed by the shadows.

Harry let out a breath he seemed to have been holding for minutes.

Drew had a worried look on his face that seemed to ask if Gage would be ok.

Dax looked at the dark line of the forest. "He always comes back," he said. He turned toward the cottage. "Come on," he said. "We have to make sure she knows this isn't what we want for her. Not like this."

Inside, Snow White sat near where they had left her, cleaned up and clutching a cup of water. Bennett sat at her side, pale and silent, as if rooted there by shock. When the others entered, she looked up, scanning their faces as if searching for judgment. None came.

Harry moved to her first, dropping to his knees by the bed. "I'm sorry," he said, not for anything he'd done, but for everything she'd just gone through. "We should have been here."

"It's not your fault," she said dully. "I agreed. I'm sorry if you think I'm a disgrace."

"No! You agreed to be ours," Harry said, coming to sit

at the foot of the bed. "Not to be left abandoned like that. He took it too far."

Her throat tightened. "We had a safe word. I could have asked him to stop. He would have listened to me. But I liked what he was doing. I wanted it. I asked him to keep going."

Silas flopped down onto the other side of her, his arm curling automatically around her shoulder. "We're idiots," he sighed. "But even we know there's a difference between rough play and crossing the line."

Snow White let out a watery laugh at that, despite herself. She rubbed her wrists where the ropes left their mark.

Dax stood at the end of the bed, arms crossed, brow furrowed. "You'll want to leave," he said bluntly. "We'll pack you food, point you toward the right road."

Her chest squeezed. "I don't want to leave," she said at once. The truth of it startled her. "I'm not angry with him. I said I wanted it. But now that it's over, and you all know what happened, I feel embarrassed—like I lost control of my mind for a moment."

Dax's shoulders eased a fraction. "If you want to stay, then you stay," he said. "On your terms. No more deal, no more free-use. And if any of us crosses a line with you, you tell us. Even if it's me."

She nodded. In that moment, still sore, still humiliated, still shaken, she realized something important: These men might break her heart one day. They might let her down, make mistakes, hurt her in ways they didn't intend. But for now, in this little cottage at the edge of the woods, they were trying. Trying to be better than what the world expected of men like them. Trying to make a place where she could be more than a body to be used and discarded. Trying, in their fumbling, flawed way, to be something like a family. She let out a long breath and lay back, their warmth surrounding her. "Okay," she said softly. "We all stay. Together."

Outside, the forest held its secrets. Inside, anger still simmered, hurt still throbbed, apologies still tangled on tongues. But under all the turmoil, the fragile threads binding them together held.

Chapter Eighteen

Claiming her Throne

T HE MIRROR WAS NOT beautiful. That was the first thought that crept into Snow White's mind when Harry pulled the reflective glass out from behind his back with a flourish. It wasn't like her mother's enchanted glass—tall as a man, its surface flawless, its frame carved with impossible detail. This one was human-made and humble: a simple rectangle of slightly warped glass set in a dark wooden frame, the edges nicked and worn. Maybe that was why she loved it immediately.

"Happy birthday," Harry announced, though it wasn't quite her birthday. He liked excuses. "Or half-birthday. Or 'we didn't get you anything last year because we were too busy ravishing you, so this is back pay.'"

Snow White's laugh was surprised and soft. "What is it?" she asked, even though she could see perfectly well.

"A cow," Harry said. "I brought you a cow. What do you think it is?"

Dax, sitting on the edge of the bed and untying his boots, snorted. Drew, hovering awkwardly near the door with a bundle of firewood in his arms, smiled a little. Harry stepped closer and held the mirror out.

Snow White wiped her hands automatically on her

apron before taking it, as if it were something delicate and easily smudged. It was heavier than it looked. The wood was solid, the glass cool beneath her fingertips. She turned it, watching the light from the window stutter across the surface. For a moment, all she saw was blur: the cottage behind her, Harry's expectant face, a hint of her own outline. Then the image steadied. She saw herself properly for the first time in years.

"I found it in town," Harry was saying, voice suddenly more tentative. "In a trader's cart. Thought maybe... I don't know. You might want to see what we all see."

"I haven't..." Her voice trailed off. She swallowed, throat tightening. "I haven't had a mirror since I was a child, when my mother redecorated the castl—" She stopped, the old word slipping too close to the tongue. "—my home," she finished. "She took them all down."

Harry glanced at Dax over her shoulder; Dax's gaze sharpened briefly, filing away that near-slip. Drew shifted, setting the wood down quietly so it wouldn't break the moment.

Snow White lifted the mirror, angling it toward her face. For a heartbeat, she didn't recognize the girl staring back. She had known, in an abstract way, that her hair had grown. She felt it when she lay down, when she washed it by the stream, when she braided it into a quick, practical plait. But seeing it now—falling in dark, heavy waves around her shoulders, the ends brushing the tops of her breasts—made something shift in her chest. It was glossy in the dim light, black as raven wings—a raven, like her father's coat of arms. It framed a face she knew and did not know: cheekbones a little sharper than she remembered, jawline a little stronger.

Her skin, though not untouched by sun and work, was still pale, still smooth. Her lips, without paint, were the deep red they had always been, the color standing out stark against everything else. She looked like her mother. The realization hit like cold water. It made her stomach drop, her fingers tighten on the frame. Only... not quite. Her mother's beauty had always felt like a blade: honed, polished, designed to cut. What Snow White saw in the mirror now had softer edges. There was a kindness in the set of her mouth, a lingering openness in her eyes that Liora had long since lost. "I..." She couldn't quite find the words.

Behind her, Harry came to stand at one shoulder, Dax at the other. Drew lingered near the end of the bed, his usual silence even heavier. "See?" Harry said, his voice gentler than his usual jokes. "Told you. We're not just being polite."

"Are you just noticing how beautiful you are?" Dax asked, one brow lifting.

She didn't answer. Couldn't. Her throat was too tight. She thought of Hunter calling her "Liora" in the forest, eyes clouded with lust and confusion. The insult of it had burned then, the way he'd tried to overwrite her with the image of the woman who had ordered her death.

Now, seeing how closely her features reflected Liora's, she understood. It stung in a different way. But there was something else, too. Something newer. Power. She watched herself in the glass as she tilted her chin a fraction higher. The small adjustment transformed the line of her neck, made her look less like someone waiting for orders and more like someone accustomed to giving them. She straightened her spine. Her shoulders slid back. The girl in the mirror shed some of her uncertainty like an old cloak. A faint, almost unfamiliar surge swelled in her chest. This is me, she thought. Not just someone's daughter. Not just someone's bargain.

Harry seemed to sense the shift. "Stand up," he said softly. "Here." He took the mirror from her and stepped back so she had space. She set aside her apron, smoothing her palms down the front of her plain dress.

"I don't remember... what I really look like," she admitted, fingers fiddling with the laces at her bodice. "Only shadows in polished pots and water."

"Well," Harry said, "lucky for you, we're about to fix that." He held the mirror at an angle where she could see herself from mid-thigh up. Dax moved behind her.

She felt the warmth of him before she felt his hands—large, steady palms settling lightly on her upper arms. He caught her eye in the reflection. "Breathe," he said quietly. "Just look." She did. Her hair gleamed, her cheeks were flushed, her eyes were bright. She looked... alive. More alive than the princess in her childhood memories, whose beauty had always seemed like a performance put on for someone else's gaze.

"Let's see all of you," Drew chimed in.

Before she could protest, Dax's fingers found the ties at the back of her dress. He worked them loose with practiced efficiency, the fabric slackening around her torso. He didn't yank it down. He peeled it. He slid the shoulders off slowly, letting the worn material drag over the tops of her arms, along the curve of her breasts. The coarse wool rasped lightly over sensitive skin, sending little jolts through her. Her nipples tightened under the thin chemise she wore beneath. The dress puddled at her feet.

In the mirror, she saw herself in nothing but that thin undergarment—white now gone off-white from countless washings, clinging to her from shoulder to mid-thigh. Dax's gaze met hers in the glass, asking a silent question. She lifted her chin fractionally. "Keep going," she told him, surprising herself with how steady she sounded.

His fingers found the hem of the chemise and drew it up, slow enough that she could stop him at any point. The fabric slid over her thighs, her hips, the dip of her waist, the underside of her breasts. Each inch of bare skin revealed felt both terrifying and exhilarating. When the chemise cleared her head, the air of the room kissed her nakedness. She stood there, bare in front of three men and, more importantly, before herself.

Her breasts were fuller than she remembered from the castle days, the weight of them pulling comfortably against her chest. Her nipples were a light rose, hardening further under their own reflection and the cool brush of air. Her waist curved into hips that had grown womanly with use and time. Her gaze dipped lower, to the dark triangle of hair at the juncture of her thighs, to the way the muscles there had firmed from riding and work. She saw the swell of her labia, the subtle gleam of moisture there that made color rise to her cheeks. She thought she would have felt shame. She felt... tall.

"Look at you," Harry crooned, awe in his tone. "If you walked into any court dressed like that, the queen would faint dead away."

"The queen already did," Snow White said before she could stop herself. The slip hit her like a slap. She swallowed. "In one story, anyway."

Dax's hands, still warm on her arms, squeezed gently. He didn't press the near-confession. Not now. He stepped in closer behind her, his chest a solid presence against her bare back. She could see him in the mirror, too, now—his eyes not avoiding hers like they usually did. He slid one hand down, over her forearm, then guided it toward her own body. He placed her palm flat against her lower belly, just above her mound. "Have you ever touched yourself?" he whispered in her ear.

She paused, considering his words and their meaning. "I—" she began, hesitation thick on her tongue. She had never touched herself intimately before—it had never really occurred to her. She felt stupid and almost silly.

Harry stepped to her other side, in view of the mirror. "Yeah, you should do this for yourself."

Drew hadn't moved from his spot near the door. His eyes were fixed on her reflection, wide and bright, his hands clenched at his sides. Snow White swallowed. Her fingers curled, then spread again. Slowly, almost tentatively, she began to move her own hand lower.

She skimmed over the faint rise of her mound, the crease where thigh met torso. When her fingertips brushed the slick fold of herself, she sucked in a breath. She was wet. Wet enough that her fingers slid easily over the sensitive flesh, sticking briefly together before gliding apart. It was different, touching herself, watching herself. She could see the way her pupils dilated, the flush creeping down her neck. She could see the small, involuntary movements of her hips as her hand explored. She could see how, when she circled gently over the place that felt best, her shoulders tightened and her lips parted.

"How do I do it?" she whispered.

"There's no wrong way," Dax said. "Just whatever feels good."

She let her fingers wander, experimenting. A stroke here that made her gasp; a firmer pressure there that made her knees want to buckle. She found a rhythm that felt good, rubbing gently back and forth, up and down, breath catching each time she hit the right spot. She risked a glance at the men. Harry's jaw was slack, his chest rising and falling faster than before. Dax's eyes were hooded, his hand still on her arm but not leading, following. Drew's arousal was visible now, pressing against his trousers, his face flushed.

"That's right," Dax assured her, then fell silent.

He stepped back half a pace, giving her space. The room went quiet. She realized no one was guiding her now. Confidence surged inside her, dizzying. She wasn't passive here. She wasn't being moved or arranged or taken. She was directing. And no one corrected her. She looked herself in the eye in the mirror and, for the first time, saw not prey or pawn, but the center of a universe made of wanting. She adjusted her feet, widening thighs a little for better balance. The new angle gave her hand more room; her fingers slipped more easily over her slick skin. Heat surged low in her body, familiar and insistent.

Drew took an involuntary step forward. She watched him in the mirror as he fumbled with his fly, his hands shaking, clearly not quite sure if he was allowed to. She smiled—sharp, sudden. "No," she said, catching his wrist just as he freed himself. He froze, eyes going wide. She spun him with more strength than any of them expected, sending him down onto the mattress. He landed on his back, startled, then stared up at her with something like awe.

Harry laughed softly. "Oh, I like this," he said, surprised by Snow White's new found agency.

Dax's mouth twitched in what might have been the ghost of a smile. Snow White climbed astride Drew, the movement slow and deliberate. She could see every inch of it reflected in the mirror: her thighs straddling his hips, the way his chest rose in quickened breaths, the way his hands hovered near her waist, unsure where to rest. She reached down and gripped his length, guiding him to her with her own hand this time.

"I'm going to ride you now," she told him. She sank down slowly, taking him into her with care. His head tipped back, a quiet gasp escaping him as her heat enveloped him. For her, the stretch was new in angle, the sensation of control as intoxicating as the physical pleasure. She could stop. She could set the pace. She could decide when and how far. She let herself slide all the way down, hips settling against his. The fullness drew a low sound from her throat.

Harry moved to her left, pressing a kiss to her shoulder. "Look at you," he said. "Sitting pretty on your throne."

Dax stepped to her right, his hand finding her breast, thumb circling the tight nipple. "You see it now?" he asked quietly. "Do you?"

She rolled her hips experimentally, watching herself grind down so that Drew's length rubbed just right inside her, the motion dragging deliciously over the place her own fingers had just worked. Her free hand—slick with her own arousal—found that spot again, thumb pressing just above where Drew filled her. The combined sensation made her gasp, head tipping back. In the mirror, she saw herself: hair tumbling, breasts bouncing with each movement, face flushed and intent. She looked wild. She looked free. She looked frighteningly, gloriously alive. For the first time, she wasn't just a reflection of someone else's vanity. She was the one in the looking glass.

Harry cupped her jaw and brought her face to his, kissing her deeply. His tongue slid against hers, hot and eager, tasting of heat and shared breaths. Dax's mouth found her other breast, tongue flicking over the peak as his hand squeezed, sending little sparks down her spine. Under her, Drew's hands finally settled on her hips, fingers digging in, eyes locked on her face like he'd forgotten there was a world beyond her. The three of them moved around her, with her, because of her.

Harry murmured in her ear between kisses, words that coiled like smoke: "Now you can see yourself. Like a gorgeous queen. Like you own us. We are yours."

Dax said nothing. He only nodded once, as if acknowledging a choice already made.

Drew, barely capable of words at the best of times, managed a single, breathy phrase: "Oh, Snow..." The look of true admiration in his eyes.

She rode harder. Her thighs began to burn, muscles fatiguing, but she didn't slow. Instead, she shifted her weight, grinding forward with each downward thrust, her fingers never leaving their spot, building heat upon heat. The pleasure rose, not in a straight line, but in waves that crashed against each other, higher each time. Her breath came in ragged gasps. Her free hand tangled in Harry's hair as he kissed her, or her nails dug crescent moons into Dax's shoulder. Her arousal surged.

She watched her transformation in the mirror: the way her mouth fell open, the way the tension in her body sharpened into something fine and bright, the way the men around her bent toward her like flowers to the sun. And she stepped into it. Into herself. The wave crested. Her vision went blurry, then white. The sounds of the room—Harry's voice, Drew's gasps, Dax's low curses—faded into a roar. Her body clenched around Drew in a strong, pulsing grip, pleasure ripping through her body in a way she'd never experienced before. She cried out loud, the sound raw and full, something breaking open inside her and spilling out. Her first. Not taken from her by someone's hand or mouth while she lay passive. Not dragged from her by accident while someone else chased their own ending. Chosen. Called. Claimed.

When the tremors finally eased, she sagged forward, bracing her hands on Drew's chest, panting. He was still inside her, trembling, eyes wide. Harry pressed soft kisses to her temple. Dax's hand stroked down the line of her back, steadying. She slid off Drew gently, with a soft wince at the sudden emptiness, and collapsed onto the bed beside him.

For a moment, no one spoke. Then Harry laughed, low and delighted. "Well," he said. "There goes any chance of us pretending we're in charge around here anymore." Dax breathed softly and looked away, giving her privacy. Drew, still flushed and dazed, reached out a tentative hand to touch her hair, his usual single word escaping again, even softer. "Snow."

Something had bloomed inside her chest. Seeing herself in the mirror, riding Drew with Harry's and Dax's hands and mouths on her, directing her own pace, claiming pleasure for herself, using them instead of being the one used... it had shaken something loose. Power and vulnerability, she thought, might not be opposites after all.

Chapter Nineteen

Seen

HER AUTHORITY DID NOT descend upon her all at once; it was forged slowly in the quiet moments. Life in the cottage still looked much the same from the outside: chores to be done, meals to be cooked, coal dust to be scrubbed from collars. But something had changed inside. She noticed it in small, daily ways, and in big, nightly ways. When a hand reached for her at night now, it often came with a question. "Can I?" Bennett would ask, fingers hovering near her hip.

"Later," she'd say sometimes, too tired or simply not in the mood. And he would kiss her shoulder and roll away without protest.

Harry, sliding into bed behind her one evening, pressed his mouth to the back of her neck. "You up for it?" he asked. "Or do you want to just sleep?"

"Sleep." The word came easier than expected as she pressed her face into the pillow. "Tomorrow, maybe."

He chuckled softly. "You got it."

Even Gage, after that explosive confrontation, was different. He attempted to apologize a few times, but couldn't find the words. He was still gruff, but a little more likely now to pause, to search her face, to pull back if she stiffened.

She began to dictate, in quiet ways, when she was touched and by whom. "If you want me," she told them once, sitting at the table with her sewing, "ask. Don't just take."

"Even me?" Silas asked lazily from his spot by the fire.

"Especially you," she said. "You're the sneakiest." They laughed, but no one argued.

The more she said no, the more confident she became in saying yes. She gave only what she wanted of herself and nothing more. The men still swooned over her, but now it was less about the wild side of lust and more about something deeper: affection, protectiveness, and shared pride.

She thought often of her father. Of his booming laugh, his warm hand around hers, the way he'd lifted her up to see the world from his height. She thought of how easily he'd been led by beauty—Liora's most of all. She thought of her mother. Of the comb, the corset. Of the way Liora had treated her own beauty like a weapon and Snow White's like a rival.

Now, standing at the stream with wet shirts heavy in her hands and her hair whipped by the breeze, she understood something terrible and important: Liora had been wrong. Beauty wasn't pain—it was power. Not because mirrors said so. Not because men did. But because when she stood in that cramped little room with three men circling her and saw herself reflected—strong, desired, unafraid—she had felt something click into place inside her, as if she'd suddenly found the hilt of a sword she'd been carrying all along.

· · · ● ● · ● ● · · ·

E LSEWHERE, IN A CASTLE that had grown a little
colder in the past year, a similar face stared into a
mirror.

Queen Liora noticed the gray hair first in the reflection
of a silver spoon. She was alone in her chamber—Captain
Hunter had left early that morning to discuss patrol routes
with the newer men. Liora picked at her breakfast. The
eggs had gone cold; the fruit tasted like ash. Her appetite,
always fickle, had dwindled further in recent months. She
lifted the spoon to her mouth and paused. There, near
her temple, glinting in the polished curve of the metal: a
pale thread among the black. Her heart stuttered. She was
just a few years beyond her fortieth birthday. Gray already?
She set the spoon down very carefully. Sudden realization
overwhelmed her—she hadn't performed the ritual with
her enchanted mirror in over a year.

She stood abruptly, the chair scraping back, and
crossed the room with quick, controlled strides to the great
mirror on the wall. "Mirror, soul of silver and glass," she
demanded, after she'd undressed and oiled, "who in this
land shall I never surpass?" She watched her reflection like
a hawk as the surface rippled. The glass shivered. The room
dissolved. For a heartbeat, she stared into a void that ate
even her own image. Then a picture formed. Not hers. She
couldn't make sense of what she saw.

A bed. Not her bed. The sheets were rougher, the

room darker, lit by a single lantern. A woman lay sprawled across the mattress, naked in the lazy form of someone utterly at ease in her skin. She was surrounded by six, tall, muscular, handsome men. One man knelt between her thighs, shoulders square, head bent in obvious devotion to some task, face below her waist. Another leaned over her, mouth taking hers in a deep, unhurried kiss. A third stood beside the bed, stroking himself slowly as his eyes drank her in. A fourth trailed reverent hands along the lines of her body, mapping each curve like sacred ground. The young woman tilted her head back and laughed at something one of them said, the sound silent but visible. She looked utterly in command of the scene, directing her own happiness and pleasure.

Liora's stomach clenched. She took a step closer. As one of the men shifted, his head moved, and the woman's face came fully into view. For a second, Liora's brain refused to accept what her eyes told her. Then the world narrowed to a single, horrifying truth: Snow... White. Not dead. Not drowned. Not devoured by wolves. Alive. Alive and beautiful and strong and adored. Her daughter. Her rival.

"Hunter!" Liora breathed, fury punching through her shock. "Liar!"

The image in the mirror wavered, then faded, leaving only her own face staring back. She saw the gray at her temples then. Saw the faint lines at the corners of her eyes. Saw the way her mouth had hardened and her cheeks had begun to hollow. She looked older. She looked... afraid.

She bared her teeth at her reflection. "I am the fairest!" she hissed. "I always will be!" The mirror did not contradict her. It never had. But now she had seen proof that it could show more than her. She whirled away from the glass, the hem of her gown snapping.

"Hunter!" she called, voice knifing through the thick silence of the corridor beyond. "Hunter!" No answer.

She stormed from her chamber, her bare feet slapping against the cold stone. The servants she passed flattened themselves against the walls, eyes downcast, sensing a storm and wanting no part of it. She flung open the door to the guardroom. Empty.

"Where is he?" she demanded of the youngest soldier there.

"Who, Majesty?" he stammered.

"Hunter," she snapped. "The captain. My... dog."

The boy swallowed. "He left a few minutes ago, my queen. On patrol and—"

She cut in. "Bastards! Bring me my captain! Now!"

As courtiers and guards scrambled, Liora paced like a caged thing. Fury and fear gnawed at her in equal measure. She had believed Hunter's lie because it had suited her as well. Because the idea of Snow White gone—removed from the board entirely—had let her sleep at night. She had given him what she promised, well, mostly anyway. She had not yet made him her king, but had occasionally rewarded him by allowing him into her bed.

Now, with one glance in the mirror, that fragile illusion was shattered. Her daughter was alive. Her daughter was grown. Her daughter had found a way to turn the curse of their shared beauty into something Liora had never truly had: intimacy that wasn't bought, power that wasn't extracted by coercion.

Liora's hands curled into fists. "If anyone is going to

kill you," she whispered, thinking of the girl in the mirror, "it will be me." She vowed, there in her chamber with the mirror watching, that she would find Snow White herself this time. No more delegations. No more trusting weak men with strong tasks. If the mirror showed her daughter once, then it could be made to show her again. She would hunt her through the glass.

• • • ● ● • ● ● • • •

B ACK IN THE COTTAGE, Snow White reached for the token at her neck while stirring the stew and felt... nothing. Her fingers met only the fabric of her dress. Her heart lurched. She dropped the wooden spoon back into the pot with a clatter, ignoring Harry's indignant "Hey!" from across the room. Her hands flew to the neckline of her dress, patting frantically. The cord was gone.

"Snow?" Silas asked, glancing up from the table where he was sorting tools. "You okay?"

"My—" Her voice came out thin. "My necklace. It's gone." The ground started moving underneath her. All at once, every breath she'd taken with that little piece of silver against her skin, every night she'd clutched it when fear clawed at her chest, every silly daydream about blue eyes and apple-stealing kisses, came crashing down.

"Where did you last see it?" Dax asked, instantly practical.

"Here," she said, pressing a palm to her sternum.

"Always here. I never take it off, I—" Her voice broke. Panic surged, irrational and huge.

"It could have just slipped," Bennett said, already pushing back his chair. "We'll find it."

Harry hopped over the bench. "All right, treasure hunt!" he said, trying for lightness, but his eyes were serious. "Everyone, check everywhere. Bed, floor, stream, stable, down your boots—I'm looking at you, Gage."

"Why would I take her jewelry?" Gage snapped, but he was already scanning the floor near the hearth.

Silas wandered toward the bed, dropping to his knees to peer under it. He checked the hooks by the door, the pile of folded clothes. Bennett moved toward the washbasin, hands sifting through the laundry pile with uncharacteristic urgency.

Snow White stood in the middle of the room, clenched and useless.

"It's just a trinket. We've all seen it on your neck while you've been indisposed. A little bird or something?" Gage muttered, glancing up. "We can get you another."

"No," she said sharply. "You can't." He shut his mouth. "It was given to me," she said, voice shaking. "By someone who... who saw me before anyone else did. Before any of you. Before..." She swallowed. "It's all I have left of him."

Dax's expression flickered for a moment, hurt. "We'll find it," he said with new conviction. "Or we'll tear this place down trying."

Time stretched. They turned up everything except the one thing that had gone missing. No silver glint by the stream. No flash of metal in the cracks between the floorboards. No telltale weight in the pockets of her dresses. At last, exhausted and discouraged, they trailed back into the main room.

"We'll keep looking tomorrow," Harry said. "Maybe you dropped it outside on the path."

Snow White nodded, numbed. She stirred the stew mechanically, appetite gone. The room seemed dimmer, the walls closer. She'd lost so much already—her father, her life as a princess, any chance at a normal existence. Losing this small, stubborn symbol of the boy who'd once looked at her like she was a miracle felt like losing that version of herself entirely.

Later, as dusk settled, Drew lingered by the bed instead of joining the others at the table waiting for supper. He knelt, small lantern in hand, and reached under the mattress, fingertips brushing through dust and the occasional forgotten button.

Something smooth and cold nudged his skin. He pinched it gently and pulled it out. A thin leather cord. A small oval of silver, etched with the worn outline of a falcon. Drew stood there for a long moment, chest tight, then crossed the threshold quietly and held out his hand, palm open towards her. The token gleamed in the fading light.

"Found it," Drew said reluctantly.

She smiled. Her fingers closed around it, clutching it to her chest. Relief surged so strong she had to blink back tears. "Thank you," she whispered. "Thank you, Drew."

He shrugged, flushing, and sank down beside her on the step, shoulder just brushing hers. The door creaked. Harry stepped out, leaning on the frame. "Found it?" he called. Snow White lifted the token, letting it catch the last light. The others spilled out one by one—Dax, Silas, Harry, Bennett, Gage—forming a loose semicircle around her.

"Good," Dax said simply.

"You look like yourself again, Snow," Bennett added, smile soft.

Gage snorted. "Told you it'd turn up."

Silas yawned and dropped down behind her, wrapping his arms around her from behind, chin hooking on her shoulder. Harry flopped onto the step below, leaning his head against her knee. Bennett took the other side, legs stretched out. Dax leaned against the wall, watchful. Drew stayed where he was, shoulder still touching hers. For a long moment, they sat like that in comfortable silence, the forest murmuring around them.

Snow White looked at the faces turned toward her, at the way their bodies unconsciously arranged themselves in a protective curve, at the steadiness in their eyes. She thought of the mirror, of the men's hands on her, of the way she'd ridden Drew while Harry and Dax and the others had bent toward her like she was their axis.

She closed her fingers around the token one more time, then let it drop back to rest against her collarbone. "Thank you," she said again, looking at each of them in turn. They didn't answer with flowery declarations or oaths.

Harry nudged her ankle. "What are we having for supper?" he asked.

"Burnt stew, if you keep distracting her," Gage replied.

Silas hummed into her neck. "As long as she makes it,"

he said. "I don't care if it's burnt."

Dax's mouth twitched. "I care," he said. "But I'll eat it anyway."

Gage rolled his eyes. "This family is pathetic."

"Family," Drew said, the rare word dropping into the circle like a stone into a quiet pond. The others stilled. Then, slowly, Snow White smiled.

"Yes," she said. "Family." Her strength was not in the mirror. It was not in the necklace. It was not even in her beauty, though that had been the door her life had always been forced through. Her strength was in this: in choosing these men, in them choosing her back, in shaping a life with them on her own terms. For now, that was enough.

Here, in the small clearing at the edge of the forest, a woman with her mother's face leaned into the warmth of the men who loved her, and prepared, without knowing it yet, to face the storm that was coming.

• • • • •• • •• • • • •

L ATER THAT NIGHT, SNOW White lay between Silas and Drew, the bed warm with familiar bodies, the air heavy with the mingled scents of wood smoke and sweat. Silas had his arm thrown over her waist, his breath tickling the back of her neck. Drew's shin pressed against her calf, his hand curled close to her own on the blanket. "Ever been in love?" Silas mumbled into her hair, voice thick with sleep.

The question dropped into the dark like a stone into a

still pond. Snow White stiffened. Images flickered through her mind. Harry's constant stream of compliments and jokes. Dax's quiet, watching eyes. Bennett's hands offering her the best piece of bread. Silas's arm around her in every quiet moment. Drew's fingers finding hers without words. Even Gage's snarled warnings and unspoken protectiveness. Caring. Attachment. Affection. But love?

Love, in her mind, had always worn a different face. Blue eyes. A stable. The warmth of steady hands at her waist. The near-kiss that had lived in her memory longer than her father's funeral procession. A silver token pressed into her palm, a promise half-joked and half-meant. The prince—as she still thought of him, though she did not know his name—occupied a corner of her heart these six men, for all their closeness, had never quite reached.

"Have you?" Silas prodded, sleep-rough but curious.

She stared into the dark. "No," she said at last. It wasn't entirely true. But it was true enough for now.

"Good," he mumbled. "Less competition." He pressed a lazy kiss to the back of her shoulder and drifted into deeper sleep, arm heavy and comforting over her waist.

Snow White lay awake longer. Power, she'd discovered, wasn't only about making others bend. It was also about knowing herself—her wants, her fears, her hidden fractures. Tonight, lying between men who would face an army for her, she realized there was one place she still sometimes hid from herself: inside her own body. Her first orgasm, in front of the mirror, had been a revelation. But it had been crowded: hands and mouths and eyes, the rush of performing her own pleasure for others as much as for herself.

Now the cottage was quiet. Silas snored lightly in her ear. Drew made soft, unconscious sounds in his sleep. The steady rise and fall of their chests filled the dark. No one was watching. Her hand, almost of its own accord, drifted down under the blanket. Her fingers found the hem of her nightdress, slipping beneath it, cool against the heat of her skin. She hesitated for a heartbeat—out of habit more than shame. Then she let herself touch.

Her fingertips brushed the soft hair, then slid lower, finding the slickness that had never truly gone away since she'd seen herself in the mirror. Her body remembered that confidence, that claiming, and some part of it hummed with leftover electricity. She circled lightly over that small bundle of nerves, testing. A tiny jolt shot up her spine. She bit her lip to hold in the sound. Her movements were unhurried. This wasn't about racing toward release to outrun fear or pain. This was about exploration, about mapping the edges of herself under no one's direction but her own.

She thought of the prince's hands in the dream—the way they'd cupped her gently instead of grabbing, the way he'd asked instead of assumed. She thought of her own face in the mirror, eyes fierce and wild as she rode Drew. She thought of the way her mother had used beauty as a cage and the way she had cracked that cage open one thrust at a time. Her breath came shallow and slow. She changed the angle of her hand, pressing a fraction harder, then easing off, learning the responses. Pleasure swelled again, slower than before but no less insistent, like a tide creeping up the shore. Beside her, Silas snorted and rolled onto his back, arm sliding off her. The sudden space made her feel both exposed and freer; she had room to move her hips now, to let them rock gently into her own touch.

She pictured herself as she must look now: hair spread over the pillow, one hand curled under her head, the other hidden beneath the blanket, moving in small circles that no one else could see. No mirror this time. Only her own inner eye. The wave built. She decreased the pressure as she circled until it was barely a touch, the hint of friction awakening her core. The lightness of her touch made the wave swell higher. When it broke, she didn't cry out. The crash rolled through her in a series of pulses, each one a soft detonation in her core. Her toes curled, her thighs trembled, her fingers pressed harder for a moment, then gradually slowed as the intensity ebbed. She exhaled slowly, shoulders sinking into the mattress. This climax was quieter than the one in front of the mirror, but in some ways it felt even more potent. There was no audience. No performance. No proof. Just her, owning her own pleasure in the dark.

Power, she realized, wasn't always loud. Sometimes it was as soft as a breath, as private as a hand moving slowly under a blanket while the rest of the world slept. She pulled her hand away, wiped it discreetly on the hem of her nightdress, and let it rest on her belly. Silas, still asleep, rolled back toward her, arm flopping over her waist again. Drew shifted, his hand finding hers loosely.

Snow White smiled into the darkness. She had learned, finally, that her body belonged first to her. The fact that she chose to share it—on her terms—with these men did not diminish that. It amplified it.

Chapter Twenty

I am Shay

"How could you?" The queen hissed, her voice almost sad.

"Majesty... I thought she was dead—I swear. She fell from the cliff into the ravine." Hunter's throat felt tight and the air felt heavy as he tried to cover his tracks. "I admit, I didn't climb down to confirm the deed—" he was cut off.

"Liar!" Liora shouted. "Did you really think you would get away with this? Did you really think I wouldn't discover your treason?" She softened for a moment, "But how? Why? You've always been so devoted. What made your loyalty to me waiver?"

Hunter froze, eyes widened. He couldn't tell her the truth. She would flay him alive. He'd never get to touch her again. He'd be banished from her life completely. His mind rolled as he spun excuse after excuse, none seemed believable.

"She got to you, didn't she? Her beauty, her body, her face—my face. She seduced you, didn't she?" Liora felt aroused at her own sharp intuition.

"My queen, I... I... I thought she was you. She looked so much like you, smelled like you, felt like you. I just wanted to touch you. I wanted you to feel me. To want me again," he explained. "I lost my mind. I lost control. She used me."

"And so you came back to me, after taking her virginity, lied to me, and then claimed your prize? You were inside me before even wiping yourself clean of her?" Liora had never felt so betrayed.

"Get out," she said.

He stared. "Majesty—"

"Out!" she screamed. "From my sight. From my halls. From my lands. You are banished. Forever!"

The word struck harder than the slap. "Liora, please," he said, the shape of her name tasting strange on his tongue. "Let me make it right. Let me find her now. I'll kill her. I'll bring you her head, her heart, whatever you—"

"Do you think I trust you to finish a task you've already failed? Do you think I would place my fate once more in the hands of a man who cannot tell the difference between his duty and his desire?" she boomed.

"But I love you!" Hunter interjected, blood rising, chest heaving. "I love you, my queen, please! I will do anything!"

Liora paused. Her breath slowed. She lowered her voice. "The day you chose her over me was the day you gave away my power and doomed me forever!"

She snapped her fingers. He flinched.

Two guards, who had had the misfortune to be in earshot, stepped in. "Escort him to the gates," she said without taking her eyes off Hunter. "See that he has his horse and no more. If he is seen within these walls again, you have my leave to put a spear through him."

"Yes, Majesty," they chorused, eyes wide. But Hunter didn't struggle. He followed them like a man walking through water, every movement slow, disbelieving. He'd given this castle his life, his blood, his bones. Now it pushed him out like something rotten.

At the great gate, the guards handed him his reins. "Sorry, Captain," one muttered. "Orders, you know."

He stepped up into the saddle, hands moving by habit. For a moment he sat there, looking back at the high walls, at the windows where he'd once stood watch, at the tower he'd thought of as a second home.

"Open the gate," he said. The portcullis rattled up and he rode through, hooves crunching over the gravel of the outer ward. But he didn't go far. Once outside the sight of the sentries, he guided his mount into a cluster of trees, tied the reins loosely, and sank down on a fallen log just off the road. He waited. The sun dipped below the horizon, turning the air biting and cold, but he did not move to build a fire. He sat on the damp log and stared at the closed gate, ignoring the gnawing emptiness in his belly and the stiffening of his limbs, waiting for a signal he had seen a thousand times before—and which had never once been for him. So many years devoted to her, so many years in love. He didn't know any other way to exist. He didn't know what, exactly, he was hoping for. Liora storming out to call him back, face softer, anger cooled. A messenger on a breathless horse, bearing some ridiculous royal summons. An apology, if he were foolish enough to dream of that. But the hours passed and none came. The sun crawled across the sky. Shadows lengthened. His horse grazed, tail swishing lazily.

Finally, when the light began to turn the color of old honey, the castle gate opened again. Hunter rose. A small cart rattled out, driven by a woman in a kerchief and patched dress. She sat straight-backed on the seat, hands steady on the reins. The rough wood of the seat bit into her velvet-soft skin, a jarring reminder that the world outside her tower was made of splinters and dirt, not silk. A basket of produce sat beside her: cabbages, some wilting greens, and a few early apples nestled like jewels in straw. It took Hunter all of three heartbeats to recognize Liora. Disguise or not, the set of her shoulders, the tilt of her chin, the contained fury in every line of her body gave her away to someone who'd watched her move for years.

He cursed to himself. He was right. He knew she would do it on her own. He waited until she'd passed, then swung into his saddle and nudged his horse into motion, keeping well back, using the trees as cover.

· · ● ● ● · ● ● ● · ·

To the west, in a cottage at the edge of the woods, Snow White sat at the wooden table with six men and something that felt more like a family than anything she'd had in years. She hadn't intended for the breakfast to become significant.

The meal started with bread. She'd set the loaf on the table, proud of the rise, the brownness just this side of burnt. Harry had stolen the heel before anyone else could, earning a scowl from Gage and a laugh from Drew. "You're getting good at this," Harry said around a mouthful. "Soon we'll all be too fat to fit down the mine shafts."

"Speak for yourself," Silas yawned, stretching in a way that made his shirt ride up.

Snow White smiled.

They passed plates, traded jokes. Conversation drifted from a beautiful large ruby found in the tunnels yesterday to Grimm's new habit of kicking over the water bucket to whether Drew would ever manage to beat Silas at cards. Somewhere between Silas's loud sneeze and Bennett's soft words, she looked around the table and felt something settle. She trusted them. The realization was simple and seismic. She trusted them with her body. With her food. With her sleep. Maybe it was time to trust them with the rest. Her heart picked up speed. "Can I say something?" she asked, fingers tightening around her mug.

Six heads turned toward her. "You just did," Harry said automatically, then winced when Dax kicked him under the table. "Sorry. Yes. Say something important."

She took a breath. "There's something I haven't told you," she said. "About who I am. Who I was."

Silas groaned. "Knew it. You've got secrets coming out of your ears. Finally going to share?"

Bennett's expression turned worried. "You don't have to," he said quickly. "Not if it hurts."

"It hurts more not to," she replied. She stood, unable to sit still under their combined gazes. "When I came here," she began, "I told you my name was Snow White. That was... not a complete lie. It was what people called me. Because of this." She gestured to her skin. "But it wasn't the name my father gave me," she continued. "He named me Shay. After the old word for snow. He said it fell the night I was born, and the world looked fresh and new, and he wanted me to carry that with me."

"Shay. It fits you," Bennett said with a smile.

Her voice wobbled. She steadied it. "There's more."

"Please continue," said Drew.

"My father was King Wilhelm," she said. "My mother is Queen Liora. I grew up in the castle."

Silence crashed over the table.

Harry's eyes went wide. "Well," he said faintly. "That's a twist!"

"You mean… *our* queen?" Drew asked.

"The one we slave for in the mines day after day? Sending her jewels and gems in exchange for scraps?" Silas asked.

She nodded.

Gage slapped Silas on the side of the head as if to say "obviously" and "shut up" simultaneously.

And so she told them. Not everything at once—she couldn't. But enough. She told them about her parents: her father's warmth, her mother's cold beauty. She spoke of her father's death, how they never found the killer, and of her mother's protection that felt more like a cage. Her voice grew flatter as she reached the next part.

Their reactions were not as shocked as she had expected. She was sure by now they suspected she was not being truthful about her past, but she thought the revelation that she was a princess might cause more of a stir.

She told them about the ball that never was for her—the corset laces drawn tighter and tighter until blackness took her. The gift of a comb, encrusted with gems from their mines, too pretty to be trusted. The sting and the plunge into sleep. She hesitated, then went on. She spoke of waking in the forest with a knife at her throat and Hunter's breath hot on her ear. Of the way he'd called her Liora in the dark. She didn't give them details. She didn't need to. The way her hand unconsciously went to her ribs, the way her mouth trembled on the word "virginity," painted enough.

"I escaped," she said. "I ran. I rode until I thought Grimm's legs would give out, and then I rode some more. I thought we'd die out there. Instead…" She spread her hands toward them. "Instead, I found you." She looked at each of them in turn. "You fed me," she said. "You taught me to cook, sew, and clean, to care for myself and for others, to feel safe, to feel loved." I was afraid if I said my real name, you'd be wary of me. You'd send me away before the queen's guard could come and for you. I'm not just a runaway stable girl," Shay said. "I'm a fugitive princess with a mother who would poison her own daughter. If she ever finds out I'm alive…" She shrugged, trying to make it seem lighter than it felt.

Dax's face had gone very still. "You think she might?" he said.

Shay started, "I trusted Hunter. I've known him my whole life. He's like a brother or an uncle to me. But his loyalty has always been to her. If she pries the truth out of him, she'll know. And if she knows, she'll come."

A muscle jumped in Gage's jaw. "Let her," he muttered.

The table was quiet. Then Harry reached across and took her hand. "We wouldn't have sent you away," he said simply. "Not then. Not now."

"Even knowing what this means?" she asked. "What

this brings down on you? The danger you could be in?"

Bennett's fingers curled around hers on the table. "You're not a burden," he said. "You're... the best thing that's happened to this place."

Silas shrugged. "I'm glad you kept the truth from us," he said. "Too much excitement for me."

Dax exhaled slowly. "We won't pretend this isn't serious. If she comes, she won't come alone. And we're miners, not trained soldiers with horses and swords. But we're strong, we know how to fight, and we know these woods."

"We'll do more than that," Gage said darkly. "If she tries to take you, she'll have to go through all of us. And Grimm."

"Yea and he bites," Harry added. They laughed, the tension easing a fraction.

"Still," Dax said. "Until then, we're not going to make it easy for her. Or anyone." He looked at Shay. "From now on, when we're at the mine, you stay close to the cottage or the stream. No wandering or riding off. If someone you don't know comes near, you run to us."

Shay nodded. "I understand."

"And Snow—I mean, Shay—don't talk to strangers," Harry added.

She rolled her eyes. "I'm not a child."

"Queens don't tend orchards themselves," Dax said. "But they do send others to do their dirty work."

The reminder sent a thin bolt of dread through her, quickly smothered by the warmth of their concern.

She felt... lighter, having told them. Saying "Shay" at the table, saying "princess," and "queen," and "murder," aloud had been like putting down a weight she'd been carrying alone. Her relief, she realized, was not just in rebuilding herself. It was in letting others see the cracks and choosing who helped her hold them together.

•　•　•　•　●　•　●　•　•　•

F AR AWAY, IN THE woods, a farmer's cart creaked along a narrow path. Liora's disguise was simple but effective: a shapeless dress that hid her curves, a scarf tied low to shadow her face, and her hands stained with a little dirt from the produce basket. No one looking at her would see a queen. Under the straw, wrapped in cloth, nestled the weapon she'd crafted. The corset had merely stolen her breath for a while, just buying time, keeping her out of sight until she could craft a poison. But she must have gotten it wrong, the elixir. The comb's poison was too weak. It had only put her to sleep for a short time. This time, it won't be a nap. This time, there won't be room for doubt. No reliance on a man to do a woman's work. A sleep that lasts forever. She had consulted apothecaries and hedge-witches in secret, trading fine jewels for knowledge. She'd tested tinctures on mice, then on condemned prisoners in the dark of the dungeons.

She'd settled on the apple. An innocuous thing. Symbol of health, of harvest, of simple peasant life. She'd coated a single fruit—shiny, red, perfect—with a distillation of everything she'd learned. A poison designed not to stop a heart outright, but to sink into the veins and send the victim to a lifetime slumber. If Snow White slept forever, she could not surpass her. A sleeping girl doesn't threaten one's power. "Sleep," Liora muttered, reins in one hand, the other resting briefly on the basket. "If I can't erase you, I will freeze you in time."

She hadn't wanted to bring Hunter. She didn't need him, she'd decided that. But habit was a stubborn thing, and she wanted eyes in the woods besides her own. She had banished him from her presence. She was finished with him. But she had not forbidden him from following. She knew him well enough to know he would.

Behind her, just out of sight, a brown horse moved through the trees as quietly as a man of Hunter's size could manage. He watched her back, jaw set. He told himself he followed to protect her. From wolves. From bandits. From herself. The truth lay somewhere harder: he didn't know who he was without her. Hunter's heart pounded as he followed Liora into the dark woods, hidden just behind the furthest tree, waiting for a moment he could redeem himself.

Chapter Twenty-One

Take A Bite

THE MORNING BEGAN LIKE any other. The men rose before dawn, the cottage a blur of half-awake grumbles and the soft thud of boots hitting the floor. Shay moved among them by habit, pressing mugs of thin coffee into hands, slapping bread onto plates, nudging Silas when he threatened to fall asleep upright. "Eat," she told him.

"Bossy," he muttered, but he took the crust she held out.

Dax checked the straps on his belt, the shine on his lamp, the state of his gloves. Silas tossed a heavy coil of climbing rope toward Gage to carry. Gage caught it instinctively, but then his hands froze on the rough hemp. He stared at the fibers for a long, sickened heartbeat before shoving the coil violently to the bottom of his pack, as if the mere thought of what he did burned him. Harry hummed a tune under his breath, trying to lift the lingering weight in the room after Shay's confession a few days before. Gage paced near the door, restless as ever, like a big dog itching to get loose. Shay leaned back against the table for a moment, watching them. They felt closer now. Knowing they knew who she was—*what* she was—and had chosen to let her stay had settled something in her bones. The bonds between them felt stronger, less like tethers, more like a net.

"You sure about this, Shay?" Drew asked quietly as he passed her, plate in hand. "Us leaving you alone?"

"You leave me alone every day," she pointed out. "And I somehow manage not to burn the cottage down."

"Sometimes," Harry added, sarcastically.

She made a face at him. "I'll be fine. I'll stay near the cottage or the stream. I'll keep Grimm nearby. I won't talk to strangers."

"Good," Harry put a hand over his heart. "We'd hate to come home and find you've run off with some handsome shepherd."

"Dimwit," Gage muttered. She flicked a crumb at him. He caught it automatically, popped it into his mouth, and scowled.

Dax shouldered his pack and stepped to the center of the room. "Same as always," he said. "We're gone, you stay close. If you hear anything off, you ride. No heroics."

"No climbing trees to see if you can spot the castle," Harry said.

Shay rolled her eyes. "I'm not a child," she said. "I understand the danger."

"We know, Shay," Bennett said quickly. "We just—"

"Worry," Drew finished, in his simple, apt way.

Her throat squeezed. "I know," she said, softer. "Now go. Before the mine caves in without your constant complaining."

They laughed, the moment easing. One by one, they filed out. Silas brushed a kiss over the top of her head as he passed. Bennett squeezed her shoulder. Drew's fingers brushed the back of her hand—a quick, shy touch. Gage was last. He stopped in the doorway, hand on the frame, and looked back. His eyes dropped briefly to her wrists, checking them for marks that had long since faded. For a heartbeat, his scowl slipped. Something like foreboding flickered behind his eyes. "Don't do anything stupid," he said. "I am no knight errant, looking for damsels to rescue."

"I won't. I've been safe here for a year now. I can't imagine any danger is out there anymore. If she wanted to find me, I'd think she would have by now," she replied. He stared a second longer, as if memorizing the sight of her framed in the cottage door: hair pulled back, skirts messy, light from the hearth painting her skin gold. Then he huffed, shook his head, and followed the others into the gray morning. Outside, the mine path wound away into the trees. The men's voices faded, swallowed by the forest.

Unseen by any of them, another figure watched from the darker line of pines beyond. Wrapped in a coarse dress and a farmer's scarf, Liora stood beside her borrowed cart, hands clenched white on the reins. Under the kerchief, her jaw was tight. She had risen before any rooster, too. She watched the six men tramp off to the mine. So these were the men from her mirror. If Snow White was able to harness her power and control these six burly men... but her thoughts trailed off as the miners stepped out of the clearing and into the woods. Snow White was left alone now. Good.

Gage paused for a moment at the edge of the trees; a chill crept up his spine. He turned, squinting back toward the cottage. From here he couldn't see her face, only a glimpse of her skirt as she moved inside, the faint gesture of her arm as she cleared plates. *You're getting soft,* he told himself. *She'll be fine.* He forced his feet forward.

Liora waited until the sounds of the men faded completely, then exhaled slowly. The path lay open, unbarred by watchful eyes. She clicked her tongue gently and guided the cart along the path that curved toward the sound of running water just around the bend.

Hunter followed at a distance, cloaked in shadow and shame. He told himself again and again that he trailed her to protect her. That if something happened in these woods—a bandit, a wolf, a loose stone on a slope—he could step in, save her, earn his way back into the queen's arms.

The trees thinned. The stream appeared ahead, bright in the mid-morning light—water tumbling over smooth rocks, banks matted with new grass. And there, just near where Liora had glimpsed her in the glass, knelt Shay. She had her sleeves rolled to the elbow, hands plunged in the cold water as she scrubbed a shirt against a rock. Her hair had come loose from its tie, dark strands sticking damply to her cheeks. An overturned basket sat beside her, already half full of rinsed linens. She looked ordinary in this moment. Ordinary and stunningly beautiful and heartbreakingly alive. Liora reined in the cart a short distance away, schooling her features into something pleasant.

Shay heard the wheel creak. She looked up, startled. The cart trundled closer, driven by a woman who looked, at first glance, like any peasant from the outer farms. Her dress was patchy but neat. A wide-brimmed hat and scarf shaded most of her face. "Morning," the woman called, voice pitched rougher than Liora's usual tones. Years of mimicking others had given her a knack for sloughing off her speech.

Shay's fingers tightened on the wet fabric. "Morning,"

she replied cautiously. *Was this a threat? Should she run?* Shay hadn't seen anyone but the men in a long time. New faces—any new face, was startling. The woman drew the cart to a halt at the bank. Up close, Shay could see the contents: a few cabbages, some wilted greens, several potatoes, and, nestled in straw at the very top, three apples so red and glossy they seemed to glow.

"You're a fair sight," the woman said, eyeing Shay's pile of shirts. "Most girls run from wash like it's poison."

"Someone has to do it," Shay said. "I live just up there." She nodded vaguely toward the vague direction of the cottage, not wanting to point too precisely.

"With your husband?" the woman asked.

Shay hesitated. "With... friends," she said.

"Mm." The woman clicked her tongue, as if that told her everything. "Hard work, keeping men in clean shirts and full bellies."

"You could say that," Shay muttered.

The woman laughed. It was a low, rusty sound, but genuine enough to disarm. "Here," she said, reaching into the basket. "Let me pay you for the entertainment. Washing is dull to watch." Her hand emerged with an apple, perfect and smooth. Sunlight slid over its skin, catching tiny droplets of moisture that made it look freshly polished.

Shay's mouth watered despite herself. She hadn't seen fruit like that since the castle. The apples they got at the cottage were usually smaller, a little bruised, stubbornly clinging to their stems in the small orchard beyond the hill. This one looked like something out of a painting.

"Go on," the woman said, extending it. "You look like you could use something sweet."

Shay's fingers twitched. She didn't move to take it. Something about the woman nagged at her. Maybe it was the way she held herself—too straight for a farmer's wife. Or the way her hands were calloused in the wrong places, not from hoe or churn but from something else. Or the way, when Shay tried to catch a glimpse of her face beneath the hat, the woman shifted just slightly, turning so the brim cast a deeper shadow. A prickle ran up Shay's spine. "Thank you," she said politely. "But I... I have to finish these. And you'll be wanting to sell those in town. I don't want to hold you up. You should continue your travels."

"Nonsense," the farmer's wife said. "One apple won't break me." She waggled it invitingly, the red skin seeming even brighter against her rough fingers. The scent of it drifted on the breeze—crisp, sweet, the exact smell of autumn markets and childhood treats stolen from the royal pantry.

Shay's stomach tightened. "I really shouldn't," she said again, more to herself than to the woman.

The woman's lips thinned imperceptibly beneath the scarf. "Look how juicy it is," she said, reaching into the basket again. Her knife flashed—a simple, worn thing, not a court dagger—and she sliced a neat wedge from the apple. Juice beaded and ran down the blade, dripping onto the straw below.

Liora lifted the slice to her own mouth and popped it in. She closed her eyes in an almost theatrical sigh. "Mmm," she said. "See? No harm in it." Shay watched her chew, waiting for some sign of treachery—the woman to threaten her with the knife, bandits to jump out of the woods and kidnap her. But the woman put the knife down and smiled.

"It looks very good," Shay admitted, tempted.

"You're working hard," the woman said. "Take a reward when it appears. That's what my mother always said."

Mother, Shay thought. The word sat wrong in this woman's mouth. Still. The apple *did* look delicious. Shay's fingers, trusting and hopeful, reached out. "Thanks," she said, taking the fruit. It felt heavy in her palm. Cool. Perfect. She turned it slowly, admiring the unblemished skin. A droplet of juice from the earlier slice traced a path along its curve.

"Go on," the woman urged. Her tone was light. Only someone who knew her well would have heard the strain beneath.

Shay hesitated one last second. Everything in her life had changed the last time she'd taken something from a woman who smiled at her. You're being foolish, she scolded herself. It's just an apple. You're far from the castle. No one here knows who you are. You watched her eat some.

Shay lifted it to her mouth and bit. The flesh was crisp under her teeth, sweeter than anything she'd tasted in years. Juice flooded her tongue, ran down her hand. For one absurd moment, her eyes stung with gratitude for something so simple. She chewed. The woman watched.

As Shay lifted the second bite, the farmer's wife made a small grimace and took the slice she'd bitten earlier from her own mouth, spitting it onto the ground behind her. Shay swallowed. The warmth from the fruit spread down her throat, into her chest. Then, abruptly, it thickened. It felt as though the blood in her veins was turning to molasses, heavy and sweet and slow, dragging her heartbeat down to a terrifying crawl. She frowned. A strange heaviness seeped into her limbs, as if someone had filled her veins with warm sand. Her fingers slackened on the half-eaten apple; it tumbled from her hand into the grass. "What...?" she began. Her tongue felt thick. The word dragged. Her vision blurred.

The woman straightened. She reached up and, with slow, deliberate care, removed the hat. Dark hair tumbled out. Eyes like polished obsidian glittered above high cheekbones. The farmer's wife's lines melted away from her posture like a shed skin.

"No," Shay whispered, the sound barely there. "No, no, no..." She knew that face. She'd seen it every day of her childhood. In mirrors. In her own features. In nightmares.

"Hello, my little snow-thing," Queen Liora said.

Shay was dizzy, like the world was spinning all around her. Her thoughts flashed through her mind—her father, Grimm, the prince, her six men. Her heart squeezed in her chest. Shay tried to scramble backward, but her legs didn't cooperate. They felt boneless, distant, as if they belonged to someone at the far end of a tunnel.

"You look surprised," Liora went on, stepping closer until her shadow fell over Shay. "Did you think you could hide from me forever in a hovel with coal dust on your skirts?"

Shay's heart pounded wildly, but her body refused to respond. She could feel every beat—thumping hard in her chest—but her limbs were heavy as stone. "Stay... away," she managed, though the words felt slurred, like she'd drunk too much wine.

Liora crouched in front of her. Up close, Shay could

see the changes the mirror had hinted at: the faint gray at her temples, the fine lines beginning to etch around her mouth. But the force in her eyes was the same as ever—sharp, unyielding, hungry. "You've grown," Liora said, tilting Shay's chin up with two fingers. "Into quite the little queen of your own, haven't you? Men at your feet. Power in your hands." Her lips curled. "How very like… me."

"Why…?" Shay's head spun. "Why are you—?"

"Because you breathe," Liora said sharply. Anger growing, she spouted, "Because every day you draw breath, you steal a piece of what is mine. My beauty. My attention. My power." She leaned closer, eyes narrowing. "Tell me," she murmured. "When you look in the glass they have there—do you see me? Or do you see yourself?"

Shay's jaw clenched. "I see…," was all she could force out.

"Exactly," Liora said softly. "And so did the mirror. And so did he." She didn't say Hunter's name. She didn't have to.

Shay's vision blurred. "Mother," she said, the word sharp like glass and sin. For a heartbeat, something flickered across Liora's face. Not quite regret. Not quite tenderness. Something more complicated and fleeting, but then it was gone.

"You always were too free with that word," she said. "You should have stuck with 'Queen.' It might have hurt less."

Her tongue felt numb. Her head lolled. The world around her started to look like a painting smeared by careless fingers. Shay's vision blackened. She felt like she was tumbling down into darkness, the world twisting into terrifying shapes around her. Liora stared into her daughter's eyes. For the briefest of instants, she caught her own reflection there—a tiny, warped version of herself in the dark of Shay's pupils. The face she'd once wielded like a weapon, now seen through the lens of someone she had marked for death. It wavered. It faded. As Shay's eyes fluttered, as the lids drooped, the last glimmer of Liora's image vanished. A symbolic passing, if anyone had been there to see it. Power, moving from one vessel to another. "Sleep," Liora whispered, fingers tightening on Shay's chin.

Shay's body obeyed. Her muscles unspooled, the last bit of tension leaving her frame. She slumped to the side, catching herself only clumsily on one hand before even that failed. Her cheek hit the soft, damp grass, eyes half-open, unfocused. Her lips were parted slightly, breath barely stirring them. The queen knew this time the poison would last.

Liora straightened, brushing imaginary dust from her skirt. A sharp pain lanced through her own chest then—a sudden, pulsing ache that made her gasp and clutch at her heart. The poison. She'd planned for it. The apothecary had warned her: "Even a drop on your tongue, my queen, will carry a price. Be swift." The bite she'd taken herself—discarded before she swallowed, but still tasted—left its mark. It wasn't fatal. Not to her. Not yet. But it was a warning. Her hand pressed to her sternum, feeling the echo of Shay's vanishing heartbeat in her own racing one. "We are bound," she murmured, half to herself, half to the trees. "You and I." She looked down at the girl—no, the woman, the princess, the daughter—she'd just felled.

Shay looked younger in sleep. Softer. For a fleeting second, Liora saw the child who had reached for her hand in the snow, who had begged to try on her jewels, who had laughed when Wilhelm lifted them both into the air. The second passed. Liora stepped back. She left Shay there on the bank, dark hair spread over the grass, damp shirts forgotten in the stream. She climbed back into the cart, fingers still slightly numb. As she flicked the reins, her gaze snagged one last time on the still form at the water's edge. "Sleep well, princess," she said. "May your dreams be kinder than your life." The wheels creaked. The cart rolled away, swallowed by the trees.

Up the slope, hidden behind a screen of brush, Hunter watched, eyes cold and calculating. He hadn't moved; he hadn't tried to warn Shay of the danger. His loyalty was stronger this time. He was determined this time. He would win Liora back, win her favor, win her hand. He had to. This time had to be it. It had to work. If he were to be cast away again he would fall on his sword, for a life without Liora was too difficult for him to stomach.

He looked toward the cart's path. How could he help her? Protect her? He made his choice. There was no rush in his descent, no panic, only the efficiency of a soldier cleaning up a battlefield. As he stood over Shay's body he felt no remorse. He felt no pity. Looking at her face, so terrifyingly similar to the face he worshipped, he felt only a twisted sense of relief. The rival was gone. The obstacle was removed. Liora was safe. But Liora had been careless. His eyes scanned the ground. The apple—red, shiny, and unmistakably out of place— lay in the grass where it had fallen from Shay's hand. If someone found it, they might see the bite. They might suspect. He used the toe of his boot to kick the bitten apple over the bank and into the moving stream.

"Sleep. Let them find you. Let them think it's some accident and I'll...." He didn't finish the sentence. He turned his back on his king's daughter and walked into the trees, disappearing into the shadows again.

In the dark below ground, six men worked, unaware that the woman who had become the heart of their strange little household had just fallen under a spell older and crueler than any bargain they'd ever struck.

In a carriage rolling toward the castle, a queen clutched her chest and smiled through the pain.

Chapter Twenty-Two

Of Glass and Gold

THE RHYTHMIC CLANG OF pickaxes against stone echoed through the mine shaft, a steady heartbeat that had become as familiar to Gage as his own pulse. Dust hung in the air like suspended memories, catching the flickering light from their lanterns and casting long shadows across the rough-hewn walls. The other men worked with practiced efficiency—Dax chipping away at a stubborn vein of quartz, Harry sorting through promising specimens, Drew humming a tuneless melody under his breath.

But Gage couldn't focus. His hands moved mechanically, striking the rock with less force than usual, his mind somewhere else entirely—somewhere back at the cottage where Shay would be tending to the garden, or perhaps sitting by the window with one of her books.

"Something's wrong," he stammered, more to himself than anyone else.

"What's that?" Harry called from across the chamber, not looking up from his work.

Silas inserted, "The air is clear in my lungs and nose. The canary is singing. Not to worry, Gage."

Gage shook his head, trying to dislodge the feeling that had settled in his chest like a stone. It wasn't just worry—it was certainty. "Not here. *Her*!" A deep, primal knowing that cut through rational thought and settled in his bones. He tossed his mine pick to the ground with a clatter that silenced the other men.

"Gage?" Dax's voice held concern now.

Gage didn't wait for questions or explanations. He turned and hurried out of the mines, his boots kicking up dust as he broke into a run toward the cottage. Behind him, he heard the scramble of the others following, their voices calling after him, but he couldn't stop. Couldn't explain. He just knew. The path back to the cottage blurred beneath his feet as he ran, his heart pounding not from exertion but from dread. When he reached the small wooden structure, he burst through the door without knocking. "Shay!" His voice echoed through the empty rooms.

He checked the kitchen first—cold hearth, untouched dishes. The bedroom—neatly made bed, no sign of disturbance. The sitting room—books arranged precisely on the shelves, exactly as she always kept them. Every room was empty, pristine, waiting for an occupant who wasn't there. The other men crowded into the doorway behind him, their faces etched with confusion and growing concern. "Gage, what is it? Where is she?"

"I don't know," he admitted, his voice tight with panic. "But she's not here." His eyes scanned the room again, searching for any clue, any sign of where she might have gone. Without another word, Gage rushed back outside and turned toward the stream. It was their favorite place, where they often sat together in comfortable silence, watching the water flow over smooth stones. If she'd gone anywhere, it would be there. The distance seemed to stretch endlessly as he ran, his lungs burning, his mind racing with terrible possibilities. And then he saw them.

Drew was kneeling on the bank of the stream, his shoulders shaking with silent sobs. Next to him lay a figure so still, so pale, that Gage's heart stopped completely before lurching back into a frantic rhythm. "No," he whispered, then louder, "No!" He ran the last few yards and dropped to his knees beside her, his hands hovering over her body as if afraid to touch her. But he knew immediately. The unnatural stillness, the bluish tint to her lips, the way her chest didn't rise and fall with breath—it was all unmistakable.

"She's gone," Drew choked out between tears. "She's gone."

The other men arrived moments later, their expressions shifting from confusion to horror as they took in the scene. "What happened?" Silas yelled.

Gage responded. "I don't know. Drew found her like this. No enemies, no wounds," he frantically checked her skin.

"We have to help her," Bennett cried. "Maybe she just fainted, hit her head." He pulled off his heavy tunic and draped it over her, tucking it frantically around her shoulders.

They tried waking her, shaking her, warming her, cooling her, rubbing her skin, calling her name. But she did not wake, and she did not breathe. Finally, as the sun began to dip low, casting long mournful shadows through the trees, Dax put a hand on Gage's shoulder. Gage was still holding her, staring at her face. "Gage," Dax said softly. "She's dead."

Gage whipped around, snarling, "She's not! Look at her! She looks peaceful. She looks like she's asleep. Does that look like death to you?"

"It's not life," Dax said, his own voice trembling. "It's something...else. Heart failure. Or..." he trailed off. "Or the queen found her."

"But there was no mark, no weapon. She must have just... passed on." Silas said.

One by one, they removed their hats and hung their heads in sorrow. The air grew heavy with grief, pressing down on them like the weight of the mountain above their mines. Harry stepped forward, his voice thick with emotion. "Her beauty was a gift for the whole world," he said softly, "and now it's gone." His mind raced back to their conversations, her laughter, the way her eyes lit up when she talked about the stars. All of it, gone.

Gage couldn't speak. He gently brushed a strand of hair from Shay's face, his fingers trembling. She looked peaceful, almost as if she were sleeping, but the coldness of her skin told a different story.

"We have to bury her," Silas said.

"We can't just bury her in some dark hole," Harry said suddenly, his voice firm despite the tears in his eyes. "She's too beautiful for that. The world should be able to see her, to remember her. Not pushed underground in the darkness forever."

"A glass coffin," Bennett agreed immediately. "We'll craft one ourselves from the crystal veins in the lower mine. She deserves to be seen, to be honored."

Dax nodded slowly, his mind already working through the logistics. They had the materials in their workshop and the skills to create something worthy of her. As they carefully lifted her body and carried her back to the cottage, Gage felt a strange sense of purpose cutting through his grief. They would honor her properly.

The next few hours passed in a blur of activity. They worked through the night. Grief gave them a terrible, manic energy. They mined the purest vein of crystal quartz they had. They worked the gold they had hoarded for years, melting it down to frame the glass and adorned the sides with gems and jewel stones of many colors. They built her a resting place not of wood and nails, but of light and treasure. Dax stood back to admire their work, his expression thoughtful. "She's a princess," he declared finally. "She deserves a royal funeral. We should take her to the castle."

"But not Queen Liora's," Gage said quickly, the words surprising even himself.

"The castle to the west," Dax agreed. "It's farther, but it's the right choice."

They prepared for the journey with solemn determination. Dax would ride ahead on Grimm to arrange the funeral proceedings with the king, while the rest of them would carry Shay's glass coffin. They would walk the long distance together, giving her the procession she deserved.

As they set out the next morning, the sun rising behind them, Gage felt a strange sensation of being watched. He glanced around but saw nothing unusual. Unbeknownst to any of them, Hunter followed at a distance, his presence hidden by the early morning mist.

The journey was long and arduous, but the men

carried their burden with unwavering dedication. At night, they camped under the stars, taking turns keeping watch over her. Each man spoke to her in quiet moments, sharing memories and promises, as if she could still hear them–Harry telling her jokes, Drew humming songs, Bennett professing her beauty even in death, Silas lamenting the loss of his spooning partner, and Gage whispering apologies. They walked through wind that howled like their own grief. They walked through nights where the only light was the moon reflecting off the glass of the coffin.

When they finally approached the western castle, they found preparations already underway. Trumpets sounded as they entered the grand courtyard, their procession drawing the attention of courtiers and servants alike. The coffin gleamed in the sunlight, showcasing Shay's ethereal beauty to all who passed. A rumbling of gossip and rumor rose from the crowd as the men passed by with the coffin atop their shoulders. Whispers of the beauty of the coffin itself and the girl inside. "The princess," they heard, "Wilhelm's heir."

At the front of the courtyard, near the grand steps where the king awaited them, the procession paused, and as tradition demanded the men carefully opened the coffin lid to allow the final blessings to be spoken directly over Shay's body. The king himself—a distinguished man with kind eyes, a fur cloak, and silver-streaked hair—stood to receive them. He had clearly been briefed by Dax, for his expression was one of genuine sorrow.

As he spoke to the crowd, giving honor and reverence to a neighboring ruler's lineage, his words were drowned out by commotion from the king's son.

Prince Jacob sat astride a magnificent grey horse, dressed in a pristine white riding coat that seemed to glow in the sunlight. His golden hair was perfectly styled, his posture regal yet approachable. No longer a boy, he was handsome, noble, and beloved by his people.

As the procession stood at a halt, Prince Jacob's gaze fell upon the glass coffin, and his breath left his lungs in a rush. It wasn't just that she was beautiful, though she was. It was a sense of recognition. He stared at the girl in the intricate coffin, heartbeat quickening. He dismounted with practiced grace, eyes never leaving the girl's lifeless face.

There was something in his expression—surprise, wonder, and a deep, aching longing. He moved closer, his steps measured but urgent, until he stood directly beside the coffin. The men bristled, hands going to their weapons, but Dax held up a hand. "Wait," Dax assured his men.

Jacob knelt by the coffin. He looked at her closed eyes, her dark hair. Then his gaze dropped to something shiny at her neck. His eyes widened as he noticed the simple necklace—a delicate cord with a small silver pendant. His hand touched the matching falcon embossed in his chest plate. Recognition dawned in his features, followed by a look of profound emotion. "This is her," he whispered to no one, his voice filled with awe. "The girl from the stables."

Bennett, noticing his matching falcon chest plate, and feeling hope and heartbreak at once, confessed, "She wore it every day. She cherished it. She said it was a promise."

Jacob looked at Bennett and then back at her. His heart beat louder. He had looked for her in every ballroom, in every court. The men exchanged confused glances, but before anyone could ask what he meant, the royal chaplain began speaking the funeral rites.

Ignoring the proceedings, prince Jacob stooped forward, his hand reaching out to gently cup her face. His eyes filled with tears as he looked down at her, his expression one of heartbreaking tenderness. "I've dreamed of your lips since that day," he crooned, his voice barely audible but carrying clearly in the hushed courtyard. A feeling of regret and action washed over him at once. Before he knew what he was doing he leaned down and kissed her cold lips in a gesture that surprised everyone present.

For a moment, nothing happened. The prince lingered, his lips pressed gently against hers, his hand still cradling her face. The crowd held its collective breath, some turning away in sorrow, others watching with morbid fascination.

Then, something extraordinary occurred. A warmth began to emanate from where their lips met, subtle at first but growing stronger. Prince Jacob felt it immediately—a softening, a responsiveness that hadn't been there before. He pulled back slightly, his eyes wide with disbelief. At that very moment, color returned to the dead girl's cheeks, and Shay's eyelids fluttered open.

Her gaze was hazy at first, clouded by the lingering effects of the poison, but it cleared quickly. *Where am I? What happened? Who is this—is that...?*

She blinked again as she tried to focus on the face above her. Recognition sparked in her eyes, followed by confusion, then amazement.

"You? You're...you're alive," Prince Jacob breathed, joyful and relieved.

Shay blinked slowly, a small smile forming on her lips. "I think I'm dreaming again," she whispered.

The courtyard erupted in cheers as the reality of the miracle sank in. The men who had carried her so faithfully stared in stunned shock, their grief transforming instantly into overwhelming happiness. Even the king looked astonished, though a proud smile soon spread across his face.

Shay's eyes searched Prince Jacob's face, her expression filled with gratitude and something deeper. "I've dreamed of you. All this time," she said softly, "I never even knew your name."

"You must be Princess Shay, daughter of King Wilhelm," he replied, his voice warm with affection. "And I am Prince Jacob." He took her hand gently, helping her sit up in the coffin as the crowd continued to cheer around them. "I never stopped thinking about you," he confessed, his eyes, still full of amazement, never leaving hers. "Even when it didn't make sense."

Tears welled in Shay's eyes. She reached up to touch his face, as if confirming that he was real—that *she* was real. "I've thought of you too—so often," she admitted. "I wore your necklace every day, hoping I might see you again."

Again, action overtook logic and Jacob leaned in quickly for another fast kiss, as if his lips would cement her in life.

Shay's gaze flew past the prince's shoulder, latching onto the six men who were slowly retreating toward the gate, eyes on the ground, heartbroken.

She scrambled to sit up further. Panic spiked in her chest. "No! Stop! Don't you dare," she cracked, her voice fierce and breaking. "You cannot leave me now," she cried.

"You have finally found where you belong, princess," Dax admitted. "You will be happier here than you ever were in our cottage."

"No! You are my family," she pleaded.

"Family," Drew responded. He nodded and turned back toward her. The other five followed suit.

The men circled them as the celebration continued. The poison that had claimed her had been broken by true love's kiss—not just any love, but a love that had endured years of separation, uncertainty, and longing. As Shay and Jacob held each other in the sunlight, surrounded by cheering crowds and six faithful friends, it was clear that their story was far from over. It was just beginning.

Chapter Twenty-Three

Vanity Shattered

T HE CELEBRATION IN THE courtyard reached a fever pitch as Prince Jacob helped Shay to her feet, her hand clasped firmly in his. The crowd's cheers echoed off the castle walls, but Gage felt a strange stillness settle over him amidst the chaos. He watched as Shay looked up at Jacob with tears of gratitude shining in her eyes, her expression one of pure wonder and relief. Gage took a deep breath and stepped forward, his movements deliberate and solemn. He walked directly to where Shay stood and knelt before her, one knee touching the stone courtyard. The five other men followed his lead without hesitation, forming a protective circle around their princess, much like the circle formed around her the first time she awoke in the cottage. Gage looked up into her beautiful eyes, his heart aching with a love that was both profound and impossible.

"Your highness," he said, his voice steady despite the emotion threatening to overwhelm him, "I pledge my loyalty to you. Not just today, but for all my days."

One by one, the other men echoed his vow, their voices strong and true. "We will protect you from the queen," Dax declared, his usual stoicism tempered by genuine devotion. "From any threat, from any danger."

Shay's eyes filled with fresh tears as she looked

at each of them in turn. She knew what they were offering—not just protection, but their hearts, their lives, their unwavering loyalty. There was love in their devotion, yes, but it was the kind of love that asked for nothing in return, that existed purely to serve and protect.

Prince Jacob watched this exchange with understanding in his eyes. He stepped forward and placed a gentle hand on Shay's shoulder. "You may stay here in the safety of the castle," he announced to the assembled crowd, his voice carrying the authority of royalty. "These six men can be knighted as your royal guards, sworn to your protection."

Shay turned to Jacob, her gratitude overwhelming. Without hesitation, she threw her arms around his neck. "Thank you," she whispered, her voice thick with emotion. "They are special to me."

Jacob held her close, his embrace both protective and tender. The crowd continued to celebrate around them, everyone distracted by the miracle they had just witnessed, by the joy of seeing their beloved prince reunited with the woman who had captured his heart all those years ago.

But in the shadows at the edge of the courtyard, a figure moved with purpose. Dark-cloaked and silent, Hunter had been watching from the moment they arrived. He had followed them all the way from the cottage, his obsession driving him forward with every step.

· · • • ● • ● • • ·

MEANWHILE, FAR TO THE east, Queen Liora returned to her castle in a fury. Her murderous errand had been completed—she was certain of it. The apple had been delivered, the poison administered. Shay would be dead by now, and the mirror would finally show her what she most wanted to see. She stormed into her dressing room, poison still subtly affecting her body. Without even taking the time to oil as she normally would, she stripped off her garments, letting them fall in a heap around her feet. She stood before her magnificent mirror, naked and proud, her body fully beautiful despite the passage of time.

At forty-three, Liora's beauty had matured rather than faded. Fine lines framed her eyes, earned from years of calculated smiles and strategic frowns. Her skin showed the gentle effects of gravity, but there was strength in the curve of her hips, power in the swell of her chest. A few silver strands threaded through her dark hair, catching the light like precious metal. She ran her hands over her body, appreciating the way her flesh still responded to her touch, still held the power to command men's attention and obedience. "Mirror, soul of silver and glass," she demanded, her voice ringing with confidence, "who in this land shall I never surpass?" She knew she would see her own reflection, triumphant and alone. She knew that Shay was dead, that the threat to her beauty had been eliminated once and for all.

The mirror rippled.

• • • ● • ● ● • •

Back in Jacob's courtyard, the shadowy figure emerged from the crowd with sudden, deadly intent. Eyes red with rabid rage, Hunter drew his sword and darted toward Shay, his movements swift and practiced. The celebration around them provided perfect cover for his attack.

Shay turned just as Hunter lunged, her eyes widening in shock as she recognized the face beneath the hood. "Hunter?" she gasped, disbelief warring with betrayal.

Gage reacted instantly, throwing himself between Hunter and Shay. He grabbed the assassin around the waist and slammed him to the ground, pinning him with his superior strength. At the same moment, Prince Jacob positioned himself in front of Shay, drawing his own sword with ease.

"Hunter! Why are you doing this?" Shay demanded, her voice trembling with hurt. "What is she paying you this time?"

Hunter struggled against Gage's hold, his eyes wild with obsession. "It's not about money! It's never been for money!" he shouted, his voice cracking with manic emotion. "It's not about the kingdom or the throne. I love her! I've always loved her! I'll do anything to be with her without regard to my own life, and if you didn't mirror her image so closely, you'd already be dead!" There was something different in Hunter's eyes—something savage, reckless.

The words hung in the air like a potent poison. Shay stared at him, her face slowly turning pale with dawning horror. "Wait. You?... It was you. You killed my father," she whispered, the realization hitting her like a physical blow. "All those years ago... you were the one? You killed the king, to be with her!"

Hunter's expression twisted with madness. "Your father walked in while your mother's naked body pressed on mine. He never should have tried to come between us!"

Shay screamed—a sound of pure anguish that cut through the courtyard like a knife. The realization washed over her. The man she had trusted, the friend who had protected her family, the man she had given her virginity to... he had murdered her father. The betrayal was almost too much to bear.

Gage's face darkened with rage as the truth sank in. This was the man she spoke about, who had taken Shay's innocence, who had damaged something precious and pure, as he had done a few months prior. With a roar of fury, he punched Hunter in the jaw, his knuckles connecting with satisfying force. The other five men immediately surrounded Gage, pulling him back before he could kill their captive. "Don't, Gage!" Dax warned. "He's a trained fighter. He'll kill you!"

Hunter laughed maniacally, blood dripping from his split lip. "I'll hunt you until you're dead, Shay! I can't have her without your head on a spear. You'll never live in peace! Never!" Hunter didn't wait for a response. He moved with the terrifying speed of a man trained to kill. He lunged, his blade aiming not for the men, but straight for Shay's heart.

"No!" Gage roared. He didn't have a weapon drawn; he had only his body. He threw himself into the path of the blade, shoving Shay backward into Bennett's arms. There was a sickening sound of tearing fabric and wet impact. Gage grunted, stumbling back, a hand pressed to his side. Blood—bright and arterial—welled up instantly between his fingers, soaking his tunic.

"Gage!" Shay screamed, struggling against Bennett's grip. Hunter didn't hesitate. He spun, slashing wild and fast. Dax drew his mining knife, but it was a tool, not a weapon of war. Hunter parried Dax's strike with a lazy flick of his wrist and sent the leader of the miners sprawling onto the cobblestones with a boot to the chest.

"Filthy rats!" Hunter sneered. He was a whirlwind of steel, driving the miners back. He wasn't just fighting; he was carving a path. He cut Harry across the forearm, sent Silas scrambling back with a near-miss that took a button off his coat. He was the Captain of the Queen's Guard, and these were men who hit rocks for a living. It was a slaughter waiting to happen.

"Enough!" Prince Jacob's booming voice cut through the chaos. Jacob stepped further forward, his own sword drawn, grip steady. Hunter spun around to face him. "Step away from them," Jacob commanded, placing himself between Hunter and the wounded Gage. Drew, Bennett, and Harry led Shay up the steps to the balcony, out of harm's way.

Hunter laughed, a wet, deranged sound. "The pretty prince wants to play? I killed a King, boy. Slit his throat right in front of his queen. Do you think I fear you?"

"I think," Jacob said, his eyes flicking briefly to Shay,

"that you have forgotten what men fight like when they have something to lose."

Jacob struck first. It was a blur of motion, metal ringing against metal. The crowd gasped and surged back, giving them a wide berth.

It became immediately clear that this would not be an easy victory. Jacob was outmatched. Hunter kicked dirt into Jacob's eyes; he feinted low and struck high. He was stronger, heavier, and fueled by a frenzied delirium that made him ignore his own fatigue. Jacob parried a blow that would have taken his head off, the force of it jarring his arm all the way to the shoulder. He retreated, step by step, forcing Hunter to chase him.

"Is this the man who will protect her?" Hunter taunted, slashing Jacob's thigh. A line of red bloomed on the Prince's white trousers. "I protected the Queen for years! I did what needed to be done! You are nothing but a child playing dress-up!"

Hunter lunged. Jacob blocked, but Hunter's weight bore down on him, locking their blades at the hilts. They stood nose to nose, grunting with exertion. "She will die," Hunter hissed, his spit flying into Jacob's face. "And I will bring her heart to the queen!"

With a roar, Hunter struck Jacob. The Prince stumbled back, dazed, blood pouring from his nose. He fell to one knee, his sword clattering a few feet away.

"Jacob!" Shay cried out from the balcony, the words cracking with terror.

Hunter loomed over the fallen Prince, raising his sword for the killing stroke. The sun glinted off the steel. Time seemed to slow. Dax and Silas rushed forward, but they were too far away.

Jacob looked up. Through the haze of pain, he saw Shay gripping the balcony rail, her face white with fear. *Not today,* Jacob thought. *I just found her.*

As Hunter brought the sword down, Jacob didn't try to block. He rolled forward, diving inside Hunter's guard. He tackled the swordsman around the waist, driving him back with a desperate surge of adrenaline. They crashed to the ground, a tangle of limbs. Hunter dropped his sword, forced to resort to his fists, raining heavy blows onto Jacob's ribs. Jacob took them, gritting his teeth, and scrambled for a loose dagger at Hunter's own belt.

Hunter's eyes were rabid. His hands found Jacob's throat, squeezing, crushing the windpipe. Jacob's vision was spotted with black. He couldn't breathe. The sounds of the courtyard faded. *Shay.*

With a final, explosive effort, Jacob ripped the dagger free. He didn't have the angle for the heart. He drove the blade upward, jamming it under Hunter's ribs, into the soft vulnerability of the gut, and twisted.

Everyone froze. Hunter froze. His grip on Jacob's throat slackened. His eyes went wide, the madness in them dimming into shock. Jacob shoved him off, gasping for air, coughing violently. He scrambled back, retrieved his sword, and stood over the assassin. Hunter curled on the stones, clutching his side, coughing blood. He looked up at Jacob, then past him, toward the East. Toward Liora. "She..." Hunter wheezed. "She will... never... love you..." He slumped forward, the light leaving his eyes.

The courtyard was silent, save for the ragged sound of Jacob's breathing. He stood there, bruised, bleeding, his pristine white coat stained with blood and dirt, his face swelling—but victorious. He dropped his sword. He didn't look at the crowd. He turned immediately to the miners. "Gage," he rasped, stumbling toward the wounded man.

Shay was already there. She had flown down the stairs, ignoring the danger, ignoring the blood. She fell to her knees beside Gage, her hands pressing over Drew's on the wound in his side. "You idiot," she sobbed, looking at Gage's pale face. "You stupid, brave idiot."

Gage managed a weak, bloody grin. "Told you," he wheezed. "No knight errant. Just us."

"Is he...?" Shay looked up at Dax, terrified.

Dax knelt, checking the wound with hands that still shook from the fight. "It missed the vitals," Dax said. "He's lost some blood, but he's as stubborn as the mountain stone. He'll live."

"Okay, you lot. Enough fussing. Bandage me up and let's be done with it," Gage ordered.

Shay turned and threw herself into Jacob's arms, her tears mingling with his sweat and blood. He held her tightly, his breathing ragged but his heart full.

She inhaled him—his scent, the sweat, the blood he shed for her. "I thought I lost you. When you had only just been found," she cried.

"I wish I had found you sooner. Your mother, the queen, never allowed me through the gate, though I tried many times. I... I just..." Jacob paused, adrenaline subsiding, reality returning. "May I court you, properly?" Jacob asked softly, his voice full of reverence. "Even if it's complicated?" he added as he looked at the six men.

His touch was innocent, his hands gentle as they

cradled her face, but it aroused her more than any previous touch in her life. There was purity in his affection, honesty in his desire, and the knowledge that she had genuine romantic love for him made every contact electric. She had longed for him for so many years, dreamed of this moment, and now it was real.

"Yes," she whispered, her voice filled with wonder. "Please." But then she pulled back, her hands resting on his chest, her eyes darting to the six battered, bloody men who stood in a protective ring around them.

Gage was wiping blood from his lip; Bennett was watching her with terrified hope. "But you must know," Shay said, trembling but firm, "I am not the girl in the stable anymore. I have been loved by these men. They are part of me now. I cannot walk away from them."

The courtyard went silent. The miners held their breath, waiting for the Prince to recoil, to demand she choose. Jacob looked at the six men. He saw the way Gage watched the perimeter, the way Harry was ready to catch her if she fell, the way their hands lingered on their weapons, ready to kill for her. He looked back at Shay and saw the fierce loyalty burning in her eyes.

Jacob was silent for a long moment. He looked at the men again—really looked this time—at their bruises, their blood, the way they never took their eyes off her. "I won't pretend I understand this yet," he said finally. Shay's heart stuttered. "But I know one thing," he went on. "You didn't survive by accident. And I won't insult you by asking you to erase your past. What do *you* want?"

She took a deep breath, afraid her next words would condemn her. "I had a dream of just you, once, but I have a new dream now. I want them with me. And I want you with me."

"Then it shall be," he replied. And he kissed her deeply, passion and love swelling from both of their hearts.

• • • ● • ● ● • • •

LIORA STOOD BEFORE HER mirror, waiting for the confirmation of her victory. But instead of her own triumphant reflection, the mirror's surface rippled like a pond disturbed by a stone. The dark glass swirled, clearing to reveal a scene that made her breath hitch in her throat. Shay and Prince Jacob, kissing tenderly in the courtyard, the six miners standing proudly behind.

"No," Liora whispered, her hand trembling as she reached toward the glass. "It cannot be! She is dead. I fed her the fruit. I watched her fall!" The image in the glass did not fade. It grew brighter, taunting her with the one thing she could not poison: love. "Stop it!" Liora shrieked. "Show me! Show me who is fairest!"

The image of the courtyard faded. In its place, her own reflection returned. Liora let out a sigh of relief, leaning in close to admire the smooth line of her jaw, the dark fire in her eyes.

But then, the reflection blinked.

The woman in the glass smiled, but it was not Liora's smile. It was a rictus of decay.

As Liora watched, paralyzed with horror, the

reflection began to change. The smooth, alabaster skin she had oiled and pampered for four decades began to gray and thin, sucking tight against the skull. Her midnight hair, her pride and joy, turned the color of dirty ash and fell out in clumps, drifting to the bottom of the frame. Her teeth yellowed and lengthened; her posture curled into a question mark.

Liora gasped, clutching her own face. Her fingers met not smooth skin, but deep, dry furrows. She looked down at her hands—they were spotted and withered, the hands of a crone.

"What is this?" she croaked, her voice a rusted hinge. "What are you doing to me?"

The mirror seemed to hum, a low vibration that shook the teeth in her head. The poison she had ingested earlier—the single bite of the apple—suddenly roared to life in her blood. It didn't put her to sleep. It accelerated the time she had stolen. Decades crashed into her in seconds. Her bones cracked and bowed under the weight of sudden age. Her heart fluttered like a dying moth.

"Stop it, dark magic! I am the Queen!" she screamed at the glass, raising a withered fist. "I am the fairest! I am Liora!"

She struck the glass with her fist in a fury of rage. It did not just crack—it exploded. With a sound like a thunderclap, the great mirror shattered outward. A thousand shards of silver glass—bright as diamonds, sharp as daggers—erupted into the room. They flew at her like a swarm of angry bees, driven by a magic that was finally done serving her.

Liora fell back, pierced by the jagged fragments of her

own vanity.

She landed hard on the cold stone floor. She tried to crawl, to reach the door, but her limbs were suddenly too frail, too old. She rolled onto her back, her breath rattling in her chest. All around her lay the shards of the mirror. In every single pointed piece, she saw a reflection. A thousand tiny, withered hags stared back at her, their eyes wide with terror, dying alone in the dark.

She reached up, trying to shield her face, trying to hide the ruin of her beauty one last time. But her hand was too heavy.

"Fairest…" she wheezed, the word dissolving into a dry rattle.

And there, amidst the wreckage of her obsession, Queen Liora took her last breath—alone, quiet, and flayed by the truth she had spent a lifetime avoiding.

· · · ● ● · ● ● · · ·

B ACK IN THE WESTERN castle, Shay rested in Jacob's arms, feeling safer than she had in years. The threat was gone, the future shining with possibility. She had found her protectors, her prince, and most importantly, herself. Two futures shimmer before her. One born of devotion. One born of desire. Shay whispered to herself, "Once upon a time, a princess lived happily ever after."

The End

Epilogue

Two possible futures. Two possible fates.
Only one can be yours.
Snow White stands at a crossroads. Fate splits. Desire
splits. Which path calls to you?
<u>Choose your destiny:</u>
Epilogue A: Devotion
Epilogue B: Indulgence
Once you turn the page, the future you choose
becomes the only one that exists.

Epilogue A: Devotion

T HE BALLROOM FELT COLD, even with the roaring
fire in the hearth. Shay traced patterns on the
condensation of the wineglass, ignoring the politely spoken
conversations swirling around her. Months. Months of
being Princess Shay again, betrothed to Prince Jacob,
months of smiles and curtsies and endless processions.
She'd anticipated it, of course. A life lived under glass, a
queen expected to be seen and not...felt.

Jacob found her near the French doors, overlooking
the frost-laced gardens. He didn't speak, simply slid his
hand over hers, the warmth of his touch instantly thawing
the chill that had settled in her bones.

"Thinking?" he asked, his voice a low rumble against
the background music.

She lifted her gaze to meet his, the familiar blue of his
eyes anchoring her. "About how easily a cage can be gilded."

He chuckled, a sound that always felt like a secret
shared. "Is that so?" He tugged her gently away from
the crowd, towards a smaller, seldom-used drawing room.
Velvet drapes muted the sounds of the party, shutting out
the performance.

A small fire crackled in the grate here, casting dancing
shadows on the walls. He closed the door, the click echoing

in the sudden quiet. He turned, his eyes never leaving hers.

"You needn't perform for me, Shay."

She managed a small smile. "I know." She shifted, restless. "It's just...difficult. Sometimes."

He crossed the room in three long strides, cupping her face in his hands. His thumbs traced the delicate line of her jaw. "Tell me."

"Everyone expects...something. A queen. A wife. Someone...pristine." The word tasted like ash in her mouth.

He leaned closer, his breath warm against her lips. "And what do *you* expect, Shay?"

Her own desires felt dangerous, illicit even after their betrothal. "I... I want to feel."

He didn't hesitate. He lowered his head, his lips brushing against hers, a tentative exploration. She responded instantly, her hands rising to tangle in his hair. This wasn't the chaste, polite kissing they'd indulged in before. This was a claiming. A slow, deliberate unveiling.

He tasted of wine and something uniquely *him*—woodsmoke and spice and a hint of the stables. She deepened the kiss, urging him closer, her fingers tightening in the thick strands of his hair. He groaned, a soft sound that vibrated against her lips.

He pulled back slightly, his brow furrowed with a question. She just looked at him, a silent plea in her eyes. He understood.

He moved with a controlled grace, his hands sliding down her arms, tracing the curve of her shoulders. He peeled off her shawl, then the delicate lace sleeves of her gown, revealing the ivory silk beneath. She felt a blush warm her skin, but didn't pull away.

"Beautiful," he whispered, his voice thick with emotion.

Her hands worked at the buttons of his waistcoat, her fingers trembling slightly. He helped her, and soon, both of them were shedding the layers of formality, revealing the vulnerability beneath. The silk of her gown pooled at her feet. They stood naked, embraced, his hands hovering near her waist.

She tilted her head back, her lips parted in anticipation. He lowered himself to his knees, his gaze traveling over her body with an intensity that made her suck in a short breath.

"I've wanted this for so long," he murmured, his voice raw.

He kissed her again, lower this time, tracing the delicate curve of her hips. Her fingers dug into his hair, anchoring him to her. He started slowly, reverently, his touch featherlight. She arched into him, meeting his touch with a desperate need she hadn't even realized she possessed.

He explored her with a painstaking devotion, mapping the terrain of her body as if she were a sacred landscape. Each touch, each kiss, was a revelation. He'd been so careful, so respectful, observing the boundaries she hadn't even known she'd set for herself. Now, those boundaries were dissolving, melting away under the heat of his desire. He kissed closer and closer to where the heat was building between her legs.

She moaned softly, her hands gripping his shoulders. His touch was sending tremors through her, igniting a fire that threatened to consume her. He deepened his exploration, his fingers following his lips, finding her wetness had already started to pool. He kissed her there, sending pleasure up and down her body at once. His fingers found their way inside her, slow and deliberate.

"Jacob..." she breathed, her voice barely a whisper. "What will your father... we're not married yet. I don't want you getting in trouble..."

"Shay," he responded, just as breathlessly. "I see the way you ache to be touched, by them, by me. You're safe now, you can relax now, and I can't resist you any longer."

He started to move, a slow, rhythmic pulse that built with each thrust of his finger. Kisses on the front of her pussy turned to deeper licks as his fingers played inside her. He put one finger in his mouth. "Mmm so sweet." he said as he licked up the rest of her wetness. He slowly kissed his way back up her body, pressing his erection into her side as he stood. He kissed her neck, his teeth grazing her skin, sending shivers down her spine.

"Tell me what you want," he urged, his voice husky.

She hesitated. Years of ingrained obedience fought against the burgeoning desire within her, but she couldn't deny it any longer." I want...I want you to take control."

He stilled for a moment, his eyes locking with hers. He saw the vulnerability there, the hesitant plea for release. He understood.

"Lie on the chaise, bring your neck up over the armrest," he commanded.

The authority in his voice made her shiver with anticipation. She draped her back over the armrest letting her legs stretch out on the couch.

"There. Now I get an incredible view while you can

take me deep into your throat." He stepped forward and Shay tilted her head back further, opening her mouth to allow him in upended. He reached down and ticked her nipples with his fingers, circling them slowly and gently while Shay closed her mouth around him and allowed him to slowly thrust his hips forward and back.

"Touch yourself," he commended. "I want to watch."

Shay was surprised, intrigued, and excited by this new side of her prince. She didn't know he had it in him. She reached down to her already soaked heat and slowly circled her clit around and around while Jacob pushed further inside her mouth with each steady, smooth stroke.

As she fingered herself, Jacob started thrusting further and harder. The feeling of his cock hitting the back of her open throat sent waves of pleasure down her body. She rubbed her clit faster, spread her legs wider. She could feel it coming. She kept going, it felt so good. The thought of how good she knew her mouth was making Jacob feel built her even closer to orgasm.

"Oh my god you're so sexy," spilled out of Jacob's mouth and those words sent Shay over the edge. She slammed her legs together and pulled off of Jacob's cock as she came, enjoying wave after wave of pleasure.

"Oh what about the chaise? We're making a mess," she said sheepishly after she regained clarity.

"Don't you worry about that. I'm not through with you yet," he replied as he sat and pulled her on top of him.

She had to ease her way down onto him slowly due to her clenched insides from the orgasm. Shay started slow, Jacob helping her movement with two strong fistfuls of her ass in his hands. He increased the tempo, his movements becoming more insistent, more demanding. She cried out, her body arching against his. He drove deeper, filling her completely, stretching her to her limits.

She tangled her fingers in his hair again. "Oh, Jacob..."

He ignored her, his focus solely on her pleasure. He kissed her mouth, ravaged her tongue with his tongue, and then continued to thrust with a relentless energy.

She began to reach for him, to pull him closer, and tried to shift the motion and the tempo.

"Oh no you don't," he growled, expertly flipping her and pinning her beneath him, his weight anchoring her. "My job is to make *you* cum, to make you forget everything but this moment. You shouldn't always have to work for it so much."

His words were both a reprimand and a promise. He continued to pump into her as her own pace began to accelerate, one hand gripping her hip, guiding her movements. She twisted beneath him, gasping for air, her body clenched tight around him.

"I love you," he whispered against her ear, his voice thick with desire. He looked her right in the eyes as he continued pumping.

The words resonated through her, a shockwave of emotion. She hadn't heard those words in a long time, but had dreamt of them frequently—but never like this. Never with such raw honesty, such consuming passion.

"I...I love you too," she breathed, the words tumbling from her lips with a newfound conviction.

Jacob leaned down to kiss her breasts passionately, not slowing the thrusts. The admission unleashed something within Shay's body. A searing heat blossomed in her core, building with each thrust. She cried out, her body arching against his in a desperate attempt to reach the precipice.

He matched her rhythm, intensifying his movements, pushing her closer and closer to the edge. He caught her gaze and stared lovingly into her eyes. "I want you to come for me," he whispered.

Her muscles contracted, squeezing around him, and then—A wave of pure sensation washed over her, obliterating everything else. Her body convulsed, her breath came in ragged gasps. She clung to him, her nails digging into his back.

He groaned, his own release building, mirroring hers. And then, he too succumbed, his body shuddering with pleasure. They clung to each other, their breaths mingling, their bodies locked in a tight embrace.

They finished together, staring into each other's eyes, overwhelmed by the force of their shared passion.

$$\cdot \; \cdot \; \bullet \; \bullet \cdot \bullet \; \bullet \; \bullet \; \cdot \; \cdot$$

MORNING LIGHT BLED THROUGH the velvet drapes, soft and gold, settling over the crumpled silk of the chaise and the scatter of clothes like relics of a private war. Shay stirred, bare shoulders brushing against Jacob's chest. He was already awake, watching her.

She turned into him, fingers tracing the stubble along his jaw. No words. None needed. Last night had spoken in gasps, in moans, in the raw truth of skin and surrender.

Outside, the kingdom stirred—duties called, councils convened, the world moving as it always did. But here, in the hush of the forgotten drawing room, time had cracked open.

She sat up slowly, the thin sheet pooling in her lap. He didn't reach for his clothes either. Just studied her, eyes warm, unreadable in the best way.

"You're quiet," she said.

"You were dreaming," he replied. "Even before you woke. I could see it behind your eyelids."

She frowned. "What was I dreaming?"

"Freedom," he said simply. "And this."

She looked down at her hand, still resting on the sheet. Her ring—the betrothal band forged from ancestral silver—glinted in the light. Not a cage. A choice. Hers.

He shifted, pressing a kiss to her shoulder. "Today, they'll expect the princess. Tomorrow, the queen."

She turned to face him fully. "And you? What do you expect?"

His hand found hers, laced through her fingers. "The same woman I've always loved. The girl in the stables, the woman who managed to survive again and again, the vixen who broke the rules last night. The one who isn't afraid to want. That's who I married in my heart long before the crown sanctioned it. I love you, and I've always loved you."

"I love you too," Shay replied.

She smiled, small, real. Not for the court. Not for the chronicles.

For him.

And for the first time, that was enough.

Epilogue B: Indulgence

T HE CHAMBER WAS WARM, thick with the scent of pine and musk. Torches cast flickering shadows on the rough-hewn stone walls. Shay lay on a sprawling bearskin rug, a goblet of spiced wine resting near her hand, mostly untouched. Six bodies surrounded her, a tangle of limbs and whispered promises.

Dax, ever the strategist, methodically stroked the planes of her stomach, his movements precise and controlled. "Relax, Shay. Let us take care of you."

"Care of me? Or tear me apart?" she teased, her voice a breathless rasp.

Harry chuckled, breaking the tension. "A bit of both, love. Can't have you thinking this is a charitable act." He nipped at her ear, sending a shiver down her spine. "Gage, you're being too gentle. This one likes a little rough."

A low growl rumbled from Gage, and his grip tightened on her thigh. He wasn't wrong. She craved the possessive aggression he offered, the way he made her feel...untamed. He traced the inside of her wrist with a calloused thumb, pressing firmly.

Silas, as usual, was content to simply *be* near her, his body heavy and languid against her side. Drew, still hesitant, hovered near her feet, his gaze darting nervously around the room. And Bennett, bless him, focused solely on her pleasure, his touch reverent and attentive.

"How are you feeling, my love?" Bennett murmured, his lips brushing against her temple.

"Warm," she breathed. "So warm."

They'd done this before, of course. Many times. The miners had been her solace, her escape, a raw, earthy connection to a world outside the demands of the palace. Each man offered something different, a facet of her desire that Jacob, in his princely restraint, hadn't known existed.

She arched her back, inviting Gage to take the lead. He needed no encouragement. He pressed himself against her, his body radiating heat. He slid a finger inside her, slowly, deliberately, testing her boundaries. She gasped, her fingers tightening in his hair. She loved the feeling of being thoroughly, gleefully defiled.

"Like that, temptress?" Gage murmured, his voice a gravelly rasp.

She didn't answer, simply intensified her movements, urging him deeper. Dax joined in, his hands exploring the curves of her breasts, kneading and teasing. Harry began to trace patterns on her stomach with his tongue, his playful chatter a constant undercurrent of stimulation.

"Oh, Shay, you're a scandal, you really are," Harry said. "Imagine the court gossips if they could see you now."

Drew tentatively reached out, his hand trembling as he brushed against her skin. She gently guided his hand, encouraging him to explore, to lose his inhibitions. He still so inexperienced but eager to explore. Silas shifted closer, his weight pressing against her, a silent reminder of his presence. Bennett continued to focus on her clit, his touch feather-light, building the pressure with exquisite skill.

She was a nexus of sensation, a swirling vortex of pleasure. She groaned, her body arching, her head falling back against the bearskin. No longer princess, not yet queen. Just Shay. Pure, unadulterated desire. All six of them there, solely to pleasure her. Each touch, each kiss, focused on her body, her arousal, her feeling.

"More," she whispered, her voice hoarse. "I want more."

The men responded instantly, their movements becoming more frantic, more desperate. Gage drove deeper, his thrusts forceful and relentless. Dax's hands became more demanding, his fingers digging into her flesh. Harry's tongue danced across her skin, igniting sparks of pleasure. Silas's weight pressed down on her, grounding her to the earth. Drew found his confidence, bringing his cock around to her mouth. And Bennett continued to worship her body, his focus unwavering.

She came in waves, each orgasm more intense than the last, her body convulsing with pleasure. She cried out, her voice echoing off the stone walls. She wasn't sure how many times she'd reached the precipice, lost count long ago. Each release was a surrender, a letting go, a dissolving of boundaries.

Then, a shadow fell across the doorway.

Jacob stood there, his expression unreadable. It wasn't shock, though there was a subtle surprise in his eyes. He knew, she was certain. They'd discussed it. He didn't understand it, but he'd observing her clandestine absences, noticing the subtle changes in her demeanor. He was amenable to their agreement but had never accidentally walked in on it.

She met his gaze, a defiant spark in her eyes. She didn't stop, didn't flinch, didn't offer an explanation. She simply held his gaze, and invited him in. "Please Jacob, my love. See me for all that I am."

A slow smile spread across his face. Not a smile of disapproval, not a smile of judgment, but a smile of...fascination. He stepped into the room, his eyes sweeping over the scene before him. Intrigue winning out over jealousy.

"Looks like fun," he confessed, his voice low and controlled.

The miners continued their work, barely pausing in their ministrations. Harry let out a whoop of laughter. "Thought you might enjoy the show, Your Highness!"

Jacob smiled, his gaze locked on Shay. She reached out towards him, her hand outstretched.

"Join us," she invited, her voice a breathless whisper. "Don't be shy."

He hesitated for only a moment, then walked towards her, his movements deliberate and unhurried. He knelt beside the rug, his eyes never leaving hers.

"I trust you know what you're doing?" he asked, a hint of amusement in his voice.

She grinned. "Absolutely."

He leaned in, his lips brushing against her ear. "Very well then. I have to admit the sight of you like this brings feelings I've never known before, but I think I want to be a part of this with you."

He reached down and unbuttoned his pants, letting them fall to the floor. He was already hard and Shay took a break from licking Drew to bring Jacob's cock into her mouth. Soon his body was lost in the tangle of limbs. The rhythm of the room changed, becoming more frenzied, more chaotic. Jacob was surprisingly adept, his movements confident and powerful.

She came again, a searing wave of pleasure washing over her. This time, it was different. She felt a sense of freedom she'd never experienced before, a liberation from all the expectations and constraints that had defined her life. She felt powerful, desirable, in control.

One by one, the men around her reached their own climaxes, their bodies shuddering with release. Groans of pleasure filled the chamber, mingling with the crackling of the fire.

Finally, they all lay exhausted, a sweaty, tangled mess. Jacob was on top of her, his chest heaving, his gaze filled with an intense satisfaction.

"You handle them well," he breathed.

"Someone has to," she joked, smiling against his lips.

They lay there for a long moment, basking in the afterglow of their shared pleasure. It wasn't a perfect fairy tale ending, but it was *her* ending. A messy, complicated, gloriously indulgent ending. And for the first time, Shay felt truly, unequivocally free.

The fire dimmed, embers pulsing like slow heartbeats in the cooling dark. Outside, the wind picked up, rattling the iron hinges of the chamber door, but none of them moved. Limbs remained entwined, breaths syncing in the silence that followed the storm.

Shay closed her eyes, Jacob's weight anchoring her to the earth, and smiled. She had spent her life being claimed—by duty, by blood, by throne. Now, she took. And it was enough.

The Prequel

Thank You for Reading!

You've reached the end of *Glass & Sin*, but the story of **The Shattered Crowns** is just beginning. I hope you enjoyed this dark journey as much as I enjoyed writing it.
Get Your FREE Prequel: *Seed & Agony*
Hungry for more? Read **Seed & Agony**, a high-heat retelling of *The Princess and the Pea*. This novella is available **exclusively** to my newsletter subscribers. **Scan this QR Code to join the newsletter and receive your free copy of Seed & Agony:**

Quiz: Which Miner is your Soulmate?

You've finished the book, you've met the men, and now it's time to confess: **Who has your heart (and who do you want in your bed)?**

1. The Royal Masquerade is in full swing. Where are you?

A) In the shadows of the balcony, avoiding the crowds.
B) In the library, one-on-one with a kindred spirit.
C) Leading a high-stakes card game in the corner and winning everyone's gold.
D) Why stay in one place? I'm rotating through the room, keeping everyone on their toes.

2. In the *Glass & Sin* epilogue, which path called to your soul?

A) Path B: Indulgence. I want the heat, the danger, and the dark obsession.
B) Path A: Devotion. Give me the slow burn and the man who would die for me.
C) Path B: Indulgence. I want a partner-in-crime who

makes everything fun.

D) I won't lie. It said choose one, but I read both epilogues.

3. A rival threatens your honor. How does your man react?

A) He doesn't say a word—he just pins them to the wall by their throat.

B) He stands in front of you, shielding you with his body and a calm, deadly grace.

C) He laughs, insults them, and then tricks them into a trap they'll never escape.

D) You don't need a man to defend you.

4. What is the one "Red Flag" you're willing to overlook?

A) He's borderline obsessive and has a bit of a "touch her and die" problem.

B) He's so sensitive he might actually break your heart while trying to save it.

C) He never takes anything seriously, even when the castle is on fire.

D) He doesn't know how to share... except with his brothers.

5. The candles are lit, the door is locked, and the tension has finally snapped. What is your ultimate fantasy?

A) I want wild passion, dirty talk, and pushing all the limits.

B) I want to be worshiped—slow, intentional, and eye contact.

C) I want it loud, playful, and unpredictable. Surprise me.

D) Why choose one when I can have it all? I want every hand on me at once.

Get Your Results!

A Small Favor

As an independent author, reviews are my lifeblood. They tell the algorithms that people are reading, which helps other readers find my work.

<u>Could you take 60 seconds to leave a review?</u> Even a few words about your favorite character or the heat level makes a massive difference.

About the Author

Cordelia Cross wears all the hats. She is a horse trainer rehabbing off the track thoroughbreds, an adjunct college writing professor, a mom of two rambunctious young boys, and now published author with *Glass & Sin*—her debut novel.

She grew up in Virginia and after grad school moved to Maryland where she currently lives. When not working or momming, she's drinking mushroom coffee, watching reality competition shows, and snuggling with her dog and cat—both frequently featured on her social media. Her favorite TV show is The Traitors, favorite movie is Saw, favorite food is cheese, and favorite place is Disney World.

She writes high-heat, dark fantasy retellings where "happily ever after" is earned in the shadows and forged by fire. *Glass & Sin* is the first book in *The Shattered Crowns* series.

Follow her journey on facebook, instagram, and tiktok at @cordeliacrossauthor

Acknowledgements

Writing a book is a solitary act, but bringing it to the world takes a village.

First, to my boys—you're the loves of my life, and this mama bear will always fiercely protect you. You're the reason my coffee is always cold, the house is always messy, and my heart is always full. To my husband—thank you for letting me disappear into the forest of my imagination.

To my friends who sparked this idea at happy hour when we said: 'fairy tale, but make it smut.' I hope you enjoy reading it as much as I enjoyed writing it.

To the many alpha and beta readers who helped me along the way, my artist Michael Diaz, editor Debbie Fogle, and social media manager Melissa Garrett.

To my readers and the community at **Bold Bandit Books**, your support turned this dream into a reality. And finally, to the readers who like their fairy tales with a bit of bite: this one is for you.

Coming Soon

SAND & GREED *The Shattered Crowns, Book Two*
In the kingdom of shifting dunes, every grain of sand has a price, and every wish has a sting.
He was a thief who wanted the world. She was a princess who wanted to burn it down. Together, they found a power that should have stayed buried in the dark.
The desert doesn't offer mercy. It only offers deals.